THE DEVIL'S DEN

A DE KYSA MAFIA ROMANCE

PENNY DEE

The Devil's Den

A De Kysa Mafia Romance
Book 1
Penny Dee

Copyright 2023 Penny Dee
All Rights Reserved

This book is a work of fiction. Any references to real events, real people, and real places are used fictitiously. Other names, characters, places, and incidents are products of the author's imagination and any resemblance to persons, living or dead, actual events, organizations or places is entirely coincidental.

All rights are reserved. This book is intended for the purchaser of this book ONLY. No part of this book may be reproduced or transmitted in any form or by any means, graphic, electronic, or mechanical, including photocopying, recording, taping, or by any information storage retrieval system, without the express written permission of the author. All songs, song titles, and lyrics contained in this book are the property of the respective songwriters and copyright holders.

Disclaimer: The material in this book contains graphic language and sexual content and is intended for mature audiences ages 18 and older. Please read Author's Note for trigger warnings.

AUTHOR'S NOTE

Dear Reader,

I'm so excited for you to read The Devil's Den. It's a Mafia romance, so you can expect some darker themes throughout the story which include assault, kidnapping, and murder. It also contains sexual acts and profanity. But the real focus of this scorching hot enemies-to-lovers romance is how love conquers all... with some high tense plot twists and lots of steam along the way.

This book can be read as a standalone.
No cliffhanger.

PROLOGUE

"You can't do this to me!" I cry.

I look at my father sitting behind his vast desk looking so calm and collected as he rips my world from under me, and I feel utterly hopeless.

"I can, and I am," he says calmly. "You will leave for New York tomorrow."

"This isn't fair."

"Life isn't fair, Bella."

"You think I don't know that? I lost them too."

My father stands. He doesn't like me bringing it up. What happened that night only six months ago tore our family apart and left me without a mother or any siblings. It stole his wife and two sons from him. It blew our family apart.

"We're moving to America, and that is that. New York will be home from now on." He walks around the desk to the drink cart and reaches for the bottle of grappa. "Alberto will chaperone you, and you will finish your school year at one of

New York's finest schools. I will follow in a few weeks once I have wrapped things up here."

"I lose my mother and brothers less than six months ago, and now I'm losing my father and everything I've known too?"

"You need a fresh start. We need a fresh start. This is it."

"No."

My father looks up from pouring his drink. "No?"

"I won't go." I cross my arms over my chest. "I'll be eighteen soon enough, and you won't be able to tell me what to do anymore."

"You're sixteen—"

"And a half."

He replaces the cap on the grappa and turns to fully face me. "This isn't up for negotiation, Bella. You will do as I say, or I will make you. Do you understand me?"

My father doesn't make idle threats. If someone doesn't do as he says, he shoots them. Or he has Alberto, his right-hand man, do it for him. Or so the rumors go. I've never seen them do anything like that, but I'm not stupid enough to think it doesn't happen. Not when you're Mafia like he is.

Not that either of them would ever hurt me.

I am the apple in my father's eye, and Alberto loves me like a daughter.

His phone buzzes and briefly distracts him when he sees someone's name on the screen. But he ignores it and refocuses on me. "We have outgrown Italy and have new interests to pursue in New York City. It's time to move forward."

"My life is here. My friends are here." I suddenly feel desperate when I think about all the things I'll be leaving behind. Who I'll be leaving behind. "You can't ask me to give it all up."

"I'm not asking, Bella."

Again, his phone buzzes. Again, he ignores it.

"You can't stop me from seeing him."

Him being Domenico De Kysa. The boy I was born to love. Son to Gio De Kysa, my father's best friend and don to the De Kysa. We were both born on the same day. Raised side by side by our mothers who were best friends. We were raised to be betrothed. The perfect union of the two houses.

My father taking me away from all of that to move to America doesn't make sense.

Again, his phone lights up with a call. This time, I see the name. *Mari*. A woman.

"Who is Mari? Why aren't you answering her?"

For a split second, I see the unease on his handsome face. It's not there long, but long enough to ignite my next question.

"Are you seeing someone?" I ask, my voice raised. "Mom hasn't even been gone six months!"

"Bella—"

"Who is she? Is she the reason you're sending me to live nine hours away? You want to spend time with her without your daughter around—wait, Mari, as in Marianne De Kysa?" The realization rumbles through me, and I take a step back. "Why would Marianne De Kysa be so anxious to talk to you?"

Marianne is Nico's mother. Wife to my father's best friend.

"Many things are in play here that you don't understand,

and I will not explain them to my sixteen-year-old daughter."

"Oh my God, are you having an affair with her?"

Mafia wives don't call their husband's best friend repeatedly.

My father's intimidating voice cuts me off. "Go to your goddamn room, Bella, and don't come out. You've got some packing to do, and I don't want to see your face until morning."

∽

I escape out my bedroom window and bolt across the immaculate lawns of the sprawling estate. Moonlight guides my way as I sneak through the apple orchards and along the row of olive trees toward the stables at the edge of the property. The little glow coming from inside tells me Nico already waits for me.

Nico.

Just the thought of him sends butterflies loose in my stomach.

"Bella." My name rolls off his tongue as I launch myself at him and bury my face into his neck.

"He's sending me away, Nico. He wants to keep us apart."

"What? When?"

"Alberto is flying with me to New York tomorrow."

In the moonlight, he looks as flawless as a Michelangelo sculpture. High cheekbones. Strong jaw. Muscles cut from marble. I've loved Domenico De Kysa my whole life. He is my best friend, always has been and always will be. Which is

The Devil's Den

why I've shared all my firsts with him. My first kiss. My first time. My everything.

He took my virginity in this barn last Valentine's Day. I had given him a paper heart with a promise never to give my heart to another boy. He had taken it and kissed me, and then we vanquished our v-cards in the light of the full moon.

Now we meet in secret whenever we can. We might be betrothed, but my virginity is expected right up until we wed.

"I won't go," I whisper.

He presses his forehead to mine. "Run away with me."

"What?"

He cups my jaw. "We'll go somewhere far away where they can't find us."

"Go where? Our fathers have eyes all over this country."

"Then we leave the country."

"They'll find us. They'll always find us."

He tucks a lock of hair behind my ear. "We have to try."

We're silent for a moment.

He kisses me, and I feel it all the way down to my soul. He is where I start and where I end, and everything I need in between.

We make love in the hay, where Nico has set out a bed of blankets. Afterward, I lie in his arms, aching with fear at the unknown that lies ahead.

"Is this how it ends for us?" I whisper against his warm chest.

Nico lifts my chin. "There is no end for us," he says with certainty. "It would be like trying to stop the tides. *Impossible.* My reason for breathing is you."

His mouth slants over mine, and his tongue strokes into

my mouth. He kisses me with such confidence, my fear vanishes, replaced by the heady throb of lust.

Nico's kisses never fail to turn my bones into liquid.

As the kiss deepens, a new need returns, and he rolls onto me again. "No matter what happens, I will always find my way back to you."

The barn door bursts open, and the silhouettes of my father's bodyguards fill the doorway. I sit up and grab the blanket to cover myself. Nico rises to his feet, unfazed by his nakedness and the thick erection swinging between his powerful thighs. Not even seventeen, he already has a body to rival any of the older adversaries in the doorway and cuts a formidable image in the moonlight.

The bodyguards part to let an older man in a suit and tie walk in.

"Bella Isle Ciccula, you need to come with me at once." The voice belongs to Alberto.

"She's not going anywhere," Nico growls.

"That's where you're wrong, Nico." Alberto steps into a beam of moonlight breaking through a hole in the barn roof. He's an intimidating man, tall with big hands and a slight scowl on his leathery face. He has a full set of hair, but it's snow white. I've known him my whole life, and he's always looked like an old man. "Bella, you need to come with me now."

Confused, I tighten the sheet around my nakedness.

Alberto leans down to pick up the pair of jeans Nico discarded after he had undressed me and shoves them into Nico's bare chest. "Put these on. We're not all hung like that... You'll make us old men feel inadequate."

Nico takes them but reaches for Alberto's arm. "Why are you here? Did her father send you?"

Alberto ignores him and fixes his gaze on me. "Bella, get dressed. You're coming home now, either by choice or by force."

Beneath the covers, I clumsily redress.

Nico pushes his hand into Alberto's chest. "Hey! No one is forcing anyone to do anything."

"Take your hand off me, *bambino*. We're not starting something here. You need to get home."

Alberto nods to the two men with him who step around Nico and drag me off the hay.

A scuffle breaks out as Nico tries to stop them.

Alberto grabs Nico and shakes him. "You need to go home. Your mother needs you."

~

Alberto drives me home but refuses to answer any of my questions, so by the time he ushers me through the front door, I'm demanding answers.

The first thing I realize when I walk inside is the frantic pace of everything. I pause in the foyer and try to make sense of it.

Sophia, our housekeeper, drags a heavy suitcase behind her while Olivia, our maid, races down the stairs carrying an armful of my father's suits in her arms. At the base of the stairs, she drops them onto the three suitcases already waiting there before bolting back up the stairs and disappearing into the bedroom.

Sophia drops the suitcase and starts hurrying me in Italian. "Quickly, child. You need to pack."

"What's going on?"

"You must get your things, and you must hurry."

"But I'm not leaving until tomorrow. Why are all these suitcases sitting here?"

"Oh, *cara mia*, there is no time for questions."

Two of my father's bodyguards walk through the front door. They look serious and somber as they disappear into the study without a word.

"Will someone please tell me what's going on?"

My father appears in the doorway to his study. "Bella, come here."

"What is happening, Papa? Why are all these people here?"

"We need to leave for America right away. There is a plane waiting for us."

"We're leaving now? Why, what happened?"

My father looks grim. "There has been... an accident."

"What kind of accident? Was anyone hurt?"

"Marianne De Kysa."

I remember Alberto's words to Nico. *Your mother needs you.*

"Is she okay?"

"No, *cara mia*, she isn't." His throat works as he swallows. "She died."

I gasp, and my hand flies to my mouth. "How?"

"She accidentally shot herself."

Another gasp. *Nico.*

"I need to see Nico," I say, turning toward the door, but my father's voice stops me.

The Devil's Den

"I can't allow you to do that."

I turn back to him. "What are you talking about? They are our friends. Nico is my best friend. I have to see him."

"I said no, Bella. You will not see that boy again. Do you understand?"

"That boy?" I stare at my father, taken aback by his words. "That boy means everything to me, and he's just lost his mama. He needs me."

"No, he needs his family. And you need to finish packing your things. Our plane leaves the tarmac in forty minutes."

"How can we leave? They're our friends, Papa. They were there for us when Mama and the boys died. We need to be there for them."

Six months ago, a car bomb meant for my father stole the lives of my beautiful Mama and older brothers. It was sheer chance that I was still inside the house trying to find my shoes when my mother started the car.

"Things have changed since then."

"No, we have to help them. It's what friends—"

"I said go to your room and gather your belongings!" my father roars, his face red and his body rigid.

My father is terrifying when he's upset, so I immediately close my mouth.

I stare at him, confused why tomorrow wasn't soon enough for us to leave.

Finally, I nod and leave the study. My father watches me as I walk slowly toward the stairs, but the moment he turns away, I run for the front door and flee into the darkness. I speed past the cars lining the driveway and through the trees bordering our estate with the De Kysa mansion. I run until my lungs burn and my muscles ache, but there is no time to

9

waste. My father will realize I'm gone within minutes, and he'll know where I am going. He'll send Alberto to get me, and then they'll send me to America, and I'll never see Nico again.

The De Kysa's driveway is lit up with the red and blue lights from the police cars. And there is an ambulance parked by the front door.

I don't pause or stop to think. All I know is that Nico needs me.

He might not be close to his mama, but this will hurt him deeply.

Out of breath and with my feet killing me, I run up the front steps and through the front door, where I slam into the chest of one of the De Kysa bodyguards.

He tries to stop me, but I fight him.

"It's okay," Nico says, appearing behind him. His face drawn. His beautiful brown eyes wet with tears.

The bodyguard leaves, and I fall into Nico's arms. "I heard about your mama, Nico. I'm so sorry."

He holds me at arm's length. "You shouldn't be here, Bella."

"Are you crazy? Of course I should be. Your mama..."

His jaw tightens, and he looks away. Tears well in his eyes. But so does something else. Something I've never seen there before. *Hate.*

"She's dead." His tone has an edge to it. "She killed herself."

I take a step back. "Killed herself?" I whisper. "My father said it was an accident."

He turns his face back to look at me. "Well, your father was wrong."

Again, his voice is sharp and hard, like a wild rage simmering beneath the surface. I reach for him, knowing he's hurting.

"I'm so sorry. What can I do?"

He pulls away. "Go home, Bella."

Even though I try not to, I feel the sting of his rejection. But he's just lost his mama, and I know how heartbreaking it feels when your world is so suddenly rocked. Sometimes you lash out or want distance from the ones you love.

And because I don't know what else to do, I tell him the terrible news.

"We're leaving," I say.

Only then does he seem to come back to the present. His brows snap together. A sudden alarm shines in his dark eyes.

"We leave tonight. Papa says he's urgently required in America." I grab his hands. "Nico, I don't know when I'll see you again."

"So soon." He frowns as if trying to make sense of the two colliding tidal waves. His mama's death, and my father's sudden change of plans to leave for America tonight. "None of this makes sense."

Suddenly overwhelmed, I burst into tears. "We'll never see each other again."

In a rush of urgency, he takes my hand. "I'll find you. I promise. On your eighteenth birthday, I will find you. No matter where you are. We will be together again."

I begin to cry harder. I want to be strong for him. But our world is crashing down around us.

He pulls me into his strong chest and holds me tight, and I can feel the rapid thud of his heartbeat against my cheek. "This isn't the end for us."

I squeeze my eyes shut and tell myself to remember this moment. His smell, the thump of his heart, the strength in his arms around me.

A set of headlights appear on the driveway, and a car comes to a screech at the door. It's Alberto and two of my father's bodyguards. All guns are drawn.

Out of nowhere, several De Kysa bodyguards swarm around us, and there is a lot of yelling and a lot of gun pointing.

"Give us the girl," Alberto demands.

I am ripped from Nico's arms.

"Bella—" he cries, but he is pulled in one direction while I am pulled in the other.

"*Nico!*" I scream.

"Remember what I said. I will come for you."

One of my father's bodyguards hooks his arm tighter around my waist and drags me away. I struggle and cry, but I'm no match for his strength. I reach out for Nico, but he is finally dragged out of view, and I'm shoved into the car, and the doors are locked.

Inside the car, I scream, "What the fuck is happening?"

Alberto looks at me through the rearview mirror and simply says, "The Isle Ciccula and the De Kysa are now at war."

1

Nico

Ten Years Later

I stand at the penthouse window and stare out at the glittering city below.

My name is Domenico De Kysa.

Back home in Italy, they call me the Heartless King of the North. It's a title I hate. But it's a title that lets my rivals know they should fear me.

I'd say it is a pleasure to meet you. But that wouldn't be true.

You don't want to meet me.

You might think you do... after all, everyone does.

But the truth is, I'm not a good man.

In my hometown, I'm feared. My surname alone holds the power to evoke terror. There, I'm known for my lack of emotion in the way I execute my brutal revenge on anyone who dares to cross me. In my world, betrayal is met with painful bloodletting, and if you are to believe the rumor, I'm very good at it.

But in this city, I am still a shiny new star, and the darkness that follows my name has yet to cast a shadow over the glittering New York City landscape.

Here I am, still revered and lusted after by those who don't know me or my capacity for vicious retaliation. My Midas touch in the business world is like honey to the ignorant fat cats who scramble to make my association, and my dark good looks send a tremor through the social circles of the upper echelon, attracting attention and making panties wet.

Invites flood my assistant's desk by the dozen every day, and accidental meetings at the gym or as I walk into my office in Upper Manhattan are becoming a nightmare for my bodyguard to fend off.

I didn't plan on taking New York by storm. Didn't plan on my business ventures becoming successful beyond my wildest dreams. Didn't plan on becoming one of the richest men in town or an object of interest because I'm rich, handsome, and powerful. They aren't the reasons I came here.

No, I have bigger plans than being the toast of the fucking city.

Ice. Cold. Revenge.

I grip the scotch tumbler in my hand as pleasure begins to uncoil in my stomach. With a growl, I reach for the hair of the woman with my cock in her mouth. She kneels before me, fucking me with her ruby-red lips and tongue, as I stare out at the glittering New York skyline with dark thoughts on my mind.

She moans, and it vibrates through me, sending another jolt of pleasure along my cock.

My fingers tighten in her hair, and she gags as the swollen head hits the back of her throat. I take a sip of scotch from the tumbler in my other hand and close my eyes, allowing my mind to drift over the night's events.

I groan. I'm close to coming. The woman whimpers eagerly and sucks harder, massaging my cock with her tongue and lips. I grab the back of her head and start to fuck her mouth harder, thrusting, groaning, straining, my head swirling with darkness. *Revenge. I want revenge.* With a growl, I rip my cock from her swollen lips and fist my release over her eager tongue, pumping and pumping until there is nothing left to give.

The cold stab of reality is immediate, and I shove my cock back into my boxer shorts and zip my black pants.

Draining my glass, I feel the darkness crawl along my spine and worm its way into my brain.

A darkness I've lived with for ten years.

The woman rises to her feet and looks at me with a wicked gleam in her eyes as she licks her lips. I briefly wonder how her lipstick remains unsmudged.

"You have a beautiful cock." Her voice is velvety smooth. "I love fucking it with my mouth."

A smile twitches in the corner of my lips. But it's all I can offer her. I want her gone.

She tries to kiss me, but I turn away. I don't kiss. I haven't kissed anybody in more than a decade.

I unfold five crisp hundred-dollar bills and drop them on the table beside her.

She looks at them, then leans into my ear. "I told you I'd fuck you for free." Her hand slides down to my zipper. "I have a feeling you could go all night."

She's gorgeous.

But I have no interest in fucking her.

"No."

Unfortunately, she ignores me. Like others before her, she thinks she can purr in my ear, and I'll be hers. But I want her gone, and her lingering presence is beginning to scratch at my nerves.

She pulls down one shoulder on her designer dress to reveal perfectly polished skin. "How about we go to your room, and you can show me just what you can do with that beautiful cock of yours?"

"I said no."

Her tongue finds the shell of my ear. "You like what my mouth can do to you. Imagine what my pussy will feel like."

"Nothing I'll remember tomorrow."

I move away from her to refill my scotch glass as my words rattle between us.

"You're cold. I've heard that about you," she says with a hard edge to her voice. "They say you're an unfeeling asshole who doesn't show any emotion. That you show no mercy in any situation."

"Apparently, *they* say a lot." I turn around and bring the scotch glass to my lips. "I paid for your mouth to fuck me, not for it to hang around and pester me for cock afterward. Show's over."

She tilts her head to the side, her interest piqued. Her

smoky eyes gleam as she watches me. Her back straightens. She knows she's beautiful. That's why men pay good money for her services. But none of them are a challenge, and I get the feeling she likes a challenge. It's written all over her face. Me turning her down is a dare she wants to rise up to.

She moves closer to stand in front of me, her seductive lips twitching with wickedness. "You and me could be good together."

"Haven't you heard? I don't play well with others," I say, taking a sip from the glass.

She runs a finger across my chest, curling her lips into a lusty smirk. "I think you'd find playing with me to be quite satisfying."

I take a step back. I don't like being close to people unless it's necessary. And I certainly don't tolerate someone touching me.

"Don't kid yourself, sweetheart." I sweep my gaze up from her bare feet with pink-painted toes to her symmetrical face and red lips. "High-traffic zones aren't really my thing."

A dark scowl deepens the lines in her face. "You bastard."

She tries to slap me, but I grab her wrist before she can make contact with my cheek.

"Let's not spoil a nice evening."

Her glare lingers on my face before she relaxes, and I let her go.

"You really are a cold-hearted asshole." She snatches up the bills on her way out and slams the door behind her. The shock wave rolls over me as I drain my glass, needing to numb my senses tonight.

A few seconds later, my front door opens, and my brother, Massimo, appears.

"Another happy customer, I see. You really have a way with the ladies." He grins.

"She'll get over it." I cross the room to refill my glass from the bar by the window while my brother makes himself at home.

He sits on the couch and stretches his arm across the top as if he owns the goddamn place. "It's not like you to bring company home."

Massimo knows my focus is the family business and not pleasure.

"She came highly recommended for her discretion."

He crosses his legs as he studies me from the couch. "How is it that you look so tense after getting a blow job?"

Massimo may look like me—with the same dark eyes, jet-black hair, and a face of stubble—but we are opposites. I'm a tense son of a bitch while he's effortlessly relaxed. But that's the price you pay when you are the king. Too many enemies want to see my head on a platter for me to relax.

"Maybe it's my present company. Why are you here?"

"I thought you might like to know there's some concern among the families."

I look at my brother. He's not one to waste time with pleasantries and small talk. "Oh yeah, how so?"

"They're uneasy with your Mr. Popular image," he says.

"They're Mafia. Of course they are."

I hand him a drink as he says, "They like things done a certain way."

"Maybe it's time to shake things up."

Massimo has been my eyes and ears in New York since long before I arrived. He blends in and has the annoying quality of being impossible not to like.

"The families don't want a glittering icon, Domenico. They want a discreet, powerful figurehead. The media treating you like you're a goddamn rock star makes them nervous. They don't like the attention you're bringing to the table."

"Hundreds of millions of dollars—that's what I'm bringing to the table. I didn't see them complain when a few extra zeros appeared in the coffers this year."

I rule over the fifteen families who serve under the De Kysa banner, while my brother takes care of our corporate interests, which range from hotels and inner-city bars to technology and media companies. Thanks to my reign, the De Kysa wealth is now in the billions. I moved our focus away from the old-school money laundering, drug running, and racketeering to a much bigger slice of the modern-day pie—corporate domination.

"You need to show them you have staying power," he says. "That you have roots in this town. Dampen the glitz and glamour with stability and commitment to the long game."

"Meaning?"

"Meaning you need a wife."

I almost choke on my scotch. "Are you drunk?"

"After I leave here, I plan to be. I have a standing date with my buddy Jack Daniel's at the club." He rises to his feet. "The families meet tomorrow. You need to appease their restlessness. The match with Bianca Bamcorda is a good one and will dampen the unrest among our old-school allies."

"You're insane."

"No, I'm the realist. We need this alliance. It's only a

matter of time before the Irish want their slice of the eastern border for their drug trade."

"Over my dead fucking body."

"Easily done if you fuck up this alliance."

"The Bamcorda will align with us regardless."

Massimo doesn't look convinced. "Luca Bamcorda wants a more elevated position in the De Kysa stronghold. The kind that will come with his daughter being married to the don."

Luca Bamcorda. Ambitious. Rich. But not as smart as he thinks he is. He's a giant pain in my ass. He's old school and stuck in his rigid ways. Giving him any more power within our ranks would make him think he's more valuable than he really is, and I'd have to manage the behavior that came with it.

"Luca Bamcorda has been chasing you to marry his daughter for months now," Massimo reminds me. "It's expected."

Bianca Bamcorda. Mafia princess. Impossibly beautiful. But needy and annoying. Not to mention vain and arrogant. I'd rather scoop my brains out with a spoon than marry the vapid bitch.

Although a wife could be a pleasurable experience.

Just not her.

"You have to act now, Domenico. Take a wife. Appease the families. We can't afford any unrest when things are so volatile with the Irish."

Fuck.

I hate it when my brother makes sense, especially when it means I have to do something I don't like. While the De Kysa is one of the largest, most powerful underworld syndicates in the world, it relies on alliances which always come at a cost—either money, power, or marriage.

My mind slips to my greatest rival, Vincent Isle Ciccula.

The man I came to New York to destroy.

The man who broke my family apart.

The man I've set up to financially ruin in retribution for his sins against my family.

His greatest love is his daughter.

The beautiful but elusive Bella Isle Ciccula.

As I recall the beautiful artist and what she once meant to me, an all-too-familiar darkness sweeps through my mood. She left my life on the same night as my mother's death.

A night that shaped me into the *cold-hearted asshole* I am now.

I already have dice on the table when it comes to her father, Vincent. A failed business venture he unwisely invested in that will see me take his kingdom from him.

But as the thought unfurls in my dark mind, I come to accept that I'm about to roll a new set of dice.

I smile darkly.

Massimo cocks an eyebrow. "What do you have to smile about?"

"I think I have a solution."

"Yeah, what is it?"

I raise my glass to my lips and smirk.

"I'm going to make Bella Isle Ciccula my wife."

2

Bella

Six months later

I hit the floor with a thud and groan. I try to breathe, but my lungs rattle, and I'm winded.

Smiling, Ari stands over me and offers a hand.

"You're distracted," he says with an amused gleam in his eyes. "You're making this too easy for me."

I reach up and accept his hand. "Too easy, huh?"

While he's distracted, I kick him behind the knees, and he drops to the floor beside me.

"What about now?" I ask smugly.

He looks up at me from the mat, and his handsome face breaks into a bright smile. Green eyes twinkle. It's no surprise all the girls in New York are in love with him. All the girls except me, of course. He's one of my best friends, and my feelings for him are too brotherly to be anything else. We kissed once, back in the early days, but there was no spark, and it weirded us both out. I wasn't surprised when he came out two years later.

Besides being one of my best friends, Ari is also my Krav Maga coach. We've been sparring for years and are both fiercely competitive. Although this is the first time we've seen each other in eight months because I've been living in London for work.

I'm an art curator for the prestigious Ulvaeus Art Gallery in London.

But whenever I return to town, we always catch up with a little skirmish on the mats, usually followed by cocktails at one of our favorite bars.

Climbing to my feet, I help him to his.

"I don't think I can teach you anymore," he says.

"I know. I just like kicking your ass." I wink at him, and he grins.

"Hey, I'm meeting Imogen for a drink. Wanna join us?"

He pulls a face. "Only two women in the world scare me, Bella. My grandmother and Imogen. She looks at me like I'm her next meal."

"So I'll take that as a no?"

"I've got to study but I'll take a raincheck."

Ari is studying to become a lawyer.

"Chicken," I tease.

"One hundred percent." He grins and presses a kiss to my cheek. "But call me before you leave town and we'll catch up for a drink then, I promise."

"Okay, I will."

After showering, I meet my slightly crazy but lovable

girlfriend at a hot new bar on the Lower East Side called Inkwood.

I've known Imogen since I was fresh off the plane from Italy and shoved into an exclusive boarding school for the rich brats of New York's social elite. She took me under her wing and made my new life bearable.

She screams the moment I step out of the cab and onto the busy New York street and throws her arms around my neck.

We hug, and she squeezes me tight. "Please don't ever leave me again. This town is such a bore without my partner in crime."

I grimace because I'm about to break her heart. "Yeah, about that. I'm only here for a few days. I have to head back to London after dad's dinner party."

I'm back in town for my father's birthday which is tomorrow night. It's one of his rules—wherever we are in the world, we always find a way to spend our birthdays together.

Imogen pouts. "I thought you were permanently relocating back to the New York office?"

"I got a promotion. I only found out yesterday."

I don't add that the promotion was something I'd been praying night and day for because I've fallen I love with my life in London. I've created a whole new life doing what I love, away from the constant glare of the media and my father's solemn bodyguards.

The downside of living there is not seeing my best friend whenever I want to. Even our frequent texts have become less and less lately because life is so full and busy, and it feels like months since we've caught up.

She sighs. "You've been away far too long. I might have to move to London to get my weekly fix of you."

"*You* live in London? You'd die the moment you left NYC airspace."

"I know, but I miss you. And now you're extending your stay abroad. What am I going to do without my best friend?"

"The promotion is too good to turn down. Besides, I'll be back for all the important things."

"You're breaking my heart," Imogen says with a heavy bottom lip.

"I know, but I'll be flying back a lot. It'll be like I still live around the corner."

"That corner is the size of the Atlantic Ocean." She pulls another sad face but then sighs. "Well, I'd better make the most of you while I have you."

She loops her arm through mine, and we enter the club. After ordering our cocktails, we find a booth along the back wall. It's twilight, and the bar is filling up with people looking to end their Wednesday with decadent after-work cocktails.

"How was your Krav Maga class?" she asks over her margarita.

"Good."

"And Ari?"

I grin at her. "You know he's gay, right?"

She shrugs and takes a sip of her drink. "A girl needs her dreams. Harry Styles is a traveling rock star with a legion of fans and would never glance sideways at a girl like me, but that doesn't stop a girl from fantasizing."

"And Ari is one of those fantasies?"

"I'll wear him down one day."

"I admire your determination." I lift my margarita to my lips. "Anyway, I thought you were seeing that sexy attorney you met at work."

"He's okay," she says noncommittally. "I dunno, I think I'm bored."

I resist rolling my eyes. This isn't the first conversation we've had about this. In fact, it's the same conversation we have with nearly every single guy she dates.

"You go through men like candy. How about throwing some my way?"

"I would, but you'd probably throw them back."

"You're right." I take another sip of my drink. "Because I'm a dating disaster."

"Wait, weren't you seeing some guy in London, some earl or lord or something?"

"We broke up."

Just my luck, the one guy who decides to stick around turns out to be an egotistical jerk.

This time, it was me who did the breaking up. Not quick enough, though. Unfortunately, his gaslighting has had a lasting effect on me, despite being the kind of girl who doesn't tolerate being treated badly.

But that's the thing about toxic behavior. Even if you're strong, some of the noxious fumes can seep through your tough outer layer and steal your confidence before you even realize.

With Simon, my confidence took a big hit.

When I realized what was happening, I dumped his egotistical ass and have been repairing my self-confidence ever since.

I've been out with other guys since then, but they never move past the first date.

I sigh. "I don't know why I'm such a dating disaster."

"Maybe it has something to do with your daddy?" Imogen suggests with a mischievous smile. "I mean, dating the only daughter of a Mafia don would have to be as intimidating as fuck."

I give her a pointed look. "You know he isn't involved in that life anymore. He left that all behind when we moved to New York. That's why we moved."

When we relocated to New York, my father gave up his Mafia ties, and the old ways got left behind in the old land.

Now he owns five highly renowned restaurants all over New York and is revered as a charismatic businessman and restaurateur.

Imogen looks wistful. "Are you sure? I mean, he looks so—"

"If you say dreamy, sexy, or fuckable, I'm leaving."

Imogen has always had a crush on my father. I mean, he is a very good-looking man, and he's charming and stylish in his Armani suits and slicked-back hair, but he's also pushing sixty.

"I was going to say he looks so mafioso. Like he stepped right off the set of *Goodfellas*."

"He's a businessman."

She wiggles her eyebrows. "A very well-connected businessman."

This time, I do roll my eyes. Imogen likes to romanticize the whole organized crime thing. The truth is, it is ugly and dark and bloody. And it took an irreparable toll on my family.

Imogen drains her margarita glass. "And there has been no one since the earl?"

"I met a guy at a work event a few weeks ago who was kind of hot. Tall. Charming. Man bun. We met for dinner the following night."

"And?"

"And then nothing."

"What do you mean nothing? No kiss? No sexy time?"

I shake my head. "That's the thing. He was into me at the beginning of the evening, but by the end of the night, I was issued with a sudden 'I'm not really looking for anything right now' talk. It was weird. It's like something happened between our entrée and desserts."

Imogen's eyes gleam with conspiracy. "You think someone paid him a visit while you were in the bathroom?"

"Like who?"

"Daddy is well-connected," she sing-songs.

"You think my father organized someone to warn off my date?" I resist a smile. "He was an entire continent away. I doubt he's even aware of when and who I date."

Thankfully, my move to London lessened the need for bodyguards—something that was stifling in New York—which meant my father knew very little about my life because he didn't have a six-foot-ten tank reporting back to him.

"Possibly. Or maybe Mr. Vanish was just a dick. Every town has a lot of those, no matter what side of the ocean you're on. But you're a stunner, Bella Isle Ciccula. Forget about the rude men with man buns. Something way better is planned for you." She winks. "I need to pee and freshen my lipstick. Be a doll and order us another round of drinks."

The Devil's Den

When Imogen leaves, I order another two margaritas from the server, and that's the moment I see him. *The man.* He's standing in the middle of the room, but he's standing very still in a sea of people moving around him. He looks like sin wrapped in a custom suit and a raven-black button-up shirt. *And he's staring right at me.*

When our eyes meet, something runs down my spine, and the hairs on the back of my neck lift. Something about him is intense. Something dark and mysterious, and a thrill of excitement ripples in the pit of my stomach.

I can't look away. For a moment, the club and the people in it are gone, and it's just me and Mr. Tall, Dark, and Dangerous looking at each other across the room.

Something stirs in my heart.

A name plays on my lips.

A name I refuse to say.

A name that belongs to a ghost.

I frown and quickly stamp the memory down.

"You want to pay for those now or start a tab, honey?" asks the server.

Startled back to the present, I look at her. "We'll start a tab, thank you."

"No problem."

When she leaves, I look back at the dance floor, but the man is gone. I scan the room, but there is no sign of him.

"Who are you looking for?" Imogen asks when she returns and slides into the booth beside me.

"No one," I say, my skin prickling with goose bumps. "No one at all."

3

Nico

The couple behind the glass window fucks slowly.

Music fills the room from the state-of-the-art sound system, a steady throbbing pulse meant to seduce. Muted light casts shadows on their naked bodies as they writhe in pleasure.

Massimo and I pay little attention to the peep room on the other side of the glass as we discuss business over good scotch.

While I watch over the family business, Massimo also takes care of our personal portfolios and runs a tight ship when it comes to our investments.

This club is the latest. It's called Lair and caters to a wide assortment of kinks, but its specialty is voyeurism. Based on the old peep shows, we've created a nirvana where, for a price, all your visual fantasies can come true in front of your very eyes.

Compared to our other ventures, it's not a multimillion-dollar adventure. In fact, money wasn't the motivation behind it. But since it opened a few months ago, it's proved very successful.

"You look tense," Massimo says as we conclude business.

"I'm always tense."

"Yes, but more so today."

I glance at the undulating bodies on the other side of the glass but feel nothing.

Usually, I like to watch. Hell, I like to do a lot of things. But lately, nothing gets me hard like my plans for revenge.

Except for last night.

When I finally let Bella see me at the club in Manhattan. In the seconds our gazes collided, it set off an unexpected eruption of dark anticipation in my mind, one that had a physical reaction I wasn't expecting.

I got hard as fuck.

I've been watching her for months without her knowing. Emotionlessly. Detached. Hungry for revenge. Yet the moment our eyes met, my body tightened with a physical longing that haunted me all night.

Later, in the shower, I made myself come thinking about it, hoping I could fuck my hand and forget.

But this morning, I woke up hard and carried the tension in my shoulders all day.

This ridiculous reaction tells me it's time to move forward before my feelings get any more twisted.

Massimo reaches over and refills my tumbler with scotch from the bottle on the table. "The families are growing restless. Not to mention, Luca Bamcorda. You will need to announce your plans to marry soon."

"I will."

He looks surprised. "Bianca?"

I scoff. "No. I'd rather perform brain surgery on myself."

He lifts his glass to his lips but pauses. "You're not seriously entertaining the idea of making Bella your wife?"

Massimo thinks my plans to force Bella into marriage is an impossible task. But I'm tenacious as fuck and generally get what I want because I'm prepared to do whatever it takes.

He doesn't know that I have been moving the chess pieces into place for the past six months. Or that I'm about to unleash havoc in the Isle Ciccula camp.

I take a sip of my scotch. "She'll be a suitable wife. She is used to the life."

Behind the glass, the man comes all over the woman's tits. She kneels before him, stroking his gigantic cock as thick ropes of cum splash across her chest.

Massimo fixes me with a suspicious look. "Last I heard, she abandoned the life and moved to London. Became an artist or something."

"She works at a gallery as an art curator. She paints on the side."

Massimo's brows disappear up his forehead. "You've been keeping track of her?"

"Now that she's the future Mrs. De Kysa, yes."

"I should've known, you tenacious fuck." He chuckles and sips his scotch. "You really think Vincent Isle Ciccula will go for it?"

"He won't have a choice."

"And Bella? I remember her stubbornness even as a kid. She won't be easy to convince."

"She'll do it out of duty for her father."

"Maybe, but she'll fight you."

The idea spins excitement through me. "Which will only make it more interesting."

He shakes his head. "You're really going through with it?"

"My plans are set," I assure him. "All I need to do is press the detonator."

4

Bella

I stir restlessly in my bed, my mind trapped in a dreamscape of broken memories.

The man in the dark suit stares at me from the opposite end of the corridor. His eyes black as night, his expression sharp and tight. There is no light in this man, and I'm sure that what lies beneath his rib cage is a heart just as dark as everything else about him.

But it's the rage I feel emanating from him that terrifies me. A cold, dark rage.

And all of it is for me.

I shiver, knowing I'm in danger.

I want to flee, but I'm rooted to the spot, frozen by fear. His dangerous expression sears my skin like he's just set fire to me.

What happened to you? I say the words, but my mouth doesn't move.

The Devil's Den

And then he's gone, and I'm running through the olive plantation where I grew up in Italy, laughing as the boy I love chases me to the lake at the end of the property. We discard our clothes as we run and dive into the tepid summer water, breaking the surface as we laugh. When he pulls me to him, his erect cock brushes against me, and my body heats with longing. He places perfect wet kisses along my neck and up to my mouth, making me want all of him. My nipples tighten to peaks as they brush against the hard muscle of his chest, and a new wave of longing spears through me.

It's the shrill of my phone that rips me from my dreams and pulls me back into reality. Eyes still closed, I fumble for it on the nightstand.

"Hello?" I mumble, my head murky.

"Bella, it's Harry."

My eyes flick open.

Harry is my boss at the gallery.

"Harry?" I look at the clock. It's 7:32 a.m., so it's lunchtime back in London. "Is everything okay?"

"I'm sorry, Bella, but this couldn't wait." I hear the tinkle of ice against glass and picture him with a scotch in his hand. "Look, I don't really know how to tell you this." More ice tinkles as he takes a sip. "But I'm going to have to let you go."

It takes a moment for his words to register.

I sit up, suddenly fully awake.

"You're firing me?"

"That's such a dreadful term, but yes, I suppose that's what I'm doing."

I push my bed hair out of my face. "But why?"

"Look, it's not you. Honestly, you're lovely, and your work is impeccable. It's the budget. You see, we need to free up some capital, and well, you were the last hired." More ice tinkling. Harry is self-medicating with scotch while he delivers this fatal blow, and I'm starting to think I might need some ice tinkling of my own. Five o'clock or not.

My mind scrambles. "I thought you were happy with my work, and I've brought in some big deals in the past six months—"

"And if it were up to me, we'd never let you go. But this has come from the top, Bella."

As the realization that I'm losing my job sets in, my stomach drops.

I clutch my phone to my ear. "I'll be back in London tomorrow. I'll come see you, and we can talk."

"There's really nothing to discuss, I'm afraid. As of today, you no longer work for Ulvaeus Gallery." Harry is a nice guy, somewhere in his sixties, regal and old school, but not a stiff upper lip. He's kind and generous, and this will hurt him.

"I'll need to collect my things." I sound dazed because I am. This has come out of nowhere. Last week, Ulvaeus offered me a promotion and an extended tenure to stay in London. Now they're kicking me out the door.

"No need, I'll have Lizzie pack up your belongings and deliver them to your home address. Or now that this has happened, will you be staying in the United States?"

No.

I love my life in London.

There will be another gallery.

"I really am sorry, Bella. This has come as quite the

shock." Harry sounds crushed. There is no more ice tinkling, so I assume he's consumed his three fingers of scotch.

"When I get back to London, can I call you, Harry?"

Maybe this can be sorted over Devonshire tea at the bakery down the street from the office. Surely if we put our heads together, he and I can figure something out. If not, at least I get to say goodbye to my friend.

"I suppose that would be lovely," he says resignedly. "Anyway, I must dash. Safe travels and all that."

He clicks off the call, and I'm left sitting in bed, staring at my phone, dazed and confused.

I've just been fired.

But why does it feel like that's not the worst thing that will happen today?

~

Unemployed.

It hardly seems real.

I want to call Imogen, but she's on a weekend away with a model she met at work, a very sexy Brazilian with rock-hard abs, biceps of steel, and a monster cock, and she won't be back until tomorrow. *Don't try calling. I'll be too busy riding the rocket launcher between his thighs to answer.*

And Ari is studying for his bar exam and won't turn his phone on until it's time for a cocktail at four.

I debate visiting my dad at the restaurant, but he'll take the news as a personal insult, and I'm not in the mood to manage his reaction. *Who would dare fire my daughter? She has more talent in her pinky finger than they have brains in their thick skulls.*

Instead, I decide to walk through Greenwich Village and let the vibrant hum of the neighborhood lift my spirit.

It's a perfect New York day. Warm. Sunny. Just enough breeze to kiss your skin and blow away the old energy and bring in the new.

I absorb it all. The sun on my skin. The pulse of the city beneath my feet.

In Washington Square, I take a seat on one of the many park benches and close my eyes. Sucking in a deep breath, I let the sounds and smells of the city calm my nerves.

But that's the thing.

My nerves aren't as rattled as I would expect after losing my job. Because I know I'll find another one. I already fired off several résumés this morning, and Harry said he'd give me a glowing reference.

It's only a matter of time before I'm back in London loving life again.

Yet a strange forebodingness scratches at the nape of my neck. Like a ghostly finger tickling my sixth sense, telling me something even bigger than losing my job is about to happen.

I've always been able to trust my instincts.

But I haven't always followed them.

And when I don't, the consequences have been like an ash cloud following a volcanic eruption. Unavoidable and unpleasant.

Like Simon.

I met him at an art exhibition three weeks after arriving in London. Blue eyes. Dimpled chin. Nice looking. We bonded over impressionism art, specifically Monet and Renoir. We had completely different views about it—I loved the spontaneity of it, while he called it chaotic and amateurish.

We debated. We bantered.

We fell into bed. *A lot.*

Something inside told me to steer clear. A warning that existed on the outer edges of my peripherals, clear to see but easy to ignore, especially when I was getting a generous amount of sex.

Granted, it wasn't toe-curling sex. But it was sex, nonetheless, and it gave my vibrator a break.

For a few weeks, it was good. He was attentive and generous. He'd lavish me with dinners at good restaurants and talk to me for hours about art.

But it didn't take long for the cracks to show.

A mean comment here. A backhanded compliment there.

You're a beautiful girl, Bella. If only you could drop ten pounds, you'd be perfect.

That's a cute outfit, Bella, but isn't it a little tight?

You're sexy, Bella, for a girl with lots of curves.

I always thought I'd see a toxic relationship coming a mile away. But I was in the middle of one before I realized it.

The final straw came when he told me I needed to change if I wanted to be with him.

What he didn't count on was me knowing I didn't need a man to tell me my self-worth. Or that I didn't need a man to tell me who I should be, either.

Two things a very red-faced Simon learned in a crowded coffee shop in Piccadilly one wet winter's day.

Leaving his jerk ass was easy. It was fixing the machine-gunned holes in my confidence after nine months with him that was hard.

All of a sudden, I was questioning the little things. My clothes. My thighs. My hair.

Maybe you would look prettier as a brunette, Bella.

Then without warning, I started to question the bigger things. My purpose. My tastes. My beliefs.

My art.

It's funny how someone not worth your time can silently destroy your confidence when they're not even in your life anymore.

It was my job that got me through it. Because for all the self-doubt in every other area of my life, at least I *knew* I was good at what I did.

But now my job is gone, and I'm not going to lie, it fucking sucks.

Clouds move over the sun, and out of nowhere, my thoughts drift to Nico De Kysa. *The only boy who ever really loved me.* Needless to say, he never showed up on my eighteenth birthday to whisk me away like he promised all those months earlier when we were ripped from one another's arms.

Looking for answers, I had googled him, and there he was, splashed all over social media—Nico De Kysa, the handsome playboy son of the mighty Gio De Kysa. In every photo, another beauty at his side.

Heartbroken, I'd slammed my laptop shut and built an impenetrable wall around my heart, believing that moving on was my best revenge. Nico didn't deserve any more of my tears. He didn't deserve anything from me, so I decided to forget him just as he forgot about me.

Art became my everything.
And now it's all I have left again.

I lift my face to the sunless sky and suck in a mind-clearing breath and smile to myself because whatever happens, I know I am going to be okay.

My life is an adventure full of friends, art, and cocktails.

And I will never let another knock take my confidence away from me again.

5

Nico

"This might be more trouble than it's worth," my brother says as we step out of the Escalade and start walking toward the back door of The Olive Grove, one of the best restaurants in the city.

The renowned food magazine *Finest Eats* calls it bold and innovative, with a menu that never fails to deliver. Apparently, they're booked out eleven weeks in advance.

I check the door, and it's unlocked.

For an old Mafia boss, Vincent Isle Ciccula's office is surprisingly easy to access.

"Are you sure you want to do this?" Massimo questions me, his brow furrowed with concern.

"More than I fucking want to breathe," I say, tapping into the rage that has kept me focused on my goal for the past ten years. "It kills two birds with one stone. I avoid the nightmare of marrying Bianca Bamcorda, and I get to break

Vincent Isle Ciccula's heart. So yeah, I'm fucking sure I want to do this."

I reach for the door, but Massimo stops me. "You haven't seen him in ten years."

"So?"

"You have a lot of anger toward this man. I just don't want you fucking shooting him because your emotions get the better of you."

"You know me better than that, brother. My emotions never get the better of me."

"Only because you don't have any," Massimo quips, opening the door and letting me walk in first. "Just don't murder him, okay? Not today."

"Scouts honor," I deadpan.

"Like you were ever a Scout," he mumbles as he follows me into the club's back entrance.

Behind us, two of my most trusted men follow, ready to bring hell with them if this meeting goes south.

We're met by one of Vincent's bodyguards who leads us through the kitchen to an office where the man who led my mother to suicide sits behind a desk. Two bodyguards stand in the corners of the room behind him. Seated in a chair across the room, Alberto Giabelli sits like a man who has no care in the world. But I know Alberto. Any sign of trouble and he'll have his firearm out of his shoulder holster quicker than Cool Hand Luke in a gunfight.

I ignore the older mobster and fix my gaze on the man I plan to destroy.

Massimo was right to be worried.

Being face-to-face with Vincent makes me want to put a bullet in him.

But I manage to control the pain and anger. It's something I've gotten good at in the past decade.

Vincent doesn't stand. He remains seated, his hands confidently folded in front of him on the desk. "And so the De Kysa cub finally shows his face. To what do I owe this pleasure?"

Outwardly, I maintain my poker face, but inside, I'm bristling at him calling me a cub. He's right to distinguish that I am different from my father. I'm far more ruthless, and if he calls me cub again, it's only fair to show him just how ruthless that is.

"Still a slave to the Macallan, I see," I say, nodding to the glass of amber liquid on the desk in front of him. Beside it is a bottle of the thirty-year-old single malt scotch. I know it well. Woody, smoky, and fucking delicious. Worth every penny of the thousand-dollar price tag.

Vincent offers me an empty smile with dead eyes. "Old habits die slowly."

"I suppose they do."

The atmosphere in the room is tight.

"I'm sure you didn't come here to discuss what scotch I like to drink. I hear you're the head of the De Kysa now that your father has stepped down." His tone is condescending. He thinks he has the upper hand, but he's going to find out just how wrong he is.

I decide to toy with him a little.

Payback for his condescending tone.

"Oh, I'm not here to walk down memory lane. I've come here for my money."

Vincent laughs at me, giving me another reason on the long list of reasons I should shoot him.

"And what money is that?"

"Two hundred million."

He laughs at me again. "For what?"

"The money you borrowed against your portfolio for the Lexington deal."

The blood drains from Vincent's face as the pieces tumble into place in his brain.

He's not laughing now.

"How the fuck do you know about that?" His voice is low and threatening.

I scoff and adjust the cuffs of my shirtsleeves. "You borrowed two hundred million dollars from Bramco & Stokes Financial. Bramco & Stokes Financial is owned by Sky Raker Corporation, and Sky Raker Corporation is owned by...?" I lift my eyebrows as if I'm encouraging a five-year-old to respond.

"You?" Vincent pales.

Smiling smugly, I give him a clap. "Well done, Mr. Isle Ciccula. Well done."

Now that's how you condescend someone, you wrinkled old cunt.

Vincent's hands curl into fists on the desk.

The temperature in the room plummets.

Beside me, Massimo's shoulders stiffen as he braces himself for what's about to unfold. Across the room, Alberto unwinds his crossed leg and sits forward, ready to interject.

Hell, you could cut the tension in this room with a blunt knife.

"And now, I'm calling in that loan."

Vincent's eyes narrow. "You can't do that. There's a contract."

Leaning down, I place two palms on his desk and look him square in the eyes as I deliver the fatal blow.

"Oh, I assure you I *can*, and I *am* doing that. You see, you were too desperate to secure the money and too certain that the Lexington deal would make you a filthy rich old man that you failed to fully understand what you were getting into. Specifically, the clause in the contract that says the financial institution has the discretion to pull the loan at any time." I straighten. "Well, old man, that time is here. I'm pulling the loan."

"This will never hold up," Vincent seethes. "My lawyer is the best in this goddamn town. There's no way he missed some clause."

I smile, but it's cold. "It's amazing what five million dollars will buy you these days."

Vincent's head almost explodes off his shoulders. "He's a part of this?"

"Five million dollars is a lot of money, Vincent." I see the shared look between Vincent and Alberto. He doesn't believe me. But when he visits his lawyer's swanky office on the Upper East Side, he'll find it empty. "Don't bother looking for him. He knows I'm here. He's probably halfway to his new life on an island somewhere in the Pacific Ocean. Under the protection of the De Kysa, of course."

Vincent looks like he's about to blow a gasket. He mutters something inaudible in Italian under his breath.

"It was a sure deal," he growls, and by the way he looks away, I'm pretty sure he's wondering how it all went so wrong.

"No, it was never a sure deal," I say, and his eyes dart to

mine. "You know what they say; if something is too good to be true, it probably is."

I give him a shit-eating grin to drive the stake in deeper to his pride, and that's when he realizes that the bomb blowing up in his face has been a setup from the start.

Vincent stands and pounds the desk in front of him. "You little fuck."

My two men take a step forward, ready to raise weapons, but I shake my head. Bullets aren't going to slay Vincent Isle Ciccula today. Financial ruin is going to do the honors. I'm going to take everything except his life from him, beginning with his fortune.

And after I wipe out his kingdom, I'm taking his daughter too.

"You set me up," he fumes.

"Yes."

"You created a phony business opportunity to try to ruin me?"

"Oh, I'm not *trying* to ruin you, Vincent. I *am* ruining you." Venom drips off every word. "And, yes, I dangled the Lexington deal in front of your greedy little eyes, and you took the bait like a rabid dog."

I started planning this the moment I found out what really happened the night my mother died. I decided Vincent Isle Ciccula needed to learn what it felt like to lose everything. So I formulated a plan to ruin him by forcing him into so much debt he would be forced into bankruptcy and lose the lifestyle he'd spent his life building.

It was never about taking Bella from him. But now that I need a wife, I'm taking her too, and well, that's just the goddamn cherry on top.

"This will get you thrown in prison. The FBI doesn't take kindly to this kind of bullshit."

I scoff. "Don't you worry about me, old man. It's not about who you know. It's about how much you're willing to pay them off."

Did he really think I didn't come prepared for this fight? That I don't have government officials eating candy out of my palm?

He sneers. "You have some balls on you."

"And you have twenty-four hours to come up with the full two hundred million or face financial ruin."

Vincent realizes I have him over a barrel. His eyes blaze with hatred as he slowly sits in his chair. He waits a moment before he speaks. When he does, his voice is gravelly. "What do you want?"

I smile, and it's smug. "You're going to give me Bella."

A fresh wave of hostility rolls off him. "Her name even slips from your lips again, *young cub*, and I will cut them off and shove them up your fucking ass."

My chuckle is cold and void of humor. I have to hand it to the old man. He's creative with the threats.

But he's going to have to do more than that to stop this barreling train. It has ten years of hatred fueling it.

Ignoring his threats, I twist the ring on my pinky finger and offer him a look of indifference. "I can make all your troubles disappear, Vincent, just like that." I snap my fingers. "All you have to do is give me your daughter."

"Never," he seethes.

"Are you sure about that? Think about it. Everything you have worked hard for, everything you escaped Italy to build will be gone. But I'm offering you an out."

"For the price of my daughter."

"Arranged marriages are not new in our world."

That's not a lie. In fact, they're more common than not, especially for his generation. I'm surprised he hasn't already ensured that Bella will marry well. But then again, if watching Bella for the past few months has taught me anything, it's that she is still a fierce heart and won't easily be forced to do something she doesn't want to do.

Her learning about this bomb will be an enjoyable experience to watch.

"She will be well taken care of," I add. "She will be under my protection and want for nothing."

By the expression on Vincent's face and the sag of his shoulders, I know I'm wearing him down. He's cornered, and inside his thick skull, he's scrambling to come up with another way out of the mess he's in. But there is no other way out.

"What was the point of all of this?" he asks.

Finally, an interesting question.

"You fucked with me and my family."

"Because I took Bella away from all the bloodshed and pain?"

"No, because you helped destroy my mother." The truth curdles in my chest. "The De Kysa and the Isle Ciccula have been sworn enemies since the night my mother died, and you escaped to America with Bella. It should come as no surprise that the moment I took the crown from my father, I would come looking for revenge."

"You know nothing of that night," he spits.

"I know my mother died, and you left. It doesn't take a genius to work out one event gave birth to the other."

His face is as cold as ice, a stark contrast to the hatred burning like wildfire in his eyes.

"You don't know shit," he mutters.

I slam my palm down, and the desk rattles beneath it. "I know that it changed everything. And now I am here for retribution."

"Retribution for taking my daughter away from you?" He scoffs and shakes his head.

"No, it goes much deeper than that." I drag my finger along the edge of his desk as I move around it to stand behind him. "You need to pay for everything that happened."

"Then why go to all this trouble for revenge when you could just kill me?"

"You're right. I could kill you and then just take Bella and force her to marry me."

"Then that is what you will have to do. Because I will never give you my consent."

I stand behind him, savoring the moment as I stare down at his sagging shoulders.

"Hmm. I don't think so. That'd be too easy for you and less satisfying for me. You see, I want you alive and kicking so you can see me take everything from you." I lean down to whisper in his ear. "And I want you to know what it feels like to lose her."

6

Bella

"You're both insane if you think I'll agree to this."

I look at my father and then at my godfather, Alberto, disgusted by the suggestion. We're sitting in a leather booth at my father's popular restaurant on West 44th Street. His birthday dinner is over and we are alone.

All evening, I knew something wasn't right. But he downplayed his sullen mood until about two minutes ago when he confessed about the meeting with Domenico De Kysa.

A heavy knot tightens in my chest.

Why the hell does Domenico De Kysa want me to be his wife?

What does he stand to get out of this ridiculous arrangement?

I assume it's to gloat about the delirious power he has over my family.

I can tell there's more bad news coming. Something my

father is struggling to tell me. "He has us at a disadvantage, Bella. He's in a position to take everything we've worked so hard for."

"What do you mean? How could he possibly do that?"

My father's jaw clenches. "A while back, I was presented with a business deal. I stood to make a lot of money. But to make a lot of money, sometimes you need to borrow a lot of money."

A tingling sensation crawls into my gut. "You borrowed money?"

He nods, and going by the grave look on his face, I know it must be a lot.

"How much?" I ask, feeling sick.

"Two hundred million."

The number hits me like a bomb going off in the room.

"Two hundred—" I sit back in my chair, winded. Who even has that kind of money? "What about the deal you invested in? Will the returns be able to pay it back?"

My father shakes his head. "It collapsed. It was a fraud."

I frown. My father is a clever businessman, but somehow, he was duped out of two hundred million. My breath catches on the figure again, wondering how the hell he could ever pay that amount back.

"How does Nico figure into the scenario?"

"He owns the financial institution, and he's foreclosing on the loan." My father's face is grim. "He can take everything, Bella, but he won't if you agree to marry him."

My head spins, and the heartache and anger I already feel for the boy who broke my heart all those years ago have just morphed into a dark hatred in a matter of minutes.

He is going to take everything from my father—from my family—unless I marry him.

I should've known the moment I saw him that he would unleash havoc on my life.

Hatred rattles my bones. "The investment... did he create that to back you into a corner?"

When my father nods, the hatred I feel toward Nico morphs into a giant monster in my chest. Every muscle in my body tenses with tight, unchecked anger.

"He set you up," I whisper, shocked.

"Yes."

I don't know why I am surprised.

It seems Domenico De Kysa is a man who gets what he wants, when he wants it.

Including me, that resentful little voice whispers.

My heart stops and dies and turns black.

"Why?" Tears prick at my eyes, but I refuse them entry. It will be a cold day in hell before I shed one more tear over the Heartless King from the North.

"He wants control of the entire eastern border. Marrying you will give him New York."

I stare at my father and then at Alberto. "What do you mean?"

My father is a businessman. How will marrying me help Nico gain control over the East Coast?

A second bomb goes off, and I sink back in my chair.

Well, fuck.

"It's all been a lie, hasn't it?" I say, feeling the onset of betrayal crawl through me. "You never severed ties with your old life. You just got good at lying to me."

"Bella—"

It's all so suddenly clear that I feel foolish for not seeing it sooner.

"You never gave up the Mafia life when we moved to America," I say. "You're still involved with all of it."

Boy, he hid it well.

"You don't leave the business, Bella," my father says. "Unless it's in a body bag."

"Even Domenico De Kysa couldn't leave it if he wanted to," Alberto adds. "The choice leaves us the moment we commit to the life."

"So all this time, you've still been involved in organized crime—"

"Bella." My father's voice is laced with warning.

It's the number one rule. You never talk about organized crime when you're neck-deep in it.

I just stare at him.

Feeling blindsided.

Feeling betrayed.

My family is still at war with the De Kysa, and apparently, now I am the key to ending the rivalry in the world I didn't even know I still lived in.

The world that took my mother and brother from me.

I'm also the only thing standing between my father and bankruptcy.

No pressure here. None at all.

"He's really going to take everything?" I ask.

He's destroying my life and ruining my father for control of the eastern shipping border into America. There is so much to unpack, I don't even know where to start.

My father nods reluctantly. "Yes."

"Surely, there are other ways for him to gain control of

the border," I say. "Forcing me to marry him seems a little over the top." *Not to mention psychopathic.*

Which is another thing I'll need to unpack later.

"Cara mia, he's not doing this just for control. He's doing this for revenge."

My eyes fly to my father. "Revenge? For what?"

He's the one who broke his vow to find me.

He's the one who left an eighteen-year-old heartbroken and confused.

"There is much you don't know," my father says.

"Then best you inform me," I reply in a harsh tone. "If I'm expected to marry this... monster. What happened that made him so vengeful?"

My father's jaw is set, his thickly lashed eyes hard. "He's a De Kysa, Bella. They're hot-headed sons of bitches. They're also prepared to do whatever it takes to get what they want, and Nico wants to control everything coming in and out of Boston and New York."

"And marrying me will give him that."

Somewhere buried very deep inside me, it hurts to know I'm nothing more than a pawn in his game of power. When once upon a time, I was his everything.

Alberto leans forward. "The Irish and Russians are making a play for the border. With the De Kysa and Isle Ciccula in an alliance, they won't try. They'll die."

Nausea crawls into my stomach.

My father sighs. "He has me over a barrel. You could refuse—"

"No, I won't refuse," I say with a rush of anger. I won't have that asshole take my father's kingdom from him. I won't give him that satisfaction. "I will marry the son of a bitch if that means you don't lose everything."

I will marry Satan. I will be his wife. I will plaster a smile on my face in public but turn away from him the moment we're out of view. I will live in London, and he can reside in hell, where he belongs.

I'll be damned if he gets anything more than that.

My father pauses, searching for the right words. "I want you to know that I would not ask this of you if it wasn't necessary. I would never put you in harm's way."

I give him a dark look. "It sounds like you've been doing that my entire life."

His eyes drop as he plays with the heavy ring on his pinky finger. "You loved him once."

"When we were children. And if I remember correctly, you destroyed that friendship. You broke my heart and then told me I had to get the fuck over it."

His eyes flick up. My father loathes me cussing. "For the sake of peace."

"There has been no peace, apparently. And now it all rests on my shoulders." I don't know who I'm more angry with—my father for all of his lies or the asshole demanding my hand in marriage.

"It's a business transaction. You'll be married in name only."

"Fantastic," I reply, unable to keep the bitterness out of my voice.

"The marriage will last for twelve months. You will appear on his arm as his wife in public. It's a role, Bella. Nothing more."

"And such a small price to pay for peace," Alberto adds.

"Says the man whose entire existence hasn't been reduced to arm candy in the last five minutes."

My father looks tired. "Cara mia—"

"Fine," I snap. "But I want an airtight agreement that this is nothing more than a business deal. And I will be filing for an annulment twelve months and one day after the wedding."

I think about the boy I had loved with all my heart.

How I thought I would die when we moved from Italy to America.

Back then, I was so in love with him.

But now I hate him.

Just as my father wanted me to.

7

Nico

I wait and watch from the back seat of the Escalade. Forty-five minutes ago, Bella entered The Olive Grove to meet with her father and Alberto.

From what my sources have told me, she has no idea her father is still involved in the old ways. Apparently, Vincent Isle Ciccula fed her a lie when they moved to the US, told her he'd shed his Mafia skin, and pursued a more honorable life as a restaurateur and visionary entrepreneur.

But it was all a facade.

Oh sure, he set up his restaurants and invested wisely in start-ups here and there, but he remained very much a part of the old world.

We've been at war ever since the night my mother died. Both sides have taken a hit. His men versus my father's men —who are now my men, now that my father has stepped down.

And Bella had been none the wiser as she etched out her safe little life in London with her safe boyfriends and her safe dreams.

Pain shoots through my jaw before I realize I'm clenching my teeth hard enough to hurt them.

Back in London, it was hard to watch her with other men, especially that asshole with the blue blood and crooked nose. He was an earl of something and utterly wrong for her. He dimmed her fire, something I don't plan on doing once we're married.

I don't want to dim her anything.

I want to ignite it and feel her hellfire sear my skin.

Inside the Escalade, there's no sound except for the steady sound of my heartbeat in my ears as I wait.

Bella's been inside long enough to learn her fate, and I figure about now she realizes how duped she's been.

That her world is about to change.

That she's about to become my wife.

I'd give anything to see the look on her face when her father tells her that he has brokered the marriage.

Like other dons before me, witnessing the moment someone realizes their fate has become an addiction of mine. That split second when they understand that everything has changed is charged with so much power and retribution, it's intoxicating.

My own came to me as a boy of seventeen, and it shaped me into the man I am today.

It's almost midnight when she finally reappears. She steps out of the restaurant looking lost in thought, and I can't help the kick in my chest when I see those beautiful curls blow in the gentle evening wind.

She hails a taxi and stops to look both ways before crossing the street and sliding into the yellow cab. When they pull away, as per my instruction, Mateo, my trusted driver, pulls away from the curb, and we follow her through the glittering New York City streets.

Several miles down the road, the cab suddenly swerves to the curb, and Bella exits and disappears inside the all-night bodega. Mateo stops on the other side of the street, and from my vantage point, I watch her select a bottle of wine off the shelf. She begins to walk away but thinks better of it and turns back to grab a second bottle of wine.

A small smile plays on my lips but quickly vanishes.

She makes her purchase, then returns to the yellow cab.

It's a ten-minute drive to her loft in Greenwich Village. By the time we arrive, it's raining, and heavy drops thrum against the roof of the Escalade as I watch her step onto the drenched sidewalk and stop.

I expect her to disappear inside her apartment building. But she doesn't.

Instead, as the cab pulls away, she stands in the rain and tips her head back as far as she can to catch the raindrops on her face. Her eyes close, and a small smile spreads across her wet lips as she holds her hands out to her side and twirls.

Inside my chest, my black heart twists at the tiny display of happiness.

I lean forward as if I'm leaning closer to her and watch her red-gold curls dampen and disappear under the weight of the rainwater until her hair hangs in long tendrils down her back.

She's soaking wet but still twirling. Though her eyes are

open now and looking up at the rain falling through the ribbons of light from the streetlight.

She laughs, and even though I can't hear it, I feel it all the way down to my dark soul. I can't look away. I'm utterly mesmerized, and the sudden ache to taste the rain on her pink lips is crushing.

I sit back.

Best not to think those things.

Especially considering what I have planned for her.

She stops suddenly, as if she's aware of my presence, and stares into the dark street, searching for what is out of place. The smile falls from her lips, and she looks unsure. *Afraid.*

And she should be.

Because I'm the monster hiding in the shadows just out of view.

And I'm coming for her.

8

Bella

"So what do you know about him?" Imogen asks, taking a sip of her wine. We're sitting in a booth at our favorite bar in the Lower East Side called Humpty's. It's a dark and moody cocktail den with masculine leather booths, terrazzo floors, and cute lanterns on the tables.

When I told her I needed to see her, I suggested we meet somewhere where alcohol was in vast supply. Humpty's is popular with the lunchtime crowd who enjoy liquid with their lunch.

"Only that he's an asshole forcing me to marry him," I reply.

"What else?"

"Do I need to know anything else?"

"Have you googled him?"

For the past ten years, I've resisted googling him.

"No." I almost drain my glass with the huge mouthful of

wine I take. "My first instinct when my father and godfather told me I was to marry a monster was to call you."

"So let me get this straight, he says if you marry him, he'll end ten years of bloodshed *and* forget the debt."

"Yes."

Her eyes gleam. "I knew your daddy was still in the business."

I cock an eyebrow at her. "You're not helping."

Imogen whips out her phone and starts looking while I finish my wine in another mouthful.

"Oh my God, Bella..." She looks at me, her face drained of all expression. "He's the most beautiful human being in the world."

I squeeze my eyes closed. "Don't say that."

"Oh wow! He owns a gazillion businesses around town." She keeps reading from the screen. "It says he's taken New York by storm since arriving in town eighteen months ago. They say he has the Midas touch because everything he touches turns to gold. I knew his face looked familiar. He's been all over the papers and magazines."

A strange tingle takes up in my stomach.

"Look!" she insists.

When I open my eyes, she holds up her phone so I can see a photo. And there he is, looking back at me from the screen in all his custom-suit glory.

My jaw tightens.

Blackmailing son of a bitch.

I signal the server for another drink while Imogen keeps cyberstalking my future husband.

Just as my drink arrives, a stunning blonde appears at our booth. She is clutching a massive planner.

"Bella?"

"Yes."

She thrusts an elegant hand at me. "My name is Anastacia. I'm Domenico's assistant."

Cautiously, I accept her hand. "Nice to meet you."

She smiles, but it's aloof. "Domenico suggested I introduce myself since we'll be spending some time together in the future."

"Nico knows I'm here?" I glance around the room but can't see him. "How?"

Her smile doesn't waver, but it doesn't reach her eyes either. "He owns this place."

Of course, he does.

She glances at one of the CCTV cameras in the corner of the room. Cameras I've never noticed before.

"You mean he's watching us?" I ask.

She looks amused as if my question was ridiculously silly. "No, he's not here. He simply left instructions for me to introduce myself when you next came in. Our security team noticed you. I'm not interrupting anything, am I?"

I glance at Imogen who is watching this encounter unfold with rampant fascination.

"No, not at all." I indicate for her to sit down.

"It's lovely to finally meet you. I've heard a lot about you." She sits down but keeps her distance. "I was hoping we could schedule a time for your wedding dress fitting."

"Sure," I say. Although a part of me still prays for a stay of execution.

"What about the other wedding arrangements?" Imogen asks her. "Can I help?"

"Oh, they've already been taken care of," Anastacia

replies, then turns to me. "When you've got time, I can go over them with you."

"They're already organized?"

Things are moving fast.

Too freaking fast.

"Of course. I started organizing things the moment Domenico told me about the..." She looks for the right word. "Arrangement."

Something about her is decisively cool.

"Getting the botanical gardens wasn't easy on such short notice, but when it's for one of the most important men in the city, let's just say the De Kysa name can make magic happen." She opens her planner and removes a glossy pamphlet, then slides it across the table to me. "I was able to get you a fitting with Magda Bianchon for next week—"

"Magda Bianchon!" Imogen gasps. Her eyes flick to mine, excited because Magda Bianchon is the fashion world's current it woman when it comes to wedding couture, and if you want to get your hands on one of her gowns, then booking at least a year in advance is a necessity.

"When I mentioned it was for Domenico De Kysa's future wife, Magda was only too happy to squeeze you into her busy schedule." She flicks her long blonde hair over her shoulder. "Oh, and I've arranged for Ken Winchester to design and arrange your hair on the day."

Ken Winchester is the it boy of hair.

Magda and Ken.

I have a feeling Anastacia could run the entire planet with her planner.

"Have you given any thought to when you'll move all of your belongings back to the States?" she asks.

Her question catches me off guard. "Excuse me?"

She glances up at the CCTV cameras nervously, then her eyes dart back to me. "It was one of the conditions in the agreement."

Beside me, Imogen's mouth drops open.

While I can't keep the edge out of my voice. "I'm not moving back to the US."

Before she can stop herself, Anastacia laughs. "But of course, you are. Domenico is a very important man—"

"I don't care if he's Christ reborn, I'm not giving up my life in London."

I might've lost my job at Ulvaeus, but I have a reputation in London. I will find a new job because I'm good at what I do.

And hell will freeze over before I give up working to be a trophy wife.

Anastacia's cool eyes remain on mine. "Well, that is something you will have to take up with him. But surely you don't expect to live in different countries when you're married. Domenico would never relocate. You'll be expected to make a life in New York with him."

Imogen and I both stare at her with our mouths agape.

Anastasia looks uncomfortable. "But like I said, you'll need to discuss that with him."

"Great. Let's get onto that."

"Now?" she balks.

"No time like the present."

"That's impossible, I'm afraid. Nico is in important meetings all afternoon."

She's lying.

In fact, the way she keeps glancing at the CCTV cameras tells me that there's a good chance he's watching.

I stand. "Where is he?"

"Excuse me?"

"Nico. I know he's here."

Her expression falters briefly but long enough for me to know I'm right.

Catching one of the CCTV cameras in my peripheral, I lift a middle finger to it and mouth the word, "Asshole."

I look back at Anastacia.

"Take me to him," I demand.

"I assure you, he isn't here."

"My ass, he isn't."

"He's not—"

"Fine, if you won't help me, then I'll find him myself."

I scoot out of the booth and storm through the cocktail den looking for anything that resembles an exit, running my hand along the walnut paneling for concealed doors, and banging on the stamped tin walls, much to the confusion of the small lunch crowd. I don't care that I look like a crazy woman.

Because I am crazy.

Crazy angry.

"Bella, please—" Anastacia calls behind me.

In my determination to confront him, I somehow manage to find the concealed doorway near the bar before security can stop me, and I push it open. It leads to a flight of stairs barely visible in the dim light, and with Anastacia and Imogen close behind me, I run up the stairs, taking two at a time like I'm an Olympic sprinter.

If Nico bloody De Kysa thinks he can tell me what to do,

then he's about to learn a very valuable lesson.

Bella Isles Ciccula is no fucking pushover.

Give up my life in London?

The man is fucking insane if he thinks I'm giving up anything to marry him.

Upstairs, it's a whole new world. Plush carpet. Marble walls. Chandeliers hanging from the vaulted ceiling. Everything in a shade of white.

But I barely take it all in as I storm down the hallway, ready to lose my shit.

I stop at a pair of closed twin doors. He's behind those doors. I just know it. I can't explain how I know or why.

I just know.

Furious, I push down on the elegant gold doorknobs and burst through the doors.

He is sitting behind a large desk looking at something on his computer screen.

"Who the hell do you think you are?" I yell.

A mean-looking man with no hair and big arms steps toward me, but Nico stops him with a wave of his hand as he slowly rises to his feet.

"Bella—"

"You chauvinistic jerk!" I spit out, slightly breathless from storming up the stairs because clearly, I am *not* an Olympic sprinter.

"Domenico, I'm so sorry!" Anastacia pants as she and Imogen grind to a halt behind me.

But I ignore them.

"You think you can snap your fingers, and I'll do what you say?" I take an angry step farther into the room. "It doesn't work that way, buddy. If you want a wife who will give up everything she has worked hard for, then I strongly advise that you find somebody else to marry. Do you know how hard I worked to get where I am today? I've worked my ass to the bone, that's how hard. I've put in hours that would make you weak just thinking about them. So if you think I'll give it all up for a narcissistic, chauvinistic asshole who wants to boss me around, then you're as delusional as you are a manipulative jerk!"

My tirade makes me out of breath.

It also makes me slightly emotional.

Nico simply stares back at me, his arms folded across his chest, his stupidly beautiful face calm and assured.

I hate him.

I hate him so much my bones ache.

Yet seeing him for the first time in ten years, my heart lets out a sigh.

"Why?" I glare at him, my anger deepening when I remember I'm standing in front of the boy who broke my heart.

Nico moves slowly around his desk and clears the room with a nod. Imogen looks at me questioningly. Silently asking me if I want her to leave. I give her a small nod, and she leaves with a pinched-face Anastacia. I turn back to glare at Nico and am only vaguely aware of the two bodyguards leaving when the door clicks quietly behind them.

"I've agreed to your sick business deal in the name of peace, at least show me the same respect and tell me why," I demand.

"Why what?"

I hate that his deep and smooth voice sounds like a sexy voice-over actor.

"Why me? If you need a wife so badly, why didn't you pick from the legion of women clamoring for the attention of the Heartless King from the North?" I glare at him. "Why pick the girl whose heart you broke?"

The words tumble out, thoughtlessly, and I regret them immediately. The last thing I need is for him to think he has any kind of power over me. Or that him failing to show up on my eighteenth birthday actually meant something to me.

Yet there they are, out in the open. The admission that he did indeed break my heart.

His dark brows pull together but slowly smooth back into place.

He opens his mouth to reply, but I don't give him a chance to respond because I'm on Angry Avenue, and it's a one-way street.

Plus, I don't think I'm ready to hear the answer.

"Expecting me to give up my career just because we're married is chauvinistic and archaic. We will be married in name only."

"But we will reside in the United States."

"Why, if it is in name only?"

"My wife is expected to be with me at all public events. And I travel a lot for business."

"I don't care if you travel to Mars for business. I'm not giving up my career to be your Stepford wife!"

"I'm open for negotiation."

"You say that like it's something I'm prepared to negotiate, and it's not." I step closer and shove a pointed finger in his rock-hard chest. "Let's get one thing straight, Mr. De Kysa. I may have agreed to marry you, but I won't be forced to do anything else. Do you understand me?"

Infuriatingly, he unfolds his arms as if he doesn't have a care in the world and takes a predatory step closer. "You're just as bullheaded as I knew you would be." His eyes are impossibly dark. His scent full of the dark notes of musk and testosterone and sin. "It's good to see some things don't change."

I don't know what maddens me more. Him looking so fucking hot, or the fact that he is completely unfazed by my outburst.

I cross my arms. "Are you kidding me? That's all you have to say?"

"I know this probably comes as a surprise. But it will all make sense in time," he says.

He's so confident, it's sickening.

"Ugh, you're so...infuriating!" My arms fall open. "What does that even mean?"

He steps closer, and I forget to move, momentarily spellbound by the look on his face. It's a mix of darkness and warning, and suddenly, I'm sucked into his orbit and unable to look away, let alone move.

I grit my teeth. "Whatever you're about to say, don't bother. Unless you're about to tell me you take it all back and I don't have to marry you. Otherwise, don't waste your breath. Nothing you can say will make any of this okay."

A hint of amusement sparkles in his eyes.

"I can see you're going to be a giant pain in my ass," he says calmly.

"Good!" I snap, turning away from him and walking toward the door. "Because I'd hate for that to be a fucking surprise."

9

Nico

She slams the door, and the sound waves ripple through the room.

She's going to be a handful.

A real pain in the ass.

Why does that excite me so much?

A smile tugs at my lips. Because she's a firecracker, and I would expect nothing less.

My body hums from the encounter. I was hard the moment I looked up from my desk and saw her standing in the doorway, her beautiful eyes blazing with anger, her wild red hair swirling around her like fire.

I had expected it. The moment she'd looked at the CCTV camera and flipped me the bird, I knew I had poked the bear, and oh, how I ached for the bite.

Another smile spreads across my lips as I think about her stomping toward me and shoving her finger into my chest.

About the way she stood up to me with so much heat in her words.

In my world, men die for less.

But she hates me too much to be afraid of me.

Because I let her down.

Why pick the girl whose heart you broke?

Anger crawls up my spine at the memory, and my smile vanishes.

Because I learned the truth.

I reach for my phone and place it to my ear. When the familiar voice answers, I say, "Follow her."

Then I hang up.

I return to my desk and sit down. Opening the bottom drawer, I remove a bottle of grappa and splash the grapey liquid into a glass tumbler. Taking a mouthful, I shake my head.

I've set something in play, and as much as I think I'm in control, I have a feeling Bella will try to ensure that I'm not.

But I hope she's prepared for a fight. Because she has no idea what I'm capable of.

10

Bella

The ridiculously large flower arrangement arrives at my apartment the following morning.

I watch as the deliveryman brings it in and places it on a table covered in brushes, spatulas, and squeezed tubes of acrylic paint.

I look at the card.

Let's start over.

N

The nerve of him. Thinking he can win me over with a bunch of flowers.

He didn't even have the balls to bring them to me himself.

Although he is right to stay away because I'd probably throw them at him.

I signal to the delivery guy not to leave before quickly scribbling my reply on the back of the card.

Let's not start at all.
B

I tuck it back into the flower arrangement. The delivery guy looks uncomfortable, and I feel bad for him, so I tip him twenty and thank him for ensuring the flowers are promptly returned to Nico.

"And make sure you bill him for the return trip."

I'm probably being childish. But fuck it. Let him understand early on that I can't be won over.

Forcing him out of my mind, I return my attention to the canvas in front of me. It's an abstract piece created in layered plaster of paris and marble dust, and colored in rust and patina hues.

The day drags by slowly, and despite being in my happy place with a paintbrush in my hand, I feel edgy and restless, and I can barely keep my mind focused.

Across the room, my laptop calls out to me.

Begging me to do what I've avoided doing for so long.

With a sigh, I concede defeat. I put down my brush and walk over to it.

Opening it, I google Nico.

My emotions immediately spin in circles when I see his photos splashed all over the internet.

Nico looking like all kinds of sin in a custom suit.

Nico looking like an international player as he arrives at a glittering social event.

Nico leaving a café looking perfectly put together in casual clothing.

A shirtless Nico covered in tattoos and looking like a god emerging from the ocean in some glamorous location somewhere in the world. His muscular body is wet and his shorts cling to him, leaving nothing to the imagination.

Domenico De Kysa is hung like a fucking donkey.

So my mind hasn't embellished the memories of those nights in the barn when he made me moan and come with his name on my lips.

I shake my head as if I can shake those memories loose forever and force them out of my head. If I could, I would set fire to those memories and bury the ashes at sea.

Exhaling deeply, I refocus on the screen in front of me. The internet contains plenty of information about him.

How he grew up in a small coastal town in Italy.

How he took over the reins of the family business when his father stepped down.

How he came to America, and everyone fell in love with him.

They even touch on his rumored association with organized crime. But it is more glamorized than condemned.

They don't even know the half of it.

He is Mr. New York.

Rich.

Handsome.

Powerful.

I shut my laptop in disgust.

I hate him.

In the living room, I whip off my bra and put on my favorite well-worn John Lennon T-shirt and a pair of faded pink bed shorts I bought back in college.

Ten minutes later, I stare mindlessly at the TV screen as I spoon chocolate fudge ice cream into my mouth, not caring that it drips down my chin.

Tomorrow night is our engagement party—a fact I only learned this morning via a rather curt email from Anastacia— and I'm praying for a miracle to stop all of this nonsense from taking place.

Maybe there will be a terrible weather event or a telecommunications outage.

Hell, perhaps aliens will land and make first contact.

Or maybe—just maybe—Nico fucking De Kysa will grow a heart and tell me the deal is off, and I can be on my merry way.

The buzz of the doorbell makes me drop the spoon of ice cream onto my T-shirt. *Dammit.*

"Hold on!" I call out, running to the bathroom to quickly rinse the ice cream off before it stains. In my haste, water splashes down the front of my shirt, completely soaking the fabric.

The door buzzer rings impatiently, so I give up what I'm doing. It'll be Imogen, and she'll have wine—hopefully lots of it.

Except when I look through the peephole, it isn't Imogen.

It's Nico.

Reluctantly, I open the door.

"What are you doing here?"

His scent hits me with the force of a tsunami. Spicy notes of sandalwood and the earthy perfume of the woods after rain. It's infuriatingly sexy. And I hate it. Just like I hate him.

"I felt bad after our encounter yesterday," he says as if he isn't a monster forcing me into marriage. "It's not how I wanted our first meeting to be."

I scoff. "Like you feel bad about anything. You don't have a conscience."

Amusement twinkles in his dark eyes, and I get the feeling he likes the way I fight him.

A self-assured smile spreads his perfect lips. "Can I come in?"

No. You. Can. Not. Come. In.

Is what my heart and head scream.

But to avoid a battle on my doorstep, I open the door the rest of the way to the enemy.

His eyes sweep over me, and I'm suddenly very aware that I have no bra on, and that my nipples have tightened to points poking through John Lennon's forehead.

"Nice shirt," he says in a voice laced with seduction and heat.

I hurriedly cross my arms over my chest. "How did you find out where I live? Let me guess, Anastacia and her trusty planner?"

He smiles, and I hate how the two dimples on either side of his full lips press into his cheeks and how his teeth are white and perfectly straight. I'm tempted to step closer so I can check to see if he has fangs.

"I know everything about this town."

I pull a face at his self-assurance. "What are you doing here? Have you come to inflict more ridiculous demands on me?"

"I know what I am asking of you is —"

"Preposterous? Archaic? The idea of an insane man?"

He raises a dark eyebrow. "I was going to say unique."

"That would be an interesting use of the word," I mutter.

As I close my front door, he casts a gaze around my modest apartment. "You sent back my flowers."

I fold my arms. "I did."

He smiles. "Nice touch."

"Thank you. Did it get my point across?"

"That you don't like flowers? Absolutely."

"No. I love flowers. But you can't bribe me with them. And just for the record, you're not going to impress me with money, gifts, or by showing me how awesome you are. All the money in the world won't change how I feel about you and this absurd situation."

"Duly noted."

The damp fabric of my T-shirt clings to my breasts, and I silently curse the fact that I'm not wearing a bra.

"What are you doing here?" I demand.

"I wanted to apologize."

"For forcing me to marry you?"

He gives me a half smile and begins to move around the room. "I thought perhaps we should start over. After all, we're going to be married."

"Thanks for the reminder."

He pauses at the canvas I was working on earlier. He leans in to study it, saying nothing as his gaze roams over every stroke of my paintbrush. Finally, he says, "You're very talented."

I don't know why it makes me angry to hear it. Probably because my art is my happy place, and he is the complete opposite.

I narrow my eyes at him. "Say what you came to say and then leave."

He looks away from the canvas, amused. "You don't take compliments very well."

"No, I don't take being bullied and manipulated into marrying someone very well."

He turns to face me, and it's hard not to acknowledge why New York has fallen in love with him. His presence is larger than life. Custom suit. Chiseled good looks. An impersonation of Satan down pat.

"I thought I should bring you this." He reaches into his breast pocket and removes a velvet box and hands it to me.

I know what it is before I even open it.

But even then, I can't stifle the gasp when I open it to see the biggest diamond ring winking at me from a bed of black velvet.

It's a square-cut diamond on a band of platinum gold. Simple and elegant. And so clear and pure that it could probably settle the national debt.

Nico removes the ring and slides it onto my finger.

"Now it's official," he says.

He smiles, and for a split second, I see the ghost of the boy I used to love, and my stomach twists into a thousand tiny knots.

No, that boy is long gone.

I sigh, worn out by my emotions. "Why are you doing this, Domenico?"

"Why do you call me Domenico?"

"It's your name, isn't it?"

He pauses. "You never used to call me Domenico. It was always Nico."

"I never used to loathe the very sight of you either, but here we are."

The Devil's Den

He smirks. "You used to love me."

I tense and take a step back, suddenly vulnerable at the mention of our past.

Him saying it with a smirk twists the knots in my stomach so tight I could double over with pain.

"I stopped loving you the night of my eighteenth birthday. You remember that date, don't you, Domenico? It was the night you were supposed to come and find me... isn't that what you said when we were torn apart as teenagers? *I will find you. No matter where you are.* Well, you're a decade too late and I am no longer interested."

"Ah, the naive promises of a naive young man who had yet to learn the truth about love and all the dark shadows that live there," he says with an edge to his voice. His eyes burn with a dark fire as he steps closer, towering over me. "Do you want to know why I chose not to come that night?"

Even though it's been ten years, hearing him admit he chose not to find me hurts. Because somewhere deep inside me, I was still clinging to the hope that maybe I'd gotten it wrong. That some wild act of God had prevented him from finding me and whisking me away to be his queen. A flood or a tornado, perhaps. A coma. *Fucking anything.* But to hear that he chose not to show up... it still fucking stings after all this time.

I tighten my jaw. "No, I don't want to know. Because your reason means nothing to me. Just like you mean nothing to me." He glares at me, and I glare back. "You might've backed me into a corner so I have to marry you. But nothing in this world will make me love you."

His eyes grow darker, if that is even possible, and they narrow. "Is that so?"

"I'm just your toy. You can bend me any which way you like, and you can play make-believe with me until the cows come home. But just like a toy, I won't feel anything toward you. It will all be in your head. Do you understand me? Nothing but the imagination of a sad little rich man."

He takes a menacing step toward me, and the temperature in the room drops dramatically.

"Make no mistake, Bella, you will be my wife," he growls. "You will take my name, my legacy, my family fortune, and in return, I will have everything you have to offer." He sweeps his gaze up and down the length of me. "Mind and body."

Goose bumps ripple across my skin.

"You're delusional if you think I'll let you touch me."

He backs me up until I feel the wall behind me. "Do you know what I do to men who don't give me what I want?" His eyes are impossibly dark. "I take it."

I grit my teeth. "Of course, you do. Because that's what monsters do."

His gaze burns, and the menace in his eyes is deep and violent.

Slowly, the corner of his lips tug. "Good to see you're a fast learner, Bella. Because that's exactly what I am."

He turns away and stalks toward the door.

"What happened to you?" I call out. "What happened to the boy I grew up with?"

He stops, his back to me.

Slowly, he turns around.

His face is tight.

His eyes impossibly dark.

His voice is low and dangerous. "He died."

And with that, he turns and leaves.

11

Nico

"You insult me." Luca Bamcorda's fat face turns red with indignation.

We're in my office above the cocktail den where Bella confronted me about our arranged marriage only three days ago in an encounter I've tried and failed to get out of my head.

"That was not my intention," I say calmly.

"I don't give a fuck if it was your intention or not. You disrespect my daughter by refusing to marry her. And you disrespect me by taking an Isle Ciccula bride."

"Might I remind you that I was betrothed to Bella long before Bianca came into the picture."

"That was before Vincent Isle Ciccula fucked your mother—"

I'm out of my chair so quick, he doesn't even see my gun until it's pressed into the spongy skin of his fat neck.

"You ever disrespect my mother like that again, and I won't hesitate putting a fucking bullet through that filthy mouth of yours. This is your only warning."

Luca doesn't move or seem flustered by the business end of my Ruger pressing dangerously close to his jugular vein. In fact, he smiles. But this close, I can see the smudge of nervousness in his watery eyes. *Is the young buck crazy enough to do it?* He's not sure.

And that, my friends, gives me an edge over the motherfucker.

"Calm down, young buck. No need to go off half-cocked. I mean no disrespect."

I stare into the murkiness of his wet, old eyes, sending him a silent warning that I mean what I say.

It unnerves him enough that the smile slips from his lips. "I have ten men ready to come in here and unload their clips into you. You kill me, and it will mean war. You should think about that before you pull that trigger."

"I admit a war with the Bamcorda would be nothing but a pain in my ass." I press the barrel deeper into his doughy skin. "The De Kysa are much bigger. Much stronger." I lean down to whisper in his ear. "And a lot fucking meaner."

The color drains from his face.

"Relax. I'm not going to pull the trigger, old man." I pull the gun away. "But just so there is no misunderstanding, if you ever threaten me or disrespect me in any fucking way from this moment forward, I won't hesitate to kill you, you disrespecting fuck."

The tension in the room is palpable.

"You need to tread carefully, Domenico," he warns. "You treat people this way, and someone who doesn't like you as

The Devil's Den

much as I do might take it the wrong way and seek vengeance."

"And that would be a very unhealthy decision."

I move to the liquor cabinet and pour myself a scotch, deliberately not offering one to Luca.

He's outstayed his welcome. It's time for him to go.

He rises from his chair and crosses the room toward the door but pauses beside me. "It would be unwise to make an enemy out of me, Domenico."

I take a sip of my drink and then smile. "Ditto."

My nonchalance irritates the old man. He drills one final look at me before walking away.

I stand in front of the massive window overlooking Central Park and consider the bullet I just dodged.

In the old days, there were four families who dominated the land. Of the four, the De Kysa and the Isle Ciccula were allies, bonded in blood and honor, and respect. The third family, the Draconi, were sworn rivals of the De Kysa and Isle Ciccula. It was a bloody rivalry that went back decades. According to my old man, the reason for the rivalry was steeped in legend and no one could really say what happened, only that the Draconi hated us, and we hated them. The fourth family, the Bamcorda, were somewhere in between. Not quite an ally but not quite a foe. When the De Kysa split from the Isle Ciccula, the Bamcorda allied themselves with us against our new enemy, and it has been like that for the last decade.

Which is the alliance I just obliterated.

But it was a necessity.

Marriage to Bianca Bamcorda would've been a nightmare match. Two demanding people. Two selfish hotheads.

It would be an atomic bomb. Explosive and volatile, followed by a life lived in a miserable aftermath.

Nothing like it will be with Bella.

Oh, she hates me. But I get off on her so vehemently fighting me that I find myself deliberately provoking her.

This shouldn't be as enjoyable as it is.

Because this is about revenge.

About that night and what really happened.

But also about the time I ran away, a seventeen-year-old boy who had been sent crazy by his love for a girl who lived thousands of miles away on another continent.

About running away from home to find her, only to learn she had moved on in her new life.

About going home brokenhearted and with my tail between my legs, only to be told the truth from my father about what really happened the night my mama died.

About knowing I had given my heart to the enemy and how I must do whatever it takes to get it back.

My hands fist into balls so tight I'm white knuckled.

The intercom on my desk buzzes, and I turn away from the view.

"Your brother is here," Anastacia announces.

The door opens, and Massimo breezes in like he doesn't have a care in the world.

While we may look the same, we are worlds apart. I'm uptight and carry the weight of an empire on my shoulders, while he views life as one fun adventure after another.

"You fucking suck as an underboss, you know that," I say, pissed at him for missing the meeting with Luca. "You were supposed to be here an hour ago."

"I needed to take care of something at the club. Did I miss much?"

"Only me almost putting a bullet in the old fuck's face. He's pissed."

"You were expecting that."

"Yes, but he's taking offense. The relationship is breaking down. We need to keep an eye on him."

"Duly noted."

I pour him a scotch and hand it to him. "What did you have to take care of at the club?"

"A portion of the roof fell in. Bad craftsmanship."

"And you took care of it?"

He waves it off. "I can assure you, the contractor will have it fixed by tomorrow morning."

"Or?"

"Or he loses his balls."

I smile. "Nice work."

"Will you be bringing Bella by for a visit?" he asks.

"Of course."

"Does she know what kind of club it is?"

"The club and what type of patrons it caters to hasn't come up," I reply absentmindedly as I try her number. It rings, then goes to voicemail.

So does a second attempt.

She's screening my calls, which is a surprise. I thought she would take every opportunity to remind me of what a monster I am, given her outburst the other evening, when she had a lot to say.

"You might do her the courtesy of explaining. I don't want a scene."

"She'll behave."

Massimo laughs. "That's what I like about you, brother. You are, at the very least, an optimist."

"She knows what's at stake."

"Yes, but she doesn't strike me as the type to roll over without a fight."

She's not.

That's what makes this even more appealing.

Her fire turns me on.

I try her phone, but again, there's no answer.

It suddenly occurs to me that perhaps Bella is fighting me as we speak.

As in, running away.

I call Damian, who is currently perched outside her apartment block.

"Has Bella left her apartment this morning?"

"No, boss."

"Are you sure?"

I hear the rustle of paper and a mouthful of food as he speaks. "I haven't taken my eyes off the entrance to her building all morning. She hasn't left."

Something isn't right. I can feel it.

"I want you to knock on her door."

"Boss?"

My irritation unfurls. "I want you to get off your ass and go knock on her fucking front door."

There's more rustling of papers and the car door opening and closing.

"And ask her what?"

"Christ, I don't give a fuck. Just fucking do it." I grit my teeth as aggravation creeps up my spine. "And call me back when you're at her apartment."

I hang up, my stomach tightening.

Impatiently, I drum my fingers on my desk in front of me while my brother watches on, amused.

Finally, my phone rings. Damian's name flashes across the screen.

"Is she with you?"

"No, boss. No one's answering. It's like no one is home."

My last drop of patience leaves me. "Kick in the door."

Damian pauses. In person, he's terrifying. Six-foot-seven and built like an army tank. That's why I hired him. He's very useful when the added muscle is needed in a situation. But his looks are deceiving. He'd sooner talk things through than throw a punch.

"You sure, boss? This place doesn't look like it's the type of place that will take kindly to someone doing that type of thing."

I rake my fingers down my aching face. "Jesus Christ, Damian. Just kick in the goddamn door."

"Fine, fine, I'll do it. But there ain't going to be an armed broad on the other side who will start firing at me the moment I break in, is there?"

"No, but there'll be a ropable don ready to kick some butt heading your way if you don't fucking kick in the fucking door."

There's a thud and a smash, as Bella's door caves in under the weight of Damian's foot.

"Well..?" I ask impatiently.

I can tell by the background noise that he's looking around, walking from room to room in search of Bella. "Yeah, she's not here."

"Is her suitcase there?"

I know for a fact that Bella brought a rose-gold hard shell case with her.

"No, there's no suitcase and nothing around to say anyone is staying here. Oh look, the fridge is off—"

Frustrated, I hang up and look at my brother, my mood darkening.

Let the games begin.

"She's fucking gone."

12

Bella

If Domenico De Kysa thinks he can take control of my life and move me around like a piece on a chess board, then he has another thing coming.

Escaping the city, I take a town car to the airport. I need to get back to my life in London, back to where life is normal and makes sense, and some gorgeous Italian billionaire slash Mafia crime lord isn't trying to force me to marry him.

As luck would have it, there's a flight to London in two hours, which means my life will be back to normal by dinnertime.

I'm not stupid enough to think he won't come after me or I won't have to go a few more rounds with him. But I can sure as hell make it difficult for him.

He needs to know I'm not a pushover and can take what he dishes out.

Pulling my suitcase behind me, I approach the airline

counter. The server is a beautiful blonde woman with flawless makeup and immaculate red lips. Her name badge reads, *Samantha*, and she greets me with a dazzling smile.

"Welcome to Skylar Airlines. How can I help you today?"

"I'd like a seat on your next flight to London, please."

"Absolutely. That will be the 11:20 flight." When she smiles again, her eyes twinkle. "I have one seat left in business class and one in coach, which one would you like?"

"Does business class come with champagne?" I ask with surprise desperation. It's not even nine o'clock, and I could finish a bottle before we even take off.

Samantha picks up on it.

"Rough morning?" she asks.

"The worst." I sigh. "Ever think someone was put on this planet to make your life harder than it needs to be?"

"Boy troubles or girl trouble?"

"Boy troubles... the worst kind. You know, he actually thinks he can snap his fingers and I'll do what he says. He has no regard for personal space. And don't get me started on his ridiculous demands." I huff out a breath, suddenly aware that I just blurted everything out to poor, unsuspecting Samantha.

But she takes it in stride, offering me an empathetic smile.

"Let's see if we can't make your day any easier. I'll fix up your ticket for you, and then you can relax in our VIP lounge, courtesy of Skylar Airlines, who definitely don't want you to have a bad day."

"I could hug you. You're a lifesaver. Thank you so much."

Her immaculately manicured nails sweep across her keyboard. "You look like you could use a little pampering.

The Devil's Den

How about we put you in coach but upgrade you to first class." She gives me a wink, then whispers, "We girls have to stick together."

I grin, grateful for the sisterhood. "Thank you."

I hand her my passport, and she slides it into the scanner.

Her smile fades, and she steals an uncomfortable glance at me before looking back at her screen again.

"Um...I'm sorry..." She picks up the phone next to the computer screen. "I just need to make a call."

"Is everything okay?" I ask. A small tingle starts at the base of my spine. A warning that an afternoon of champagne and first class is about to fall out of reach.

The look on her face doesn't help matters. In fact, it's alarming. Gone is the dazzling smile and the twinkling eyes. Instead, she looks nervous and concerned. *Uncomfortable.*

When she doesn't answer me, I ask again. "Is something wrong?"

I expect reassurance from her. You know, considering we're in the sisterhood and all that. But what I get is her silencing me with a held-up finger just as she answers the person on the other end of the line. "Yes, this is Samantha at counter 2. I have a Code Pink."

My brows knit together.

Code Pink?

What the hell is that?

I look around to see if a situation is unfolding, but everything seems to be in order. Families, couples, and lone travelers line up behind me to check in while people move about the airport calmly. Everything seems normal.

Except for at counter 2 where there is an apparent Code Pink.

I turn back to Samantha, who still hasn't managed to make eye contact with me since she picked up the phone and began talking to the mysterious person on the other end.

Finally, she hangs up.

"Miss Isle Ciccula, if you could please follow me." Her tone is stone-cold professional. Gone is the warm tone of our newfound sisterhood.

"Follow you where? Look, I really need to get my ticket to London."

Another beautiful blonde in a Skylar Airlines uniform appears at the counter to take over for her. She looks equally as uncomfortable but manages to give me a soft smile.

"I need to escort you to one of our security rooms," Samantha says, walking around the desk.

She expects me to follow, but I'm not going anywhere.

I remain rooted to the spot and fold my arms.

"Something is going on, and I'm not moving a step until someone tells me what the hell is happening here. Are you going to sell me a ticket or not?"

"I'm sorry, Miss Isle Ciccula, but I've been instructed to do otherwise."

"What do you mean you've been instructed to do otherwise? By who?"

She leans forward and whispers, "Please, this will be so much better if you just do as I say."

The way she says it—with hectic desperation—sends a chill through me, and it's enough for me to pick up the handle of my suitcase and follow her across the airport.

"Please tell me what is going on?" I ask as we walk

through a security door leading to a long, brightly lit corridor. "I really need to get to London tonight."

Samantha's high heels *clickety-clack* on the linoleum floor until we stop outside a blue door.

"I'm sorry, but my instructions were to bring you to this room."

She opens the blue door, and we step into the empty room. Inside is nothing but a table and four chairs in the middle of the room. No windows. No other furniture. No people. *No explanation as to why I'm here.*

"Please take a seat. Can I offer you a water or a coffee perhaps?"

"No, what you can offer is an explanation." I'm more angry than confused now. A man appears in the doorway. He's wearing a Skylar Airlines uniform but with a vest that screams SECURITY across the front.

He steps into the room, and I'm about to unleash my displeasure on him when someone steps in behind him, and my head almost explodes off my shoulders.

Nico.

Of course.

I glare at Samantha.

So much for us girls sticking together, Sammy.

She gives me a regretful smile, and I suppose it's not her fault.

It's all him.

I glare at the bane of my existence standing in the doorway looking like he's just stepped off a runway in all that Armani darkness and will fireballs to shoot out of my eyes so he explodes into flames. His perfectly sculpted face is tight with annoyance.

As if he has any reason to be annoyed. It's not like he's being detained at the airport security room like a drug smuggler.

"This takes stalking to a new level," I say, folding my arms against my chest.

The security officer speaks to Nico. "I take it this matter will be resolved quietly and with no disturbance to any passengers or visitors."

Without taking his eyes off me, Nico nods, and the security officer and Samantha leave, closing the door behind them.

"You bastard," I snap. "You've got airport staff paid off now?"

A small smile brushes his lips followed by a chuckle, as if my accusation is ridiculously minor compared to the actual truth.

"When are you going to understand how far my net is cast? You run, and I will find you. Do you understand me?"

"You can't do this to me."

"I can, and I just did."

My frustration gets the better of me. "I just want to go home," I cry.

Nico doesn't flinch. He just drills me with those black eyes and perfect features.

"This is your home now. With me. You can either accept it or fight it. I know which one will be much nicer for you."

"Don't kid yourself. Neither of them offers anything nice for me. I'll still be your prisoner."

"Yes, but one comes with harsher consequences."

I stare at him in disbelief. "Are you threatening to punish me? You think I'm going to cower down to your demands

The Devil's Den

and just roll over because I'm afraid of you?" I let my arms free and take a step toward him. "I'm not afraid of you, Domenico De Kysa. I just don't fucking like you."

The muscle in his jaw ticks, and his shoulders tense. "You talk like you don't have a choice. But you do. You can stay here with me, dutifully stand by my side as my wife, and all your father's worries will disappear. Or you can fight me, return to London and your old boring life, and your father will face financial ruin when I take everything from him."

I can only stare at him in disgust.

This man.

How was he ever the boy who used to kiss me until I was love drunk? Who used to make me feel safe and warm and loved whenever he wrapped his strong arms around me?

I want to cry because I know that boy is lost forever. Replaced by this monster.

But also, how dare he call my life back in London old and boring?

"I have a good life back in London. One I'm sure you couldn't appreciate. But I have friends, and a good job—"

"Not anymore."

My mouth pauses open mid-word when I suddenly put two and two together.

I gasp, horrified. "You *did not* get me fired."

"No, I didn't get you fired," he says calmly. "I'm the one who fired you."

I stare at him, my mouth agape.

"You own the Ulvaeus Gallery?"

"Yes."

My skin feels clammy, and I have an overwhelming urge

to sit on the floor and cry. "You bought the gallery so you could fire me?"

I can't tell you how *fucked with* I feel.

"Surveillance takes many forms, Bella. And when I want something, I will go to any length to make sure I have every card I need up my sleeve when it comes to taking it." He cocks a confident brow at me. "Not that I'd call owning a little gallery in London an extreme."

I take the insult personally. Ulvaeus is a respected gallery, and I take great pride in my work there. Now he's admitting to using it as a pawn in his stupid game. Like it's nothing. Like my career is nothing.

"You're evil," I whisper with disbelief.

He remains expressionless. "I've been called worse."

"Oh, I don't doubt it."

"So what's it going to be, Bella? Are you going to come home with me or are you going to be on the next flight to London?"

All I can do is glare at him.

But inside, I'm already calling defeat. He will destroy my father if I don't agree to his evil plan, and if I can stop that from happening, then I have to do it.

My shoulders sag, and it's all he needs to know he's won.

"That's what I thought." He leans down to take my suitcase from me. "Do I need to call security to escort you back to the car with me, or can I trust you will behave yourself?"

"I'm not a child, Nico," I say wearily.

"No, but you forget I know you well enough to understand that I haven't frightened the fight out of you yet."

"Good," I say, walking toward the door. "Because you have to fall asleep sometime."

I turn my back on him, but not before I see the ghost of a smile on his lips.

We drive back to his apartment in silence. I stare out the window the entire time. I'd like to say that I was planning his murder, but truth be told, I was mourning the loss of the Nico I knew back in Italy. *My Nico.* The boy who loved me more than his own breath and would never fuck with my life like this. The boy who encouraged me to paint and draw and go after my dreams.

I want to ask him why he hates me so much, but I can't bring myself to do it because I don't trust the emotion that would spill out of me when I did.

And the last thing I want is for this version of Nico to think I care.

Because when it comes to him, I have nothing left but contempt.

13

Bella

We start arguing the moment he pulls into the parking garage of an apartment building.

"Where are we?" I demand.

"You will live with me from now on."

"Live with you?" I look at Nico in horror. "You're delusional if you think I'm going to live with you."

"Again, with the assumption that this is negotiable." He swings the car into an empty parking space and climbs out, taking my suitcase with him as he walks toward the elevator.

I follow him, teetering on my heels to keep up. "You know you're basically abducting me, right?"

He doesn't flinch at the accusation. In fact, he remains expressionless and unresponsive like a robot.

Wordlessly, he presses the UP button. The elevator doors open, and we step inside where silent robot man continues his impersonation of a mannequin.

The Devil's Den

"The silent treatment isn't going to work," I say. "I will wear you down."

"By all means, give it a try."

"I have a lot to say about this current situation."

"Feel free to call our complaint line," he says, watching the floor numbers on the panel begin to ascend.

"If you think I'm going to let you barge into my life and start ruling it then you're going to be sorely disappointed."

"Duly noted."

The doors open, and he steps out. I'm ready to keep arguing as I follow him into his penthouse, but... *holy hell, this place is huge.*

I stop in my tracks, trying to absorb the magnificence I'm seeing.

Sweeping panoramic views of the city fill the penthouse from every direction.

It's stunning. Open-planned with a chef's kitchen to the left and a dining area and lounge room to the right. It's the perfect balance of modern lines meets industrial chic.

It's almost too much to take in as I stare at all the fine furnishings and artwork.

He really is the king on the hill looking over his kingdom.

"This place is amazing..." I turn around slowly, taking in the high ceilings and expensive furnishings. In the lounge area is a massive TV sitting above the stone fireplace. The couches are leather and look like they'll give you a hug the moment you plonk yourself onto them. Not that a lot of plonking goes on here, I'm sure. Nico is too uptight to plonk.

Speaking of which...

"Listen, you've made your point."

He holds up his hand to silence me. "No, you listen. This

is how it's going to play out. You are going to live here with me from now on, and you will obey me—"

"Obey you!"

"And then in two weeks, you will marry me—"

"Two weeks!"

Again, with the silencing hand.

"And you will perform your duty as my wife obediently and diligently."

My eyes narrow. "What duties?"

He takes a step closer. "I'm a powerful man, Bella. Everyone needs to see the stability of my marriage or else there is no point to it. When people see us together, they're going to see two people who are in love. No one is to know that this is—"

"Forced? A fucking joke?"

He takes a predatory step closer. Heat radiates off him. Or maybe that's me burning up because of the way he's looking at me. His handsome face is tight and oh, so fucking striking. It's not fair that the monster is as gorgeous and well put together as this because it makes him even more dangerous. His good looks and power draw people in, and they don't realize what a demon he is until it's too late, and they're already snared in his web.

I wonder how many women have fallen prey to his poison, and a strange stab of jealousy sweeps violently through my wildly beating heart.

I don't doubt there have been many women since me. Did he love any of them? I look into the darkness of his eyes. No, he didn't. Because the man standing in front of me is incapable of such a thing.

He drags the pad of his thumb across my chin, sending a bolt of lightning zigzagging down my spine.

"Let me remind you what is at stake here." His low and smooth voice is dipped in fifty-karat gangster. "If you don't pull this off, then I will take everything your father has built over the last ten years and destroy it. Those restaurants of his—I'll close them. That house he loves—I'll burn it to the ground. That shiny reputation he has—I'll make sure everyone knows who he really is, a Mafia underboss who has blood on his hands. I'll bankrupt him in every sense of the word if you give me a reason to.

My blood chills in my veins.

He reaches over to push a stray curl behind my ear. "Do you understand me?"

I can only nod, frozen by hate and disgust.

But also by the way he looks at me, and the gentleness in his touch. It's a stark contrast to the harshness of his words.

And I have to stop myself from leaning into his touch.

He lets his hand fall to his side. "Where is your engagement ring?"

"I pawned it for tickets to London. First class. A girl has to have her standards."

Unimpressed, he gives me a dark look.

"Fine," I say, retrieving it from my purse. I slide it on and hold up my hand. "Happy?"

"That doesn't leave your finger from now on. Got it?"

Again, his eyes flare with warning.

"So many rules," I mumble, wondering what the hell is wrong with me.

I shouldn't want his touch.

I should want to run as far away as possible from it.

He turns and walks toward the kitchen.

That's when I make a break for the elevator. Because I need to get away. To process the havoc he's wrecking on my life and I can't do that here. I need my apartment. My art. My things.

The ding of the doors opening alerts Nico to my plan, and he gets to me so freakishly fast, I have to wonder if he's half wolf.

With a growl, he winds his arm around my waist and pulls me back, spinning me around to face him.

I pummel his chest.

"Let me go, you fucking monster."

"Stop fucking fighting me," he barks.

"I'll never stop fighting you," I scream as I continue to pound on his muscular chest despite it being fruitless.

Nico is way stronger than me.

Through his suit, I can feel his powerful arm muscles and the rock-hard expanse of his chest.

Strong fingers wrap around my wrists with vise-like strength, and he forces me back until my shoulders hit the wall. He pins my hands above my head and cages me in his arms.

Our faces are close, his breath warm on my cheek.

His strong body holds me against the wall, and it's muscular and powerful.

His grip tightens when I struggle, making me gasp.

Yet it's not a gasp. It's more like a moan.

Nico's eyes flare, and his lips part. I struggle to swallow, but my mouth is dry. I wet my lips, and Nico's heated eyes drop to them, tracking my tongue. The vein on the side of his neck throbs while my heart pounds wildly in my chest.

"Is this the way it's going to be?" he asks, his voice rough. "You fucking fighting me every step of the way?"

To answer, I struggle against his hands, pinning my wrists to the wall, but again, I am no match.

He leans closer, his lips brushing my ear. "Because right now, I'm really fucking enjoying it."

Another attempt at a gasp leaves my lips. But again, it's a moan.

He leans deeper into me so I can feel everything, and whispers, "And I think you do too."

I suck in a deep breath to calm my crazy heart and my racing pulse.

"There's nothing about this I like..." I croak.

"No?"

He loosens his grip just slightly, so my wrists are still clasped in his but not as tight. I could break free, but I don't.

"No," I manage to breathe out the word. Because I don't know what's happening inside me.

"You don't like feeling me this close to you? Pinning you to the wall because you've been a bad girl." His eyes become hooded and hot. "You say you don't like punishment, but I think a part of you aches to be punished."

The way he says *aches* makes me think there is something to what he is saying. Because my knees weaken, and it's then that I realize I *am* aching for him.

His cheek brushes my cheek, and my breath escapes me. My head swims with desire. My lips part. I want to taste his lips. His skin. *His punishment.*

Who even am I right now?

I'm out of control, and when his lips brush my throat, I let out a desperate groan.

His hands slide down the length of my body, sending goose bumps sweeping across my skin.

He moves his lips up my throat to the sweet spot below my ear, and my knees go weak. Lust pools between my thighs, the sweet throb beating in time with my heart.

"Is that what you want, Bella?" he moans in my ear. "You want me to punish you?"

I gasp as his hands slide behind me to cup my ass and hold me against his body. He's hard, and I can feel every glorious fucking inch of him.

"No," I moan, but I'm lying. Every part of me except my mind wants more of what is happening, although my mind is starting to cloud and fog with need.

I need to stop this.

Before I can protest, his lips are on mine, and his tongue fills my mouth. His kiss is exactly what I need, and I respond hungrily, taking the kiss deeper and deeper until I can't breathe. He grabs my ass, pressing me tighter against the rigid outline of his cock, and I moan into his mouth, desperate for more.

And then it happens, my brain gets ahold of herself, and I come crashing back to earth.

Nico is the enemy. He's forcing me into a marriage I don't want.

He's trying to hurt me just as much as he's trying to hurt my father.

Now he's using physical pleasure to, what, amuse himself?

I rip my lips from him and shove him in the chest.

"You asshole."

He looks amused. "That's not what you were thinking a few seconds ago."

I shove him again as humiliation burns my cheeks.

"You don't get to kiss me." I wipe the back of my hand across my mouth.

"Correct me if I'm wrong, but you were kissing me back." He smirks. "Rather hungrily, I might add."

Embarrassment spreads across my skin. "Call it a momentary lapse of reason. I assure you it won't happen again."

He sweeps his gaze up my body and sets his impossibly dark eyes on my face, the heat in them forcing me to step back because I know I need distance from this man. He's dangerous for me in every sense of the word.

He chuckles as if he knows better, and again, my cheeks burn with humiliation.

I turn away from him and press the elevator button.

"You really are trying my patience," he growls.

Effortlessly, he throws me over his shoulder and carries me down the hallway to a bedroom, and once inside, he discards me onto the bed.

Excitement and fear go wild in my chest as he looms over me, and all I can do is stare up at him.

"You need to understand that you can't win in this situation. All this effort you put into fighting would be much better put into obeying me. You might actually enjoy it."

"Don't hold your breath," I mutter as he walks toward the door. "Wait, are you leaving?"

"You need some time to think things over. This door is lockable from the outside. You'll stay in here until I say otherwise."

I sit up. "You're locking me in here?"

"You making a run for the elevator every time I turn my back would be exhausting for us both, so yes, I'm locking you in here."

I stand. "You can't do that."

"Oh, Bella, when are you going to understand that when it comes to you, I can do whatever I fucking like?"

He closes the door, and the lock clicks.

I race over and pound on the door. "This is fucking kidnapping and imprisonment, you asshole."

"Probably not the worst thing I'm going to do today, so count yourself lucky," he replies as he walks away. I hear his billion-dollar leather shoes disappear down the hallway.

Pressing my head to the door, I take in a deep breath to calm my racing heart and work out my next move.

I lift my head and spin around, scanning the room for a means to escape.

The room is stylishly flawless, a ridiculous thing to notice as I search for my way out of it, with a massive bed in the center of the room, a bookcase along one wall, and furniture along the other. Stretching the length of the other wall are floor-to-ceiling windows hidden behind gauzy curtains.

On the dresser is a statue of Hera, and it looks heavy enough to clonk Kidnapping Joe on the head when he comes back. But when I try to lift it, I can barely get it off the table. Feeling desperate, I search the drawers for something to pick the lock, but they're empty, which seems sad because a beautiful room like this deserves to be loved by somebody. Yet it's empty and void of any emotion or personality.

Just like Nico fucking De Kysa. Pretty on the outside, void on the inside.

A check of the bookcase nets me a pencil, but that's about it.

Blowing out a huff of breath, a new plan forms in my mind.

Picking the lock isn't going to happen with a pencil, and breaking out the window isn't going to be an option. We're thirty floors up over Manhattan, and unless I have spidey skills I didn't know about, I can hardly scale the side of the building all the way down to the street.

No, there is only one way out of this room.

Compliance.

And if Nico fucking De Kysa wants compliance, then I'll give it to him in spades.

14

Nico

Loosening my tie, I pull it off and throw it across the back of a dining chair, followed by my jacket.

I'm not going to lie. My body is still buzzing after my exchange with Bella by the elevator and how she struggled against me as I took her to her room. Seeing her on the bed looking up at me like that, fuck, it would've been too easy to give in to what I really wanted to do and make her whimper some more.

The need to have her was overwhelming.

When I think about the way she kissed me back, my body thrums and my cock throbs with a need that's been there since the moment my lips took ownership of hers.

You're getting into dangerous territory.

It's been ten years since I last tasted her, and after just one drink from the poisonous chalice, I'm starting to think things I shouldn't.

The Devil's Den

Like how good it felt to run my hands up her body and feel her tremble with equal amounts fear and desire.

How brutalizing her lips with my kiss made me harder than I have ever been, and how she drank it in thirstily, wanting more, *wanting me.*

How delicious her skin tasted as I slid my tongue across her throat and the soft moans that left her parted lips at the touch of my hard cock pressed against her.

How I want more.

How I want to make her pay.

How I want to bury my cock balls deep inside her perfect pussy.

None of which is a part of my plan.

I walk to the refrigerator and remove a bottle of water, twisting the top and gulping it down.

Nothing good can come of this, I remind myself.

The best thing I can do is wear the pain she gave me as armor whenever she's nearby and let her see just how cold-hearted and brutal I can be.

Not that it will be hard. Now that the Irish are making a move to breach our borders, and Luca Bamcorda has his panties in a twist about my upcoming nuptials to an Isle Ciccula bride, it won't be long before we're at war once again.

And war brings out the demon in me.

If Bella doesn't like me now, then she'll like me even less when I'm leading a campaign against my rivals.

In my den, I focus on the computer screen displaying the live feed from the camera in the bedroom. This entire penthouse is rigged with cameras, inside and out, because I can't afford not to know what happens in my home while I'm away.

By the looks of it, Bella is frantically searching for something to pick the lock with. *Or to stab me with.* She's going through the drawers and closet, but she won't find anything. No one lives here but me and a handful of bodyguards in the staff wing.

Next up is the bookcase. She pulls out books and frantically checks behind them as well as inside them. I have to give her credit because she seems determined to succeed. Bella has never been the type to take anything lying down, which excites me because I like a challenge.

Oh, I know she hates me. After all, I fired her, kidnapped her to stop her from fleeing the country, and now I have her locked in a bedroom screaming bloody murder at me through the doorway.

My phone rings. It's Massimo.

"You'd better get down to the waterfront," he says.

"Now?"

"The fucking Irish have set fire to it. Six warehouses are already alight. So yeah, now."

Fuck.

Leaving now when I need to talk to Bella is an inconvenience.

But this needs my immediate attention. Not to mention all of it. Playing push and pull with Bella, while enjoyable and, at times, pleasurable, is not where my head needs to be right now.

I pull up a new number in my phone and make a call. In two rings, a familiar sweet voice answers on the end of the line.

"Domenico!"

"I need you to come over," I say roughly, my body still

tight with need from the argument with Bella earlier. The hollering down the hall has quieted, and a quick glance at the computer screen tells me she's sitting on the edge of the bed, calm and motionless. *Thinking.*

I'm not sure what she's playing at, but I don't have time to babysit her tantrum.

"Now?"

"Yeah, now." I pause and think for a moment. "And bring an overnight bag."

15

Bella

Somehow, I manage to fall asleep, and when I wake up, someone is standing over the bed looking down at me.

Blinking, a beautiful face comes into focus.

"Hey, sleepyhead." The beautiful brunette smiles. She's holding a tray of food in her hands. "I brought you something to eat."

I recognize the face.

Nico's sister.

But it can't be.

She was the sweetest girl in the world. She would never be a part of this.

I sit up. "Arianna?"

Her beautiful smile widens. "You remember me."

"Of course, I do."

She was only eleven when I last saw her. But the sharp

De Kysa jaw, big brown eyes, and lashings of long dark hair are unmistakable.

Nico's baby sister has grown into a stunning woman.

Nico and I used to babysit her and Massimo when our parents were out for the evening, and I would spend hours brushing her hair in front of the movies we'd watch in their media room. She was the baby sister I never had, and we were close.

"I thought you might be hungry," she says, offering me the food tray. "The calzone is Mama's recipe. I remember how much you used to like it."

"You're a part of this?" I ask, confused that the sweet girl who used to sit on my bed and watch me put on my makeup is now an accomplice to her brother's crimes.

She places the tray on the bedside table and sits on the edge of the bed. "I don't agree with it."

"Then why go along with it?"

"He's my brother, Bella, and I trust him."

"You think that keeping me prisoner in this room is something you should trust your brother about? He kidnapped me, Arianna, and now he's keeping me locked up here like I'm fucking Rapunzel."

"He said you came here of your own free will—"

"He escorted me back here. There was very little free will involved."

"He said things got heated when you argued, so he put you in here to calm you down."

"With the door locked from the outside."

"That was unintentional."

"*Unintentional?*" I can't decide if Arianna has blind faith in her brother and will believe anything he says, or if she is a remarkable spin doctor and this is her telling me how it will be perceived by law enforcement should I go running to them.

She smiles again, and it's sweet and kind. "It's so good to see you again. When you left…" Her smile fades, replaced by sadness. "Well, Nico was heartbroken. We all were. You were such a big part of our lives. And to lose you at the same time as our mother—"

"I didn't want to leave," I say, suddenly needing her to know that because for some reason, I don't want her to think I left her behind.

"I know. But I thought you were coming back. Then Nico went to America to find you—"

My eyes dart to her. "Nico came to the States? When?"

"A few months after you left, he ran away and flew to America to see you but came home not long after. Not a lot was said. My father and my brothers always kept things from me because they thought I was too young to understand. But I wasn't too young to realize he was brokenhearted."

Rocked by the revelation, I frown. "I didn't know. He never came to see me."

"He never spoke to me about it. But one night I overheard him telling Papa that you had moved on."

I shake my head. "I'm so confused right now. He was supposed to come and find me on my eighteenth birthday, but he never showed."

She huffs out a breath. "Boy, by eighteen, he was a different person," she says. "I don't know what happened when he came to America the first time, but it changed him."

Social media isn't an option when your parents are

Mafia. Even more so for ex-Mafia. My father's defection was seen as a betrayal to some, and he made enemies out of families who were once allies, people who might try to get to him through me.

Because of this, I wasn't allowed a phone or email. Which of course only made me feel like more of an outcast. When you're the new kid in town and have no socials, your classmates wonder what you have to hide.

Imogen tried to help me once. She set up a fake profile on Facebook, but my father's bloodhounds discovered it within hours. Same with the email and the Instagram account she created for me.

Instead of helping us keep in touch, technology formed an impenetrable wall around Nico and me being able to communicate, and it didn't take long for that gulf to widen.

Frowning, I try to figure out what he saw that made him so brokenhearted.

Then I remember that he has kidnapped me, and I'm his prisoner, and I decide I don't care.

"Please let me go," I whisper.

She looks surprised. "You don't want to eat?"

I look at the calzone, and my stomach rumbles. Marianne De Kysa used to make a mean calzone, and I could never pass one up, and this one looks just as good as what she used to make.

I mean, *I am* hungry.

"If you're feeling better, we can eat in the kitchen," Arianna says.

I look at her, surprised by the suggestion. "You're letting me out of this room?"

She laughs like it's ridiculous that I'm even asking.

"Oh course, silly. As I said, you're not a prisoner. This room wasn't supposed to be locked."

"So I can go home?"

"Nico said you'd ask. Told me to remind you that you have a deal, whatever that means, and he'd take you leaving as breaking that deal. It comes with consequences." She shrugs. "My brother speaks so cryptically sometimes, but I guess you'll understand what that means."

I roll my eyes and reach for the calzone.

"Yeah. Unfortunately, I do."

~

We sit at the massive kitchen table. Arianna drinks red wine while I devour the calzone and cannoli she prepared for me earlier.

"You're right. This tastes just like your mama's," I say, stuffing another mouthful in. I didn't realize *how* hungry I was. "You're a very good cook."

Her smile beams across at me. "Thank you."

Marianne De Kysa was tough on her kids and never had much time for them. Only when she was in the kitchen teaching them to cook would her usually stern face soften and her body language relax. It was almost as if she became someone else when she showed them how to make everything from silky pasta to the most luscious tiramisu you ever tasted.

Come to think of it, it was the only time I ever saw her smile.

"Tell me more about Nico coming to America," I say, swallowing another mouthful of calzone.

Arianna bites down on her lip. Now that she's had time to think about it, she probably realizes she's already said too much. "I probably shouldn't have told you about that."

Bingo.

"It's just... as far back as I can remember, it was always you and Nico, you know. I thought you two were soulmates. Star-crossed lovers." She shakes her head dreamily. "I know I was young, but even back then, I saw how you looked at one another, and I remember thinking that was exactly what I wanted when I met the right boy."

"Did you meet the right boy?" I ask, biting into the cannoli.

"Not yet." She raises an eyebrow. "Can you imagine what it's like with two older brothers like Nico and Massimo? It makes dating difficult. The moment any potential date finds out who I am and who my brothers are—poof, they vanish quicker than you could say *I don't want to date the sister of the most powerful don in the city.*"

I raise my glass of wine. "I hear you, sister." I take a mouthful, and goddamn, it's the nicest, berriest wine I've ever tasted. "It's hard to be the sister or daughter of powerful men. But finding a guy who rises to the challenge will happen. You're smart and sweet, not to mention stunningly beautiful."

"Did it happen for you?"

A sarcastic chuckle leaves me. "Haven't you heard? I'm about to marry the most powerful man in the city."

She goes very still, thinking very hard about what she'll say next. A small frown deepens between her brows.

"I can't explain why Nico is doing any of this. All I can do is trust him." Her voice is almost a whisper. "He loved you so much."

A long-forgotten memory of Nico kissing me by the pond on his family's estate drifts across my mind's eye, and I shove it back into the deepest recess of my mind.

"*Loved* is the optimal word here. Now he hates me." I take another mouthful of wine and force the scorching kiss out of my head. "And the feeling is very mutual."

16

Nico

When I arrive home late, Arianna is asleep on the couch with a blanket over her legs and the TV down low.

Shaking off my jacket, I loosen my tie and undo the top button of my shirt as I make my way toward the bedrooms.

In my study, I flick on the computer screen to check the security camera in Bella's bedroom and find her waiting for me, standing in the middle of the room, hands on her hips, narrow eyes glaring up at the camera.

She knows I'm watching.

She would've heard me walking down the hallway and knew I'd check the cameras to see what she was doing.

The expression on her face tells me she hates me.

But the kiss on my lips tells me she is not all barbed wire and thorns.

I rub my lower lip with my thumb, feeling the lingering effects of her lips on mine. And it's not just my lips that burn with the memory. My whole body hums with the aftereffects like I've been zapped by lightning. Not even the Irish attempting to burn down the waterfront was enough to temper the heat in my blood.

Switching off the computer screen, I leave my study and walk toward Bella's bedroom.

"You asshole!" she snaps at me the moment I unlock the door and walk in. "You know you're breaking a thousand laws by keeping me here."

"Do you really think that concerns me?" I ask, keeping my expression emotionless. "Do I look like a man who abides by any law that doesn't suit him?"

"You're right. You don't. You look like a raging psycho who thinks he can get away with whatever he wants."

"I do get away with whatever I want. It's good to see you're learning."

I smirk, which earns me a burning glare.

Which I've decided I like.

Because when the fire in her vibrant eyes burns hot, it turns me on, knowing I'm the reason.

She narrows her eyes. "Only a fiend would make his sweet, innocent sister lock me in here when she so clearly didn't want to. I saw her face when she took that phone call from you telling her she had to lock me in the bedroom against my will. You're a beast. I only complied because I didn't want to see her cry. You should be ashamed of yourself."

"I'll take that into consideration," I say with a smile, infuriating her more.

She squeezes her fists tight and lets out a frustrated growl.

My gaze sweeps over her.

She's wearing a pair of bed shorts and a tank top, and to my delight, no bra. Her nipples are hard and obvious, but she's too angry to notice what they're doing to me. She's tied her hair into a messy ponytail, and I have to tighten my hands into fists to stop myself from grabbing it and yanking her head back so I can devour her mouth.

Urges like that could unravel everything.

Yet tell that to my cock.

"You've taken away my phone and my freedom," she states.

"And your point is?"

"You're a monster."

I chuckle, but it's humorless. "Good observation."

I'm winding her up, and she looks like a volcano about to erupt.

"How long do you plan to keep me locked up like a captive?" she demands.

"As long as it takes for you to comply with our agreement."

Exasperated, she exhales roughly. "Fine, you have my word. I'll comply."

"Good, because the alternative will be a lot more painful."

The expression on her face tells me she would shoot me given the chance.

"Grant me the freedom to live at my apartment, and I won't cause any more waves."

"And let you flee the country the moment I let you out of my sight? I don't think so."

She takes a step forward.

"I'm not going to flee the country." She folds her arms. "You see, I've had time to think while I've been locked up in here, and I think I'd much rather stick around and make sure your life is hell. And what better way to do that than to marry you?"

17

Bella

The following morning, I'm making coffee in Nico's palatial kitchen when he walks in dressed for racquetball. Last night he refused my pleas to move back to my apartment but conceded I no longer needed to be locked in my bedroom.

"Good morning, husband-to-be," I say gaily, going up to him and hugging him.

He stiffens against my embrace. "What the hell...?"

Unwinding my arms from around his muscular body, I pick up the Americano coffee from the sleek marble bench top and hand it to him.

"It's black. Just like your soul." I smile sweetly. "Did you sleep well?"

"No," he growls.

"Awwwww." I pull a sad face, then smile brightly. "Well, don't you worry about a thing, I'm here to look after you now."

I swipe invisible dust from his shoulders.

"Why the hell does that concern me more than your combative attitude?" he asks, escaping my hands and moving to the other side of the kitchen. He holds up his coffee cup. "Poisoned?"

"Plain, I'm afraid. I didn't have time to run to the store for poison."

He lifts the cup to his lips, and I watch the masked pleasure shimmer in his expression as he tastes it. Nico always did love his coffee.

And I make a damn good cup of coffee, even if I do say so myself.

"Good?" I ask with another sweet smile.

"Very," he says.

"Then my job here is done."

He notices the ring on my finger. "Nice to see you're wearing your ring."

I hold out my arm to study the gleaming diamond. "What kind of fiancée would I be if I didn't wear the ice rink my future husband gave me?"

He lifts an eyebrow. "You're actually complaining about your diamond being too big?"

I gasp dramatically and clutch it to my chest. "Never! It's perfect. Just like my fiancé... even if he is a Mafia murder man."

"What's with the split personality?" he asks gruffly.

I lean a hip against the counter. "Like I told you last night, I'm one hundred percent committed to this arrangement."

I've decided if he wants a wife, then he's going to get the

wife of all wives. The overattentive, over-the-top wife I know will drive him crazy.

Soon he'll be begging me to move back to my loft.

When I wink, he pulls a face and turns his back on me to spoon protein powder into a shaker.

"I know what you're doing," he says, screwing the lid on the shaker and popping it into his sports bag. "And it's not going to work."

"What am I doing?" I feign innocence.

He turns around. "Killing me with kindness, trying to drive me insane with overattentiveness, or at the very least hoping I will let my guard down and let you move back to your apartment."

I give him a sugary smile. "You're being paranoid."

"No such thing in my world, honey." He throws his bag strap over his shoulder. "But you go right ahead and play your little game. It'll be a waste of time, but if it makes you feel better, who am I to stop you?"

"My kidnapper, that's who," I snap before I can stop myself. But I quickly shake it off and plaster a big smile on my face. "But that's all semantics. We won't let a few awkward details get in the way of this beautiful union of ours."

He pulls a face. "Now I know you're up to something. And it's not going to work."

I shrug, unfazed.

Because he has no idea who he's dealing with.

I'm tenacious as fuck when I want to be.

I gesture toward the racket lying on the countertop.

"You still play," I say, changing the subject.

"Three times a week." He drains his coffee cup. "Do you?"

"Hmmmm, considering you've been stalking me for the past year, I think you know the answer." I take a sip of my coffee. "Are you any good?"

"I'm very good at everything I do," he says with the assurance of the raging narcissist that he is.

"Of course, you are." I look at him over my cup. "For the record, so am I."

One perfect, dark eyebrow shoots up. "Are you saying you want to play?"

"No, I'm saying I want to kick your ass."

He scoffs. "You really think you can beat me?"

I hate how he looks so fit and confident, and the urge to wipe that smirk off his stupidly beautiful lips tunnels through me with the force of a freight train.

"Oh, I know I can."

Dimples flicker on either side of his mouth. "Then you're in for a world of disappointment."

I take my empty cup to the sink and rinse it. "We'll see about that."

"Care to bet on it?"

I turn around and narrow my eyes at him. "What were you thinking?"

"Loser has to give the winner whatever they want." As he says it, his eyes flare with wickedness. "Within reason, of course."

"Fine, when I win, I want to go home."

"I said within reason."

"If you're as good as you say you are, then you won't have anything to worry about."

The Devil's Den

He smirks. "And when I win, I want a date."

I feel caught off guard. "What kind of date?"

A strange feeling lights up in my stomach at what those two little words might mean.

"Dinner. Wine. Conversation."

"And that's all?"

He looks amused. "Do you want more?"

I get the feeling that it wouldn't be a problem if I did.

But then I remember that this is Nico, and this date is probably some sick part of his evil plan that I won't see coming until it's too late.

"No, dinner and wine sound perfect," I say lightly.

"Not the conversation?"

"Like I said, dinner and wine sound perfect." I grin while he looks at me like I exhaust him. "Give me ten minutes to get ready?"

"You have five."

I scoff because we both know he'll wait as long as it takes for me to dress since he thinks he can annihilate my ass on the court. I race upstairs to change.

The closest thing I have to workout clothes is a pair of shorts and a tank top with a sugar skull on the front, although I did pack my sports shoes. I pull my hair back into a high ponytail and can't resist adding a touch of gloss to my lips because I want to look hot when I kick his ass.

As I leave my room, Nico watches me from the kitchen. I feel his eyes sweep up and down my legs and linger on my chest. His face is impassive. Blank. But his dark eyes don't hide the heat. He likes what he sees, and it annoys him. Which makes me happy.

Kinda makes me feel like I've already won.

I grin. "Ready?"

Nico drives us to the gym. Today's car is a sleek, midnight-blue sportscar with a gleaming dashboard of chrome and leather. It's lit with blue backlights and reminds me of a spaceship.

"Wow," I say, sliding in. The leather feels buttery and opulent. "I've never seen anything like it."

"There isn't. This is custom." With a push of a button, the engine purrs, and we glide through the parking garage like we're traveling on angel wings.

"They made this car for you? I didn't realize car companies did that sort of thing."

"You can have anything for the right price." He slides on a pair of sunglasses. "And I can afford the right price."

"Of course, you can." My sarcasm isn't lost on him, and as we enter the busy Manhattan street, a ghost of a smile flickers on his lips before it quickly vanishes.

The gym is in the Sky Tower in Manhattan. It's on the ground floor, and the moment we step inside, people begin to fall over themselves to acknowledge Nico.

A fit, middle-aged man in shorts and a tight polo shirt opens the door for him. Behind the reception counter, two beautiful blonde women offer him their sunniest grins as they enthusiastically welcome him. Not us. *Him.* Because it feels like I've just walked into this place with a rock star. Every head is turned by his arrival. A group of women sitting in the little coffee area to the left of the reception area all look up and stare as we walk by. Even the men at another table stop talking to watch.

"Hello, sir," a petite brunette says shyly as she walks past. *Sir?*

Oh, please.

Nico offers her a wink, and her cheeks flush.

As we pass through the reception area and into a hallway, two women in activewear can barely contain their excitement as we walk past. If Nico notices, then he doesn't show it. His poker face is firmly in place.

On the other hand, I can't help but notice all the eyes on us as we walk by the massive workout room and into a hallway leading to the racquetball courts.

Nico leads me to a court separated from the others. It is only accessible through a glass door and has a private viewing room.

"Let me guess, this is for VIPs only," I say, dropping my bag on a leather chair. It even smells nice. Not a hint of sweat in the air. More like wealth and power with a smidge of pompousness.

"No, this is my private court," he says, placing his gym bag on the sleek glass table and removing his gym jacket.

"You have your own court?"

"Like I said, Bella, for the right price, you can have anything."

Including me, I suddenly think.

An all-too-familiar resentment tightens in my chest, and all of a sudden, kicking his ass becomes the most important thing in the world.

"You ready?" he asks.

"To mop the floor with you? Hell, yes."

Again, a ghost of a smile plays on his lips and quickly vanishes.

I follow him onto the racquetball court.

Nico serves with so much power the ball ricochets off the wall and flies past me with impossible speed.

He snickers, and I glare at him. "I'm just warming up."

His next serve is just as powerful, but this time, I'm ready for him, and I hurtle it back to the wall. It doesn't take us long to find our rhythm. He's good, very good, but I don't have any problems keeping up. If I didn't hate him so much, I would actually admit to enjoying it.

Sweat gleams on his smooth forehead, and his shirt clings to his muscular body.

He calls a time-out and walks to the side of the court, where he lifts his shirt over his head, revealing a rock-hard chest and a stomach of deep dips and grooves.

Nico has the body of a perfectly sculptured Benvenuto Cellini statue. Golden skin gleams with sweat, and as much as I try to keep my eyes off him, the little traitors go rogue and sweep over his athletic form thick with slabs of muscle.

I turn away, determined not to give him the pleasure of knowing I'm looking, but not before I take in the powerful shoulders and bulging arm muscles pumped with blood.

I know what he's up to. He's trying to distract me. Get me off my game.

Cheater.

When he walks back onto the court, I decide to beat him at his own game and lift my tank over my head and throw it to the side.

His gaze drops to my shoulders and slowly inches down to where my heart beats rapidly behind my breasts. With excruciating slowness, his gaze trails lower, down to my belly button, and back up my body again, landing on the white lacy bra. His eyes flare, and his Adam's apple bobs as he swallows.

When he finally lifts his gaze, I smile sweetly.

He cocks an eyebrow. "Are you trying to distract me?"

"Is it working?"

"Not in the slightest."

My smile is fixed in place. "Hmm."

"Scared I'm going to beat you?"

"We're tied, remember."

"And you think this will stop me from slaying you?" He gestures to my near-naked torso. "That's a cheap trick."

"Says the man who took off his shirt first."

"It's a new shirt. I've put on more size since I bought it, and now it's too tight. It was hindering my game."

"You know, a poor sportsman blames his equipment for his poor game."

He looks at me like I am the bane of his existence. "Can we finish the game?"

"Sure." I lift my arms above my head to adjust my ponytail, knowing it pushes my boobs higher. Nico can't help himself and watches. I flash him a winning smile. "Pervert. It's your serve."

His serve is violent and powerful. In fact, the tempo of our game is fast and intense. He grunts with every hit of the ball, and I feel every single one of them land right between my thighs.

We volley violently. Both grunting. Both increasing our pace. It's like wild and intense fucking. We both want to make the other come undone and use all the energy in our bodies to make it happen.

I lurch for the ball, but my foot lands badly, and I crash

to the court with the grace of a bus going over a cliff. Pain shoots through my ankle as I roll it and land on my ass.

"Dammit." I sit up and begin to rub it.

Nico drops down next to me. He reaches for my ankle to inspect it. "You've probably twisted it."

"No shit, Sherlock," I mutter, the pain easing a little as I continue to rub it.

Before I realize what is happening, Nico lifts me in his arms and carries me toward the door. "What are you doing?"

"What the hell does it look like I'm doing? I'm helping you."

The way he holds me so effortlessly in his arms. I feel... *secure.*

"Put me down," I demand. Because it will be a cold day in hell before a De Kysa ever makes me feel that way. "Or so help me God, I will scream bloody murder."

"Fine, have it your way, princess." He drops me to my feet, and pain shoots through my ankle. When I wince, he swiftly lifts me into his arms again. "Happy?"

Without another word, he lifts me up again and carries me into the viewing room and sets me down on one of the leather chairs while he retrieves an ice pack from the refrigerator. Crouching, he takes my foot in his hands and wraps the ice pack around my ankle. His touch is soothing and tender, and I watch silently as his tattooed hands move around my foot so he can inspect it.

He's taken lives with those hands. He's made people pay for their crimes against the De Kysa name with those hands. Probably squeezed the life from his rivals with those strong fingers. Yet against my skin, they feel soothing and comforting.

The Devil's Den

"You'll live," he says, lifting his gaze to mine. "For today, anyway."

I can't help but laugh through the pain. "Is that your attempt to distract me from the pain—a threat on my life?"

"It worked, didn't it? You're laughing."

He walks back to the court to pick up my shirt from the sideline and hands it to me. "You might want to put this back on."

"Why, are you finding it too distracting?"

"What if I am?"

His answer surprises me, and tiny pulses take up between my thighs. His dark gaze sweeps over my chest and across my stomach. I like him looking at me like that because I can see what it's doing to him. It's written all over his face. He wants to touch. But he's fighting it. Not to mention, he's annoyed by it.

Our eyes lock, and the moment stretches between us.

It's his phone that breaks the spell.

He opens his sports bag to retrieve it, and I catch a glimpse of the gun sitting on top of his towel and come crashing back to reality.

While he takes a call, I stare at the gun in the bag.

Then I lean forward and pick it up.

18

Nico

Fuck.

There is one rule I live by.

Don't make stupid mistakes that will get you killed, and damn if I didn't just smash that one to smithereens.

Distracted by a barely dressed Bella, namely the way those shorts curve around her luscious ass and the fullness of her juicy breasts in that lacy bra, I left my gun and her unattended together when Massimo called.

Now she's pointing it right at me.

"I'll call you back," I say into my phone and hang up.

I glare at my wife-to-be.

"You need to be careful with that," I warn her.

I seem calm, but I'm not. A gun in anyone's hand is dangerous, friend or foe. She might only be trying to prove a point with no real intention to shoot me, but one accidental slip of her finger and it's lights out.

The Devil's Den

Especially since the safety is off.

"There you go, underestimating me again," she says. "If you think I don't know how to use this, then you really need to talk to the stalkers you had following me. I've been visiting gun ranges in both the US and London for years."

I'm tempted to tell her that in the past year I didn't have anyone watching her except me.

But I keep it to myself because if I don't, she'll read something into it that isn't there. Like I did it because I didn't want anyone else watching her because I'm a possessive asshole who doesn't want someone else knowing the intimate details of her life as well as I do.

She stands, gingerly putting weight on her foot.

"Nice to see your ankle feels better," I say.

"Lucky me, it's feeling better and better by the second."

I raise my hands out to the side. "Now that the ball is in your court, what is your plan?"

A smile twitches on her lips. "I could shoot you."

"Yes, you could. But what would you gain from doing that?"

Her gaze sweeps over me. "My life would be two hundred pounds lighter for starters. Then there is the whole being held captive thing. I could live where I want."

"Yes, you could. But what would you do with my body?"

Her brows knit. It was something she hadn't considered.

"The killing is the easy part," I say lightly. "It's the mess you have to clean up afterward that's the real pain in the ass."

"Don't think I wouldn't consider it worth the inconvenience." A wicked smile curls her lips, and I feel it all the way down to my dick. "Or maybe I'll get creative and invent a dastardly villain who broke in here and killed the mighty Domenico De Kysa in front of my very eyes. *No, officer, I didn't see what the killer looked like. It all happened so fast.*"

The damsel in distress voice she puts on is kind of hot. My eyes slip to her breasts again, and a new wave of lust curls in my groin.

"There's only one flaw in your otherwise perfect plan, my love." My eyes remain on her as I gesture to the cameras in every corner of the room. "The camera doesn't lie."

She looks up at the ceiling, and seeing the cameras, she sighs and lowers the gun. "Fine. I won't shoot you. Not right now, anyway."

She puts the safety on, clearly familiar with a Ruger.

I put my hand out. "Give me the gun."

She narrows her eyes. "I'll trade you the Ruger for more freedom."

Irritated, I clench my teeth. "What kind of freedom?"

"I want the freedom to come and go as I please."

"You know I could just grab the gun off you, right?"

"And you know I could just flick that safety off before you reach me and shoot you right between the eyes."

"Again, cleanup issues."

"Again, I am a good actress." She bats her lashes. "*Officer, he came at me. I thought he was going to hurt me, so I fired the gun. I didn't mean to kill him. Really, I didn't.*"

Christ, I wish she'd stop doing that voice because I'm so fucking turned on right now. I don't know if I want to punish her or fuck her. *Both, I want to do both.*

She sounds innocent, but the mischievous smile on her face and the nefarious flash in her eyes tells me Bella is just as wicked as I am.

And damn, why does that feel so fucking good?

"You want to negotiate the terms of our arrangement," I say, calmly folding my arms across my chest.

"More like the terms of my imprisonment, but yeah."

"Fine," I grit out. "Obviously, you have something in mind. What is it?"

"I want to be able to leave the apartment when I want and do things when I want to do them."

"Fine, but you'll take one of my men with you at all times. And the only vehicle you drive from now on is one of my cars. They're custom-built to protect the interior from bullets, shrapnel, and certain explosive devices."

She cocks her hip. "Fine."

"Fine?"

"Yes. Does that mean we have a deal?"

"Looks that way."

Her eyes narrow. "You're not going to renege on our agreement the moment you get the gun back, are you?"

"No."

"How do I know? Maybe we should pinky swear it."

I shoot a raised eyebrow at her. "If you even try to make me pinky swear, I'll shoot myself in the head."

"Well, you need a gun for that, and will you look at that? I'm the one with the gun."

I know when I'm cornered. I mean, I could grab her, pin her to the wall, and wrestle the gun out of her hand. But that would lead to more than retrieving a gun from her hand, and I need that shit not to happen. I'm already too distracted by her. Letting my cock take charge will gain me a bullet in the head quicker than you can say *don't mix pleasure with business unless you want to lose.*

So when she offers me her hooked pinky, I fucking take it, and we shake.

Looking smug, she hands me the gun back.

"I wasn't really going to shoot you," she says sweetly.

My chuckle is humorless as I take it from her. "If you ever try something like that again, I'll make sure you wish you did."

19

Bella

"Hells bells, Bella. Look at the planet you're wearing on your ring finger." Imogen grabs my hand to get a better look at my engagement ring as we wait for our coffees at a quaint bakery on Charles Street. "It's sparklier than a vampire in Forks."

She's not wrong. Every time the gigantic gem catches the light and sends a billion tiny spangles around the room, I get all gooey.

I love this ring.

I just don't like what it stands for.

"It's so big it should come with its own weather system," she says with a beaming smile. "Do you get to keep it after the divorce?"

"We haven't discussed it. But I'm keeping it. I'll consider it payment for time served."

A server brings us our coffees.

"How are you feeling about tonight?" Imogen asks, adding sugar.

"Like I'm walking the plank to a slow and torturous death. It's my engagement party, and I can't stand the groom."

"Correction. It's not an engagement party. It's an engagement gala."

She's right.

We're not celebrating our impending nuptials with family and friends in a cute restaurant somewhere. We're parading it in front of New York's social elite at a gala being held in the Grand Ballroom at The Plaza.

I have a feeling it's going to be over the top.

"You'll definitely be there?" I ask.

I'll need a friendly face.

"Of course. I wouldn't miss it for the world." She takes a sip of her cinnamon cappuccino. "I'm sorry I have to meet you there, but Aladdin is losing his mind about the show coming up. There's no way I can get away any earlier."

Imogen works for the newest darling of the fashion world, Aladdin Duran, and he has a big show at Clarkson Square in less than a week.

"Listen, are you sure you're okay with everything? I mean, this is an unusual situation, and… I guess I just want to make sure you're okay."

"You don't need to worry about me. It's a business transaction. Granted, it's a ridiculously unusual one, but it's only a twelve-month tenure. And it's in name only. Time will fly by."

"I know, but as your best friend, I need you to know that I'm here if you need to talk, or vent, or hide a body."

The Devil's Den

"Definitely. You'll be the first person I call and ask to bring a shovel." I finish my coffee and look at my watch. "Oh hell, I'd better go. I have to get ready."

I haven't seen Nico since we returned to his apartment from the racquetball courts two days earlier. He left not long after and has stayed away ever since.

It's almost like he's avoiding me.

Which is fine by me.

I'm praying he'll avoid me for the entire length of this ridiculous marriage.

Instead, I've been hanging out with Arianna, who has been staying at the apartment, and James, the bodyguard Nico assigned to protect me.

I glance at him sitting alone at a table across the room. Handsome with short blond hair, broad shoulders, and big hands, he has kind eyes, isn't gruff like a certain billionaire Mafia boss I know, and is permanently on alert.

But as nice as he is, having a shadow still takes some getting used to.

Another annoying thing about the situation? Feeling a tug against my heart every time the elevator doors open and seeing someone other than Nico walk through them.

When I asked Arianna where he was, she simply said, *business*, and when I pushed for more, she added cryptically, *there's currently a struggle for power, and he's ensuring that power sways in favor of the De Kysa.*

Whatever that means.

Then she clammed up like a dutiful Mafia princess should.

"I'll see you tonight," I say to Imogen.

I kiss my best friend and race out of the bakery.

Nico will probably be furious at me for being late.

But it's not Nico waiting for me.

It's Anastacia.

"You're late." She rushes toward me as I enter the suite. "The car will be here in under an hour."

I see the dress I had delivered is hanging on the back of the bedroom door. Well, it's not exactly a dress. It's a black jumpsuit that will make my boobs look awesome. "Relax. I'll be ready in twenty minutes."

Anastacia looks at me with rampant disapproval. "You don't get it, do you? You're about to become Mrs. Domenico De Kysa. Do you understand what a big deal tonight is going to be? He's showing the world whom he intends to marry."

There's something in her voice. A terseness. An edge. I can't really put my finger on it.

"If it's such a big deal, then why isn't he here?"

"He's working. He will meet you at the gala." Her eyes sweep over me. "And you're wrong. It's going to take a hell of a lot longer than twenty minutes to get you ready."

"Excuse me?"

Anastacia doesn't like me very much.

"Come on, we've already wasted enough time." She ushers me into the dressing room, where a short woman with pink hair and a tall, flamboyant young man wait for me by the mirrored dresser. "Isla and Ziggy are going to help you get ready."

I'm nudged toward my chair and forced to sit. Immediately, the pink-haired lady, whom I now know as Isla, starts wiping my face clean with little cotton pads while Ziggy frees my hair from its ponytail and shakes it around my shoulders.

"Gorgeous!" he coos, his eyes meeting mine in the mirror and winking. "What are we going to do with these luscious locks tonight, honey?"

I open my mouth to reply, but Anastacia beats me to it.

"Nico likes it down. Accentuate the curls." She turns her attention to Isla. "She'll be wearing the yellow Valentino dress. Make sure you choose a makeup palette to match."

I glare at Anastacia in the mirror, but if she notices, she doesn't show it.

"Don't I get a say in any of this?" I ask.

She gives me a sharp look. "Domenico has already chosen the outfit, and he's insistent about your hair. So no, Bella, you don't get a say in it." She turns back to Isla and Ziggy. "The yellow Valentino. And her hair down. Got it?"

She glances at the big gold watch on her wrist. "I have to go."

"You're not hanging around to micromanage?" I ask. "How will they know what to do in case of a fashion emergency?"

Her expression is cool. "Some of us don't have the luxury of floating about as if they have all the time in the world. I'm due at the gala in fifteen minutes, and unlike other people, I like to be on time."

Two jabs in one reply. She's on a roll.

She looks at her watch again. "Your car will be here in exactly fifty-nine minutes. Make sure you get in it."

When she leaves, I apologize to Isla and Ziggy for keeping them waiting.

"I didn't realize it was going to be such a production to get me ready. I usually just run my fingers through my hair and put on some lip gloss."

"Oh, don't you be apologizing, baby doll. I can't wait to get my hands on your glorious red hair. Mmmm-mmmm-mmm! That is some color. Like West Virginia in the fall."

"Thank you. My mom was Irish. Red hair is strong in our family."

"Honey, it's gorgeous!" Ziggy plays with a strand of curls. "Now forget what Madam Micromanager says. How are you wearing your hair tonight?"

I give Ziggy a wicked look. "Well, I'd like to try something. But I'll have to collect something from my apartment."

I could send James to get it.

I tell them my idea, and the three of us share conspiratorial looks before Ziggy grins. "Let's do it."

20

Nico

She's late.

But then I had expected she would be.

From the mezzanine on the second floor, I watch her walking through the crowd like she's parting the Red Sea, and my fingers tighten on the railing in front of me until I'm white knuckled. Every pair of eyes in the room is watching her as she makes her entrance. But none more than mine.

She has defied every wish I had asked of her tonight.

The dress.

The hair.

The jewelry.

And she looks stunning.

In place of the yellow Valentino, she wears a black jumpsuit, strapless, with a belt tight at the waist, and a pair of heels so high I'm not sure how she walks in them. She isn't wearing any jewelry, but she doesn't need it, and it would only be lost on her because she is so fucking beautiful.

And her hair. It's a wig. A platinum blonde bob. Even if it isn't her mass of red-gold curls, it looks good on her.

She pauses, her large eyes scanning the room for me. When a server walks past with a tray of drinks, she swipes a glass of champagne and gives him a wink.

God, she's fucking perfect.

I bring my own glass to my lips. Watching her. Trying not to picture those long legs and stilettos wrapped around my hips as I fuck her on the kitchen table for defying me.

Beside me, my driver Matteo raises his eyebrows. He's been a trusted friend and one of my lieutenants since I came to America. He's one of the few men I let into my inner sanctum.

"Good Lord, she's an angel," he murmurs, watching her intensely.

"If that angel is Satan," I mutter under my breath.

He chuckles. "I hope you know what you're doing because she doesn't look like the type who will take anything lying down."

"No, but that's never stopped me before."

"She's going to be a handful." He's amused because he thinks I've bitten off more than I can chew.

A smile tugs at my lips. "I'm counting on it."

He steals another look at her. "She's definitely stunning."

The rest of the guests think so too. Men track her with their appreciative gazes, while women watch her with either envy or fascination as she passes them by. Her presence attracts much attention.

And she's got mine.

The Devil's Den

I take the stairs from the mezzanine to the party.

I'm just about to walk over to her when Anastacia steps in front of me, her face pinched. "I'm sorry, Domenico. I was very, very specific about your requests." She is clearly flustered. No, not flustered. She is furious. "It's like she gets pleasure out of being so defiant."

I can't help but grin, which seems to upset Anastacia more. "Relax, Anastacia. If Bella had turned up wearing what I requested, I would be disappointed."

"You mean, this was a test?"

"No, a test would be a ridiculous waste of time. It was simply a suspicion." I glance at my fiancée walking through the crowd, shining like a diamond in a room full of people all dressed the same. "She would never stand for being told what to do."

"I wish you had told me." Her voice is strained.

I drag my eyes from Bella to look at my assistant, my jaw tightening. Sometimes Anastacia steps too close to the line. She forgets that I am her boss and acts as if I am her friend, not her employer. She can be arrogant. Almost possessive. But it only takes a dark look—like the one I am giving her now— to put her back in her place.

She draws in a deep breath. "I apologize."

Anastacia is a classic example of an overachiever. She takes the falls terribly hard. So I ease up on her, knowing her mood is about to plummet.

I surprise us both and let it go.

I cup her shoulders. "Relax. Stop taking everything so seriously. You're at a party. Enjoy yourself."

I leave her before she can reply but feel her eyes on me as I move through the room to find Bella.

I find her standing with her back to me, studying one of the ice sculptures.

"Nice hair," I say.

She swings around, and her eyes narrow when she sees me.

"Thank you. I was thinking of making it a permanent thing."

"You are?" I ask lightly.

"Yes. After all, blondes have more fun and all that."

She's goading me, and I like it.

People spend so much time kissing my ass. It's a breath of fresh air to be with someone who doesn't.

I lead her onto the dance floor.

When I pull her into my arms, to my surprise, she doesn't try to fight it. In fact, she slides her arms around me like it's the most natural thing in the world.

"You look stunning," I say as we start to dance.

"You're not mad that I defied all your very specific instructions?"

"Not at all."

A small smile tugs at her lips. "Interesting."

"Why?"

"I thought you'd get all possessive and controlling when you saw me." She gives me a wicked smile that goes straight to my cock. "I did it to prove a point, you know."

"You don't say."

She glances around the room at the other people on the dance floor, then asks, "So where have you been?"

"Why, have you missed me?"

"No, just curious."

I twirl her, then pull her back to me. "I've been working."

The Devil's Den

"Ah yes, world domination. Tell me, how is that working out?"

"I'm winning," I say, enjoying the feel of her curves against me as we dance.

"Of course you are." She slides her arm back around me. "Kidnapped any other unsuspecting tourists lately?"

"No, the last one was a nightmare."

"I heard she had good reason to be."

"No, she's just one of those hard-to-please types."

"Perhaps, she'd be nicer to you if you didn't try to boss her around so much."

I shrug. "Perhaps."

"I hear she's tenacious as fuck," she says. "With a woman like that, you won't win, you know."

I stifle a laugh. She has no idea what I'm capable of. "We'll see."

Before she can reply, a stunning blonde woman in an elegant, red-sheath gown interrupts us.

Amélie La Trobe.

To put it bluntly, my one-time fuck buddy.

We had a very passionate summer together when I was in college. Then, a year ago, we met up again and quickly became friends with benefits. But I put an end to it months ago. People call her my ex-girlfriend, but the simple truth is we were just two people who had a lot of sex together.

Emotions were never involved.

Her eyes flicker over Bella with gleaming interest.

"I'm sorry to interrupt your dance, but I just couldn't resist the chance to introduce myself," she says, reaching out to touch Bella on the face. The touch is almost sensual, which is no surprise. Amélie likes to touch. "You are very beautiful."

"Thank you," Bella replies, unfazed. "Your dress is stunning."

Amélie smiles broadly. "Thank you, that's so kind of you to say." Her eyes flash up at me. "Nico, darling, you never told me how beautiful your fiancée is. I must admit, I'm quite caught off guard by her beauty." She reaches for Bella's arm and leans closer to her. "When he told me he was getting married, I was picturing one of those model-types he is so fond of, you know, tiny waists and legs that go on forever." Her eyes sparkle over Bella's face. "But you are something quite different."

I'm not sure if Amélie is being genuine or if her words are a cloaked jibe. It's more than likely the latter.

But Bella remains unaffected. "That's such a lovely thing for you to say. Thank you."

"You're welcome. Now if you'll both excuse me, my date has been trapped by the CEO of some Swiss bank and looks bored to death. Best I save him before he falls asleep in his Negroni."

Amélie floats off into the crowd, and Bella watches her with a small smile on her ruby-red lips. When she turns back to me, her scent hits me like sunshine, and it's like a goddamn drug. The dopamine levels in my brain skyrocket.

"Your ex-girlfriend is very attractive," she says lightly.

With a grin, I take her hand and lead her back onto the dance floor. "What makes you think she's an ex-girlfriend?"

"The look in her eye. The way she studied me. The tone of her voice."

"Are you jealous?"

"Not in the slightest."

"Good. Because you have no reason to be."

"I know because you're forcing *me* to marry you and not *her*. Or is she going to be your piece on the side during our marriage?"

It's a comment to show me how much she doesn't care about me. But it doesn't bother me because I know it's fake. This whole tough outer shell thing is phony.

My gaze locks on her. "I promise all my attention will be solely on you."

She doesn't look impressed. "Lucky me."

I think for a moment. "You know, I could give you anything you want."

"Great, I'll take some freedom and a side order of divorce, thanks."

I smile, and then she surprises me and smiles back.

"You have a beautiful smile. You should do it more often," I say.

"If I did, you might think I'm enjoying myself."

"Oh, you're enjoying yourself. You're just too stubborn to admit it." I lean closer. "Careful, *wife-to-be*, I might start to think you don't hate me after all."

She smiles up at me sweetly. "Oh no, I still hate you."

I lift an eyebrow. "You don't kiss like you hate me."

Her cheeks flush, and she stiffens a little in my arms. "What can I say? I'm a great actress."

"You're not a bad dancer, either."

"Yes, I'm very talented."

In a low, rough voice, I reply, "I look forward to learning just how talented you are."

She gives me a look that suggests she'd rather poke out her eyes with a fork than let that happen.

"Slow down, buddy. Our marriage will be in name only."

Her body language and words tell me she hates me. But I know I also unnerve her and not because I've forced her into this situation. No, I make her nervous because she doesn't trust a part of herself to be around me—the part that kissed me back when I pressed her against the wall in my penthouse.

"You make sure you let me know if you change your mind," I say lightly.

Her eyes gleam wickedly. "Sure. How about you hold your breath until then."

Fighting the smile on my lips, I pull her tighter. I have a feeling this will be a lot more interesting than I could've imagined.

As we dance, Bella looks around the crowded room. "I didn't realize I had so many friends. Do you think anyone bought us a toaster?"

"I don't think they're toaster-type people," I say.

"Hmm, I think you're right. They've probably bought us silverware. Or diamonds." Her gaze finds mine. "A vineyard, perhaps?"

"Do you care?"

"Not particularly."

"Material things don't matter to you, do they?"

"Not in the slightest." She smiles. "How perceptive of you."

"Being very perceptive is what keeps me alive. Observing people is what I do best. Well, one of them." I raise an

The Devil's Den

eyebrow at her, and she rolls her eyes. "I probably know you better than you know yourself."

She simply scoffs.

"You don't believe me?" I ask.

"No, I don't."

"Well, let's see about that."

Her eyes sparkle with a challenge. "Okay, Mr. Perception, tell me about myself."

My eyes fixate on hers.

Challenge accepted.

I hold her tighter. "I know that right now you're trying your best to look unaffected by me."

"I *am* unaffected by you." She looks away, but I can see her pulse racing in her neck.

She's affected as fuck by me.

Just as I am with her.

"You're playing it cool, but inside, your heart is dancing wildly in your chest because being this close to me means something."

Her throat works as she swallows thickly, her eyes looking everywhere but at me.

I put my mouth to her ear. "I know that more than once during this dance, you've wondered what it would be like to feel me inside you."

She stiffens in my arms, visibly telling me that I'm right.

"Don't," she hisses. She tries to pull away, but I lock her to my body with my arm.

"I also know that if I was to slip my fingers beneath those tiny little panties you like to wear, I'd find an ocean between your thighs." Again, she struggles. But she doesn't deny it. "It would only take one word, Bella, and I'd give you more pleasure than you'd know what to do with." My cheek brushes against hers. "Just say *yes*."

My cock is fully hard now.

He and I are both having too much fun.

So the tap on my shoulder couldn't come at a worse time.

It's Anastacia.

"You have a phone call," she says, holding up her business phone.

"It can wait," I say, not taking my eyes off Bella.

"It's Tate from Green Scope. It can't wait."

Green Scope is a company I'm acquiring. It's a deal worth millions if it goes through. But it's time-sensitive, so I have no choice but to take the call.

Both my cock and I feel the disappointment.

I look at Bella. "Do you mind?"

She shrugs like she couldn't care less, and it annoys me.

Because you want her to care.

I walk her over to the ice sculpture and take the phone call outside on the balcony. I talk business for a few minutes, important shit, but I am too distracted to give it the full attention it needs because I want to get back to Bella, knowing full well the chaos she could be causing while left unattended.

I finish the call as quickly as I can, and when I return to the ballroom, I see Bella dancing with Senator Fitzgerald—a rapacious squirrel of a man, but a good-looking one at that—and my jaw clenches.

I don't like the way he's looking at her. Or the way she's looking up at him with a beautiful smile on her face.

Fuck, is she flirting?

Jealousy spikes in my blood, and my mood plummets, a volatile darkness crawling into my brain.

Just as I'm about to storm over to them, Amélie steps into my line of vision and hands me a scotch. "I see you might have some competition. Here, this should help."

I grit my teeth, and my fingers tighten around the scotch tumbler in my hand as my thoughts darken.

"Looks like you picked a bad apple, Nico," she says spitefully. "It's not too late to back out and choose a more appealing option."

Amélie is the only person I know who would suggest I find a new fiancée at my engagement party. It aligns with the venom that falls from her lips on a regular basis.

Throwing back the scotch, I drop the glass onto the tray of a passing server and stalk across the vast room.

Interrupting Bella and the senator, I sear my blazing eyes onto Fitzgerald.

"I think it's time you take your fucking hands off my fiancée."

21

Bella

Despite my protests, Nico ushers me out of the engagement party and bundles me into the limousine.

"What the hell do you think you're playing at?" I seethe, skimming across the leather bench seat.

"I won't let you embarrass me in front of my friends," he growls, sliding across from me.

"I pity you if you think any of those people are your friends," I huff. "Anyway, I didn't do anything wrong. All I was doing was talking to him."

"Are you interested in him?"

"Are you insane?"

"Good, then you won't mind when I cut off his hands."

I roll my eyes to let him know his threat has crashed and burned. It takes more than that to intimidate me.

"If talking equates to interest, then I should have a

problem with you and Amélie. Every time I turn around, you seem to be with her."

I make every attempt not to sound jealous. Because I'm not. I simply hate the one rule for him and one rule for me bullshit.

"Amélie is no threat to you."

"Of course, she isn't," I reply coolly. "To say she is would imply I have some kind of romantic interest in you. And I don't, just so we're clear."

The storm deepens in his eyes. "But you are my fiancée, and my fiancée does not dance with another man while staring up at him like a lovesick teenager."

"Lovesick teenager—oh my God, you're like a selfish child who doesn't like to share. One guy asks me to dance, and you turn into a possessive caveman. I'm surprised you didn't club me over the head so you could drag me back to your cave."

"Don't think I didn't consider it."

As I turn to look out the window, something suddenly occurs to me. I look back at Nico.

"Why have you never asked me about Ari?"

"Ari has never been a threat," he says, his jaw tight.

"Why?" An inkling slowly crawls up my spine. "How can you be so sure?"

"You're not interested in him."

"I'm not interested in Senator Fitzgerald either, but that didn't stop you from putting two and two together and coming up with ten." My suspicion grows. "How do you know I'm not interested in Ari?" This time my voice has an edge to it.

His gaze returns to me, and that's when I realize why he's not concerned about Ari at all.

"You son of a bitch. Exactly how long have you been following me?"

"As long as needed."

"How long is that? Weeks, months?"

"The latter."

I feel the air leave my lungs. The violation of my privacy is extreme, and I feel the intrusion so profoundly.

Another thought occurs to me. "I've been on dates during that time. They never worked out because my dates suddenly got cold feet. Was that you? Did you warn them off?"

"A man bun. Seriously?" he says.

My temper blows through me like a wild storm. "You scared him away? You asshole!"

"Think of it as collateral damage," he says calmly. "I had plans for us, Bella. Anyone else would've been in the way. I would've gotten to the Earl of Ego too if you hadn't dumped him first."

I can barely believe it. He even knows the nickname Imogen and I gave my ex-boyfriend. "You know about Simon as well?"

He's so calm it's infuriating. As if meddling in my private life is nothing. But then again, why am I surprised? He's an asshole.

None of it should come as a shock.

"You've been fucking with my life without me even realizing." I hate him so much right now that if I had a gun, I'd probably shoot him. "Who the fuck do you think you are?"

He sits across from me, relaxed as if he doesn't have a

care in the world. Face passive, legs spread, hands resting on the leather seat beside him. I have to resist the urge to jam my heel into his balls.

"I'm your fiancé." He raises an eyebrow as he says it. "Whether you like it or not."

He's composed while I feel positively murderous.

"You're unbelievable!" I seethe with clenched fists.

Feeling angry as hell, I don't think before I act when the limousine pulls up to a red light. I push open the door and make a break for it, disappearing into the crowd on the busy sidewalk.

Not only am I being forced to marry the asshole, but he's also a stalking jerk of an asshole.

I need to get away from him.

From this.

From everything.

A few yards into my escape, my feet cry out in pain, so I stop to take off my shoes, then continue fleeing on my bare feet. Not ideal but better than having my caveman fiancé catch up to me.

I hear Nico call out my name, so I begin to run. He's far behind me but close enough to see me in the crowd.

I duck down an alley, dodging cardboard boxes and cans, and jumping over puddles before turning down another alleyway, and then another.

It's darker down here. The shadows are longer, and the dusk light barely makes it past the tall buildings. I run down a flight of stairs leading into an underground garage and pass row after row of cars before running up a set of stairs leading out of the garage and into another alley.

I'm winded, but I'm too mad to stop. It's not until I find

myself in a dark dead end that I finally stop and look around to get my bearings. Brick buildings circle me and soar so high they almost block out the light.

Fuck.

I'll have to go back, but I'm not sure if I've gained enough distance from Nico to lose him.

But it's the only way out of this dead end.

I start to backtrack, but as I round the corner, I bump into a wall of muscle. It's a man. A big man. Bald with tattoos crawling up his neck.

"Whoa there, little lady. Leaving so soon?"

He grabs me with his big meaty hands as I try to walk past him. I attempt to yank myself free, but he's got a good hundred pounds on me, and it's like trying to shake off the Terminator.

"Get your hands off me," I demand.

"Why you in such a hurry, baby?" He has bad breath and an accent I can't place. "You ain't got no time for me?"

Again, I try to yank myself free. "I said let me go."

"I don't think so." He forces me against the damp brick wall and presses his nose into my cheek. "See, I saw you run down here, and I thought to myself, why not sample a taste of that fine piece of pussy?"

"You try tasting anything, and I'm going to make sure you never taste anything again."

He laughs, and the stench of his breath makes me want to gag. "Oh, you is fiesty. I like it when they fight."

"Yeah, but do you like it when they do this—" I twist my body and drop an elbow into his forearm, then thrust it upward into his face, cracking his nose. It's enough for him to release me and for me to take off like a lightning bolt. But for a big fucker, he's fast, and with a lunge, he grabs me around the neck and yanks me backward. I lose my footing, and he shoves me against the damp brick wall again.

I slam my knee into his groin, and his grip on me loosens again but only for a moment. I try to flee, but he shoves me back and forces his forearm under my chin, cutting off my air supply. "Fucking bitch, just for that, I'm going to make this hurt extra bad."

He forces me higher so my feet are just off the ground. I fight him. But I don't have anything solid beneath my feet, just air. I try to plant my feet against the bricks, but they keep slipping. Stars begin to dance before my eyes.

His grip on me suddenly loosens, and my feet hit the ground with a thud that rattles my bones. I'm only vaguely aware of the blood and brain matter spattering across my cheek as the man falls to the ground. *Very dead.*

Nico stands over him and fires another three rounds into his chest. His rage ice cold.

Slowly, he turns to look back at me.

"Are you okay? Did he hurt you?"

The danger in his growly voice sends a tremor through me. I shake my head.

Headlights appear at the end of the alley. Nico eats up the space between us and grabs me by the elbow to hustle me toward the limo. I'm in shock. I don't resist. Or speak. I cast a look over my shoulder at the dead man lying on the ground. Twilight stretches across the sky in shades of indigo.

Still shaking, I climb into the limo, and Nico slides in beside me. He taps on the glass partition, and we start moving. He pulls out his phone, and whoever is on the line answers almost immediately.

"We need a cleanup." He issues our location and some vague details with a cold detachment I'm sure only psychopaths can pull off. "Deal with it and let me know when it's done."

When he hangs up, I stare at the man I am due to marry in mere days, and another wave of unease washes over me as his heated gaze bores into me.

"You killed him," I say shakily.

He removes a handkerchief from his jacket pocket.

"I will kill any man who dares to put his hands on you. Nobody touches what is mine." He leans forward and hands me the handkerchief to wipe the blood off my face. "You would do well to remember that."

22

Nico

She doesn't talk during the ride home. She sits in the corner and stares out of the window, her face tight, her eyes wet, while I sit across from her, my jaw tense and my mood dark.

If she is to survive this, she needs to understand that putting herself in harm's way will result in some consequence. Either she'll get hurt, or someone will die trying to hurt her. It's the way of my world, and she's a part of it whether she likes it or not.

I glance at her, and a minuscule piece of my anger thaws when I see the lone tear slide down her smooth cheek. Christ, doesn't she know what would've happened if I hadn't found her?

But then, the quiver in her chin tells me that perhaps she does.

Anger seeps into my marrow when I think about what that *asshole* wanted to do to her. He was a Draconi soldier. A sworn enemy to the De Kysa. The eagle tattoo I saw a few seconds before I planted a bullet in his skull told me he was aligned with the Draconi family. Knowing the Draconi are in town is bad news.

Which is another reason my mood is so palpable.

It's almost dark when we pull into the underground garage. I climb out, but Bella doesn't move. Instead, she forces herself as far into the corner of the limousine as possible as if it can protect her. *Like anything can protect her from me.* I walk around the car and open the door beside her, shoving my hand into the car for her to take. But to my annoyance, she doesn't.

"Bella," I growl.

She looks up, and another infinitesimal piece of my anger melts when I see the look of fear on her face.

Somewhere inside me, a dormant part of my heart kicks its first beat in more than ten years, and I have to swallow back the sudden need to lift her in my arms and soothe her.

But she doesn't need soothing. She needs to know that fighting me will only put her life in danger. She needs to do as I say. This is her life now. She will be my wife, and me wrapping my arms around her and wiping her tears will not help.

"Take my hand," I demand.

Reluctantly, she reaches for it, and I help her out of the car.

We walk in stone-cold silence toward the elevator, but I can feel the storm brewing with every footstep, and I don't doubt that once we reach the privacy of the penthouse, our storms will collide violently.

In the quiet of the elevator, I steal a look at her. Her

blonde wig came off in the struggle, and her wild red curls fall unchecked around her polished shoulders.

Her curls have always fascinated me. As a young man falling in love, I had loved her hair, the color, the scent, the softness of it as I buried my face into it when we made love.

Now I picture wrapping thick strands around my wrists as I fuck her violently against the wall.

My cock stirs, and not for the first time tonight. She might be the bane of my existence, but she effortlessly turns me on.

The door to the elevator opens, and I wait for her to walk through, which she does, but she stops just as I step into the apartment and turns around to slap me hard across the face.

I have to hand it to her. Not too many people can get the jump on me like that, and if they do, it usually ends with me putting a bullet somewhere in their body.

"That's for dragging me into this despicable world of yours," she fumes, her words shaded with anger.

I grab her wrist and yank her to me. "You will do well to remind yourself of who you are dealing with, cara mia."

"How could I forget," she seethes, "when it's burned into my day-to-day life like a horror story."

"Do you have the faintest idea of what that Draconi soldier was going to do to you if I hadn't shown up? He wasn't just going to violate you in the most despicable, ugliest way. No, once he'd finished defiling and torturing you, he was going to cut you up into tiny little pieces and send them to me, piece by piece, as a fucking Christmas present."

If it's possible, her face pales even more. "You knew him?"

"The tattoo on his neck belonged to the Draconi." I pull her to me so she's tight against my chest and glare down at her. "This town is crawling with my enemies, Bella, and now you are in their crosshairs."

"Thanks to you and your disgusting blackmail."

I squeeze her wrist. "They will hurt you every chance they get. Whether you like it or not, I am your best protection, so stop fucking fighting me."

"I'd rather die than live in this fucking gilded cage."

"Not the way they would kill you, you don't. The Draconi take pride in their sadistic creativity." When I think about what almost happened, I feel real fear. "Consider your freedom to come and go as you please revoked."

"You can't do that," she cries.

"Don't you get it, Bella? You're a target now."

Fear flashes in her eyes and I want to take that fear and set fucking fire to it.

Another dormant part of my heart awakens and I let her go with a growl.

I cross the room to pour a drink and throw it back in one mouthful.

When I pour a second, Bella appears beside me and snatches it from me. Her wild eyes fix on mine as she raises the glass to her lips and hungrily devours the scotch.

I watch her throat work as she swallows, aching to drag my tongue along her smooth, milky skin.

I lick my lips, needing to taste her.

She holds up the glass for me to take. Her full lips wet and glistening.

There is only so much one man can take.

The Devil's Den

I take the glass and discard it on the floor. Shattering glass fills the room as I grab her and crash my lips to hers.

She fights me at first, of course she does, but as my tongue fills her mouth and my lips command a response, she moans into the kiss and responds with surprising hunger, kissing me back like a woman starved of kisses.

And I kiss her like a man who hasn't tasted another woman's lips in ten years, despite the amount of them that have filled his bed.

Christ, my cock will bust open my zipper I'm so damn hard.

I walk her backward until her butt hits the edge of the dining table. I don't want her getting frightened and pulling away from me like the little dove she is because nothing will feel as good as sliding my cock inside her again.

I'm not giving her time to overthink this. I'm going to fuck her here on the table.

Although her moans and her feverish kisses tell me she's not going anywhere.

It's the masculine clearing of a throat that stops us both.

Kiss drunk, we both swing our faces in the direction of the couch where Massimo sits with a shit-eating grin on his face.

"Thanks for the performance, but seeing as it's about to get X-rated, I really feel like you should know I'm here. Don't get me wrong, you know I like to watch." He flashes another grin. "But you're my brother, so it could get kinda weird if you go any further."

"Fuck..." I growl.

Nothing like a cock block from your brother.

"I would've announced my presence earlier, but when

the two of you argue, no one else can get a word in... and that slap..." He lets out a whistle. "I have to admit, it was kinda hot to watch."

He rises from the leather lounge seat and crosses the room.

His eyes sparkle as he takes Bella's hand and places a kiss on it. "Bella Isle Ciccula, it's been far too long."

Her eyes widen. "Massimo?" A big, beautiful smile spreads across her kiss-swollen lips.

He gives her a wink. "The one and only."

"I didn't recognize you," she cries.

"I know, I've gotten so handsome it's only natural for you to be blinded by it."

She throws her arms around my brother, and a hot electric bolt of jealousy courses through me.

Not one to miss driving a knife in deeper, my brother smiles at me over her shoulder, and I want to shove that grin down his throat for flirting with my fiancée and giving me blue balls.

Why the hell did I ever give him a key to this apartment?

"What are you doing here?" she asks.

"That's a good question. What the fuck are you doing here?" I glare at my brother. "You couldn't make it to the engagement party, but you could make it to my apartment and interrupt at the worst time ever?"

Bella's cheeks dust with pink. Her lust has cooled, and the embarrassment and remorse have set in. She thinks we're done, but she's wrong. I'm getting rid of my brother, then I'm removing every item of clothing from her luscious body and burying myself so deep inside her she'll feel me for days.

"You know I hate to interrupt." It's a lie. This is amusing him greatly. "But I heard what happened. Draconi soldiers are in the city?"

"And what do you know, it just happened to be my AWOL bride-to-be who found them." I glance at Bella, who fails to resist an eye roll, before turning back to my brother. "But let's talk about this tomorrow. I have more pressing matters to attend."

Again, I glance at my fiancée. She straightens at the innuendo and going by the stiff shoulders and awkward expression on her face, all that fierce hunger she felt for my cock earlier has abandoned her completely.

Not that it will take much for her to find it again. I'll make sure of it, no matter how much she fights her urge. I'll evoke that thirst out of her and have fun doing it.

She backs out of the room. "I'll leave you both to discuss business."

"We haven't finished *our* discussion," I growl.

"Oh, I assure you, we have." It seems not only has her passion cooled, but her hatred for me has also returned. "I'm going to bed."

She walks away.

"Then I'm coming with you," I call after her.

"No, you're not," she calls from down the hallway.

"That's my cue to leave," Massimo says.

"Oh, you think?" I say roughly.

The moment I had Bella pressed up against that table would have been the better time to extract himself from the scene entirely, not just announce his presence.

A new wave of lust rolls through my pelvis at the

memory of Bella's lips on mine and the little moans she made as I kissed her.

The way her tongue slid into my mouth and her nipples tightened against my chest.

"We'll talk tomorrow," I say.

He gives a casual salute as he disappears through the elevator doors.

Once he's gone, I loosen my tie and walk down the corridor toward the bedrooms. I knock on Bella's door, but she doesn't answer.

I check the handle, and it's locked.

"Don't think I won't break this door down," I warn through the layers of timber.

The lock unclicks, and the door opens. Not wide, just enough to see Bella's face.

"What do you want, Nico?" She sighs.

"I thought that was fucking obvious when it was pressed up against you ten minutes ago."

Her mood is frosty. "That was a mistake."

"You didn't kiss me like it was a mistake. In fact, you kissed me like it was very, very right."

"No, it was very, very wrong. I'm not interested in you that way." She bites down on her lip, which does nothing to cool the raging lust sweeping through my southern regions. "Or are you going to force that on me too?"

Except that does.

It's like a water plane dumping an ocean of ice-cold water onto a wildfire.

Anger tightens my jaw, and my teeth clench. I may be a bad man, but I'm not a raping son of a bitch. Rape is for pond scum.

"I might take a lot of things I want, Bella, but I don't ever take that." My voice has an edge to it. "When a woman rides my cock, she rides it willingly and with great enthusiasm."

"Well, I'm not riding anything."

"You don't know what you're missing out on."

Her eyes flash with heat and hatred. "You forget, I've already seen it. In fact, I was the first."

Foreign emotion soars through my heart at the mention of our past encounter. But I send a missile up after it to destroy it.

"You'd be surprised how much you can master something in ten years, cara mia."

"Something I don't care to know about." Her blue-green eyes narrow. "You're right, you can master a lot of things in ten years. A decade is a long time to fall out of love with someone and surprisingly easy when that someone let you down."

Her words gouge through my armor easier than bullets and blades ever could.

I grab onto my loyal friend revenge to respond.

"You can't run from this," I say.

"And you can't keep me locked up in this devil's den like a prisoner."

"You'll learn very quickly that I can do whatever I like," I say, unable to keep the threat out of my tone. "It would bode well for you to accept that."

She shakes her head and looks away for a moment, biting down on her lower lip again. "You're really going to make me do this, aren't you?"

"Yes, and it would be wise for you to find some way to be happy about it."

She looks at me through her lashes, her jaw defiant. "How am I supposed to be happy when I'm being forced to marry a monster?"

The disgust in her voice grinds against what little conscience I have.

I grab the door to prevent her from closing it in my face. "I suggest you try very hard because this will break you down a lot quicker than it'll ever break me."

I let go of the door, and she closes it without another word.

"Do not try to escape," I remind her through the closed door. "Or there will be consequences."

But she doesn't reply.

As I walk away, I remind myself of all the reasons I'm doing this.

And how those dormant areas of my heart that wake up whenever I'm around her are better off lying dead in the dark corners of my very black heart.

23

Bella

I pace the bedroom, barely holding my tears at bay.

How could I be so stupid and kiss that arrogant, kidnapping caveman?

I'm so mad I want to scream, and for a second, I consider doing it just so Nico will come back, and I can punch him in his smug, arrogant face.

It wouldn't change my situation. I'd still be a prisoner, and his kiss would still linger on my lips like warm, sweet poison, but it would at least make me feel a hell of a lot better.

It also wouldn't change the fact that tonight could've ended a lot worse if he hadn't found me in that alleyway with a six-foot bald alien attached to my throat.

And while I'd prefer to set myself on fire than admit he's right, I know I have to be wiser when it comes to my safety and not run down dark alleyways in a less-than-innocuous neighborhood.

I sit on the edge of the bed and look around the room. *My prison.* I can't complain. Apart from the whole kidnapping and forced into a marriage thing, my situation is quite comfortable. Nico has made certain that I want for nothing.

Well, except freedom.

And my phone.

Otherwise, he makes sure I'm being looked after. Five-star meals. Luxurious surroundings. Expensive toiletries. Even the towels in the bathroom attached to the bedroom are the softest, fluffiest towels in the world.

Lying on the bed among a sea of pillows, I contemplate my next move. Murder is out of the question. As is escaping out the window. And I've probably got zero chance of finding a phone and calling 911.

No, escape requires some careful planning.

I have to be careful with my next move.

I wish I had my art supplies here. I could spend the rest of the night taking my frustrations out on the canvas and lose hours in a creative trance until I forget a gun-wielding psycho piranha has kidnaped me.

I stretch and yawn, but I'm too wired to sleep.

Or so I think.

Because the next thing I know, a knock on my door rouses me from a deep sleep. I blink my eyes open and am surprised to see a blue sky pressing against the windows.

Groggy, I sit up.

So much for being too worked up to sleep.

The bedroom door opens, and Arianna walks in carrying a tray of food.

"Good morning, sleepyhead." Her smile is full of sunshine. "I brought you pancakes for breakfast."

I had planned on going on a hunger strike in protest against my incarceration, but looking at the triple-stacked buttermilk pancakes dripping with maple syrup and garnished with strawberries, I decide I'll start tomorrow.

I accept the tray from Arianna, and she sits on the side of the bed.

"You know, you don't have to bring me food each day," I say, feeling a little bad that Nico has her babysitting me. "Although I am very grateful."

"It's no bother." She shrugs with a smile. "I like spending time with you again."

I pause a forkful of pancake midair and smile back at her. "Yeah, me too."

And it's true. Arianna is lovely to be around, and I enjoy her company. I mean, I'd probably enjoy it more if I wasn't being held captive, but beggars can't be choosers.

"Where's his royal highness?" I ask, tucking into a pancake.

"He's at the office."

I chuckle. She uses the word *office* as if her brother leaves the house each day to go to work at an advertising agency or as an insurance broker, not as a Mafia don who sits in a wing-backed chair in his office above a cocktail den and whips up batches of chaos to inflict on his enemies.

"So you pulled the short straw and have to guard the prisoner," I say.

"You're not a prisoner," she reminds me. "And hanging out with my soon-to-be sister-in-law is not drawing the short straw. In fact, we've got something very exciting on the agenda today."

"We do?"

"Yes."

Her beaming smile is infectious, and I can't help but grin back at her. "Are you going to tell me or make me guess?"

Her eyes light up, and her hands flutter together with an excited clap. "You're being fitted for your wedding dress at the House of Bianchon at ten o'clock."

My immediate reaction doesn't match her enthusiasm. In fact, it's pretty much the complete opposite. For me, an appointment to fit my bridal gown for my wedding to a man I despise is about as appealing as being fitted for a dress made of razor-sharp nails.

"It's going to be so much fun, Bella. Magda Bianchon is so talented, and she's going to make you the most beautiful dress."

I force myself to smile because I don't want to dampen her excitement. And right now, that seems more important than hating on some dress fitting.

"Oh shoot!" Arianna says, checking her watch. "I have a Zoom meeting in five minutes."

"A Zoom meeting?" It suddenly occurs that I've been so busy fighting my situation I haven't even bothered to learn anything about Arianna and what happened to her during those years between her being a shy tweenie and growing into a stunning woman. "For work?"

She nods. "I'm in high-end real estate, and I'm brokering a purchase for a client. He's buying a castle."

"How the hell do you buy a castle?"

She gives me a little curtsy. "Through me, of course."

She leaves for her Zoom meeting, and I'm alone in my cell once again.

Bored, I look around the room for something to do. If I had my paints and canvases, I could use this time creatively. I could sketch or paint and get lost in my world of color and textures, and my time here would pass quickly and unnoticed.

My previous ransack of the room told me there was nothing other than books, and I'm all read out and feeling restless. I need to create, or I might just murder Nico out of sheer boredom the next time I see him.

I try the door and am surprised to find it unlocked.

Do not try to escape. Or there will be consequences.

Nico's warning from the night before weaves in and out of my conscience.

But what if I'm back before anyone realizes I'm gone?

I step into the empty hallway. The only sound I can hear is the low whine of a vacuum cleaner coming from the kitchen.

The cleaner is here.

She has a cart.

A cart big enough to fit a small person inside.

Then I realize the ridiculousness of that plan. I'm not a small person. I'm five seven with double ds and hips made for childbearing. Well, according to some. *Cough, Jerkface Simon, cough.*

Another idea bounces in. Does the cleaner know I'm a prisoner?

I could walk out with her. Pretend I'm simply a normal person leaving her house to get art supplies. Not a prisoner using her as a means to escape.

I doubt Arianna would stop me. Although she would call Nico—her blind faith in him would be admirable if it wasn't so misplaced—and he would have a hissy fit of all hissy fits.

And it's guaranteed that the bodyguards would try to stop me, and no doubt they're lingering nearby.

But as I sneak down the hallway, I can't see anyone but the cleaner finishing up in the kitchen.

"Good heavens, you scared me, child," she says as I magically appear beside the kitchen counter.

"I'm sorry," I say, trying to hide my nerves. "Are you finishing up?"

"All done and dusted." She winds up the electrical cord on the vacuum cleaner. "I'll be back next Tuesday."

"Oh great, I'll walk out with you," I say brightly as if I wasn't in the middle of a great escape. I glance over my shoulder to check for any looming bodyguards or Arianna, but the hallway remains empty.

"That would be lovely, but I just need to give Miss Arianna my invoice for Mr. De Kysa."

I step in front of her. "That's okay. I'll make sure he gets it. In fact, I'm on my way to see him right now."

For a second, I think she'll insist on speaking to Arianna, which wouldn't bode well for my escape plans. But then she relaxes. "Are you sure?"

"Actually, Mr. De Kysa asked if I could bring it with me. He even mentioned something about a pay raise?"

Her eyes widen. "Well, he certainly is already generous."

"Not generous enough," I say, taking the invoice from her and guiding her and the vacuum cleaner toward her cleaning cart by the elevator. "He's a squillionaire. I assure you, you deserve it, and he can afford it."

She looks pleased with the idea, and I vow silently to make sure she gets the pay raise from him as promised. It will be my first job as Nico's wife.

The elevator doors open, and we both pile inside.

"That really is very generous of him," she says as we ride the car to the basement.

I smile at her. "I know he looks like a big ole meanie, but really, he's just a big ole softy."

Which is a big ole lie.

When the door dings open, I walk with her to her van and help load her trolley and cleaning products into the back. And when she drives out, I escape out the garage door and disappear into the busy street.

∼

The door looks new.

And it throws me off guard.

Did someone kick it in?

Oh my God, has someone been inside my apartment?

A surge of anxiety rolls through me, and my instinct tells me that if I were a smart woman, I would turn around and leave.

But I stare at it long enough to talk myself out of leaving and shove my key in the lock.

Thankfully, it still works, and I'm able to let myself in, and the moment I step inside my apartment, I instantly relax. I sag against the door and suck in a deep breath, enjoying the airy scents of vanilla and patchouli, and the subtle hint of artist paint. This is my happy place. I feel safe here.

There is nowhere they won't find you.

Nico's words dip into my thoughts, and a cold shiver runs up my spine. He'll be pissed if he finds out I did this, but he can't keep me locked up like some precious gem because he's afraid of what could happen. He needs to let me have some freedom.

Still, I'm not naive to the dangers his world brings, and now that he's dragged me back into it by the hair, I have to be careful, whether I like it or not.

I'm tempted to spend the day in the village. To walk through Washington Square and take a moment on the bench seat and let the spring sunlight kiss my skin while I listen to the buskers.

But despite my desire for freedom, I don't want Arianna worrying about me. When she realizes I'm gone, she will panic and call Nico, and he'll probably send out the National Guard or do something equally over the top. Besides, Arianna is sweet and kind and doesn't deserve the worry.

A foreign noise in another room pulls me out of my thoughts, and my head snaps to the bedroom as an uncomfortable tingle works its way up my spine.

It's probably just the pigeons that like to hang out on my window ledge. But it's unnerved me enough to make me hurry and collect my things quickly.

I grab my art bag off the coatrack and fill it with art supplies. My sketchbook and some pencils, a case filled with charcoal and pastels. I'd like to take a few canvases and paints with me, but my canvases are huge, and I'm not sure I'd get them into a cab.

Plus, I'd be lying if I said I didn't feel a little rattled being here alone. It's quiet and unearthly still, and I can't shake the

The Devil's Den

unease gnawing at my gut. It's an uncomfortable feeling. Like something is watching me. I try to shake it off, but it's unnerving, and I know I need to get out of there.

Satisfied I have the things I need to stave off the boredom of being locked in Nico's apartment for God knows how long, I leave my apartment and hail a cab.

Luckily, one pulls up immediately.

As I open the door to climb in, a strange sensation crawls up my spine, and I instinctively turn my head to look up at my window.

Fear bursts through me when I see something in the glass.

Is that a face?

"You getting in, lady?" the cabbie asks.

I turn away from the window to nod, but nothing is in the window when I turn back.

Was it a face or just the light playing tricks on me?

I drop my head back against the headrest and close my eyes.

It seems everywhere I turn, Nico's world fucks with my head.

∽

Arianna paces the sidewalk where the cab pulls up to the curb. She's on the phone. When she sees me, her eyes widen, and she ends the call.

"Oh, thank God, you're safe," she says the moment I step out of the cab. "I've been so worried."

Guilt spreads through me when I see how panicked she is.

"I'm sorry, Arianna. I only wanted to collect a few things from my apartment." I hold up the bag of art supplies.

"Nico is going to be so mad," she says.

"You told him?"

"No, I was just talking to Anastacia. We were supposed to be at your wedding dress fitting fifteen minutes ago, and when we didn't arrive, she called me."

Dammit. I'd forgotten about the dress appointment. I glance at my watch. We're only twenty minutes late. We can still make it.

Before the cab can pull away, I open the door and turn to Arianna. "Come on, we can still make the appointment."

She slides in beside me. "You must have some kind of death wish. Nico is going to lose his shit."

I look at my soon-to-be sister-in-law and smile. "Then best we don't tell him."

She lifts an eyebrow. "Oh, you can guarantee he already knows."

24

Bella

The House of Bianchon is unrivaled in its designer couture, and Magda Bianchon is the queen of bridal splendor.

Somewhere in her early sixties, she has the limber abilities of a teenage gymnast as she kneels and bends her body in uncomfortable positions to fit and pin the fabric in precisely the right places.

"I'm sorry we're late," I apologize again, feeling guilty. I might not want this wedding to take place, but it doesn't mean I'm prepared to waste the time of the people helping put it together.

"The traffic in this city can be a nightmare to navigate," she says diplomatically, dress pins sticking out of her mouth. "Now straighten your back and move these hips so I can get the seam just perfect."

She moves me into place like I'm made of Play-Doh, then pierces the fabric with the pearl-ended pins.

It takes about an hour of her prodding and pinning until the dress finally sits perfectly around my body.

"Your figure is beautiful to work with," she says, standing back to observe her handiwork. Her eyes float over my body as she studies me in the dress like I study my canvases. "The fabric loves your curves."

"Thank you."

"Have you thought about what you'll wear underneath?" Magda asks, checking every inch of her work of art.

The dress is so tight, I'm not sure anything will fit under it.

"I'm open to suggestions."

"Good, because I have two must-haves for your big day."

She whispers to her assistant who disappears out of the room and returns moments later with two sets of hangers in her hands.

"This one is for wearing under your dress," Magda says, handing me a hanger with a barely-there thong and nipple pasties. "Seamless, simple and functional. It will look as if you're not wearing anything underneath."

I touch the silky satin of the thong, and it feels luxurious against my skin.

"And this one is for your wedding night. It's from La Perla's latest collection." Magda holds up the second set, then hands it to me. "Incredibly soft, elegant, and decadent."

My first inclination is to say no to the La Perla. My wedding night is not going to require sexy lingerie.

But just because Nico won't be seeing it doesn't mean I can't enjoy wearing it.

"I'll take them both," I say. After all, every woman deserves a nice piece of lingerie.

"Would you like to try it on before my assistant wraps it up?" Magda's eyes twinkle as she hands me the set.

On the hanger is a white satin and lace bra, a matching thong, and a suspender belt.

Yes, I would like to try it on very much.

Inside the luxurious dressing room, Magda helps me out of my bridal dress and hands it to her assistant who quickly takes it away like it's a newborn.

"I leave you to try on the La Perla." Magda smiles as she hands me a pair of silk stockings. "To complete the look."

"Thank you."

She goes to leave.

"Magda," I say her name. "I really am sorry about being so late."

She pauses in the door.

"I designed that dress to look stunning. You've made it extraordinary. Thank you." She smiles, and it's warm. "I'll be out here if you need me."

As I dress, I take my time, handling the expensive lingerie as if it were a fragile piece of art. I pull on the satin panties and secure the suspender belt around my hips. I slide on the silk stockings, enjoying the silkiness as it glides up my leg, and clip each one to the belt.

The bra is easy to put on and fits perfectly around my ample chest, and when I check my reflection in the mirror, I feel a rush of satisfaction.

Magda was right. The La Perla set is stunning.

I look and feel the sexiest I've ever felt.

I brush my hand over the white satin bra that barely contains my nipples, and they tighten.

Something about wearing beautiful lingerie is empowering and sexy, but I have never felt it until now, standing in front of a mirror in this flawless mix of satin and lace.

A commotion in the boutique draws my attention away from the mirror. It's Nico, and he sounds like a storm whipping through the dressing rooms.

"Where is she?" his booming voice commands.

I roll my eyes in the mirror. Clearly, he knows about this morning's jailbreak.

The curtain yanks open, and a fuming Nico appears in the doorway. But the moment he sees me dressed in lingerie, he stops, and his wild eyes sweep over me.

Several times.

I think I've just discovered my superpower.

"What the fuck?" Lust shimmers in his expression, fusing with his anger. "Are you trying to fucking kill me?"

I offer him a sweet smile. "While the thought is tempting, no, I'm not trying to kill you."

His uninhabited gaze sweeps over my body again. "I beg to differ."

I pose so he can see how great my ass looks. I may not be thin and slender, but I don't need to be. My juicy ass looks great in this silky-smooth thong. And the thighs that I'm a little too critical of because they carry a bit more weight than I want, they look amazing.

And let's not even get started on how fucking great my boobs look.

Simon once suggested I get a breast reduction because my double Ds make me look fat.

Fuck you very much, Simon.

Nico steps into the dressing room and yanks the curtain closed.

The Devil's Den

"No please, make yourself at home," I say, looking at his angry face in the mirror.

He looms up behind me. A powerful force, a muscular frame, eyes that burn with anger and lust and all the things he wants to do to me while I wear this lingerie. It doesn't scare me. It excites me.

He spins me around to face him. "You deliberately defied my orders and left the apartment."

"I'm not one of your soldiers. You can't order me around like one."

His fingers grip tighter on my arms. This close, his heat wraps itself around me like a blanket. If that blanket was on fire.

"You defy every order I give you. I've killed men for less."

"Then you need anger management." I struggle against his hold. "Now let me go."

He grips me harder, and it sends a wave of heat through me.

His anger rolls off him. "Not until you understand how much is at stake here. You're about to be my wife, and my enemies won't think twice about getting to me through you. You need protection, and I can't do that if you keep fucking running away from me."

"You drag me into this life and force me into a marriage I don't want and then expect I won't resist being locked up like fucking Rapunzel?"

I'm yelling at him, yet why am I so fucking turned on?

It's the lingerie, my rational brain whispers.

Which is a lie.

It's the deep, consuming passion rolling off Nico that

makes my pulse race and my thighs clench with anticipation.

He forces me back until my shoulders collide with the wall. "You need to understand that I'm going to be your husband, and from the moment that was decided, you became mine. So you will do as I say, or there will be dire consequences."

"Is this how you plan to treat me when we're married?" I bite out.

"And how's that?"

"Rough handling me. Pushing me up against a wall."

Dark promises flare in his eyes. "Something tells me you like it that way."

My retort dies on my lips as he runs the back of his fingers down my cheek.

"Is this why you provoke me?" His voice is low and dangerous, and too fucking sexy. "So I'll be rough with you?"

My skin pebbles and my pulse races.

And he notices.

"Do you like it when I'm this close to you?"

I lick my lips. "No." *Yes.*

His eyes gleam. He knows I'm lying.

"Is that why you defy me? To get my attention?"

Holy fuck, do I?

"No," I whisper.

He drags his knuckles down my neck to my breasts and my nipples tighten to taut peaks.

"Or does the idea of me losing control turn you on?"

He fixes his gaze to mine and a wicked smile plays on his lips as he strokes one nipple through the lace, before doing the same to the other. "You should be careful what you wish for, little one, because when I lose control I can be very imaginative with my punishment."

A violent need throbs at my core, aching to be quenched. And Nico knows it. Because I can't hide it.

Just like he can't hide what's going on behind his zipper.

He drags his knuckles lower and lower until they find the satin between my thighs, and I jolt and hiss in a shaky breath.

Heat swirls around us as one finger hooks the satiny edge of my new La Perla panties.

My whole body quivers with anticipation.

"I'm waiting for you to say *don't*," he rumbles.

And I'm desperately waiting for you to touch me there.

I sink my teeth into my lip to stop myself from moaning.

"Don't hold your breath," I say, like I'm not giving in.

Amusement tugs at his lips but quickly vanishes as he slips a finger beneath my satin panties and slides it through the most intimate part of me.

I let out a rough exhale... because *damn*.

"*Fuck*." His amused glazed eyes find mine. "No wonder you enjoy arguing with me. Look at how wet it makes you."

The pad of his finger brushes my clit, and my bones liquefy.

He begins to rub and tease, stroking and brushing my clit with relentless pressure, and I arch my hips, needing the friction.

"Do you have any idea how much I want to fuck you right now?" He growls. "Its taking everything I've got not to fuck you up against this wall."

His finger slides from my clit to dip inside me again, and I groan, arching my neck and pressing my head into the wall.

"Jesus, you're so fucking wet. So fucking tight."

I begin to rock against his hand, getting off and not giving a damn. My muscles tense violently, chasing my orgasm, my heart beating rapidly against my rib cage as my moans fills the space between us.

"That's it, little hell cat. Take it from me. Take your pleasure." He groans and its primal. "Are you going to come for me?"

"Not... for you." I crush my teeth into my lower lip. "I'm going to come... for me."

Nico smiles wickedly. "Then we both win."

On the other side of the curtain, Magda sounds nervous. "Is everything alright in there?"

As I teeter on the edge of an orgasm, it takes everything I have not to moan out my response.

"Yes... I'll be out... soon."

My orgasm hits, and I melt into the wall of the dressing room as it consumes me. Streams of bliss funnel into my limbs, and I have to put my hand over my mouth to stop from crying out.

Groaning, Nico buries his face in my neck as I come undone.

"You look so fucking hot when you come." His lips brush the tender spot beneath my ear. "You wear things like this for me, and I'll make sure you come every single day for the rest of your life."

Blanketed in afterglow, I can barely lift my eyelids.

"I don't wear this kind of thing every day," I say, still high. "This is supposed to be for my wedding day."

He smiles into my neck. "Then I promise you our

wedding night is going to blow your mind. This outfit makes me want to get very creative."

Starting to come down, I push my hand into his chest to create some space between us.

He's dangerous to be around. That mind-blowing orgasm tells me I need to protect myself from getting caught in his web, and to not feel the thrill of his wedding night promise tighten in my stomach.

This is not supposed to be a sexual arrangement.

Barely regaining the use of my legs, I move away from him to look at the woman in the mirror. Sex will only complicate this already ludicrous situation.

"I'm not wearing it for you, I'm wearing it for me," I say, my body still flushed from coming. "I might not get a say about my fate. But I can at least walk to my sacrificial altar wearing La Perla."

"And so my queen should."

He grins, but it's dark as he comes up behind me and drops a kiss on my neck. "Tonight, we're going to the club Massimo and I own in Manhattan and I only have one particular demand." His breath sends a warm shiver through me. "Don't wear any panties at all."

And with that, he vanishes just as quickly as he appeared, leaving my skin warm and my body throbbing for more.

25

Nico

I don't know what the fuck I'm going to do with her.

One thing I do know for sure is she'll probably be the death of me.

After making her come in the dressing room this afternoon and knowing how my little hellcat can purr beneath my touch, I'm so fucking desperate for more, it's all I can think about.

Which is definitely not part of the plan. And when I make plans, I run a tight ship. If something gets in the way of them, I usually just eliminate the obstacle. But this is a new hell I've landed myself in.

I drum my fingers against the kitchen countertop, sucking down scotch like a thirsty man as I impatiently wait for her to appear.

Beside me, Massimo and Mateo are talking about something that happened at the club last night, but the noise in my head is drowning them out. They don't notice the agitation radiating off me in dark waves. Or if they do, they don't show it.

Which is a healthy idea for them.

We're going to the club tonight, and I'm not sure if it's a good idea to take Bella or if I'm setting myself up for a violent tumble through hell. Because if I want this arrangement to work, then I can't afford to touch her again. And after today, I think we've already seen that not touching her isn't exactly my strong suit.

Massimo and Mateo stop talking, and it makes me look up.

Bella appears in the hallway across from the kitchen, looking like something out of my dreams, and I feel the gates of hell opening wider beneath my feet.

She looks fucking stunning.

I don't know what I was expecting, but she's exceeded it and more. She stands at the edge of the kitchen, and I have to grit my teeth to stop my jaw from dropping open.

She steps into the room, and I can't take my eyes off her.

Silver silk flows over her body like water, hugging her luscious curves and setting off her deep tan. The hem of her dress is short but not too short, just enough to show off her firm thighs. She's not wearing a bra so there's nothing between the silky fabric and her luscious breasts, making the outline of her perky nipples more than evident.

Black knee-high boots, diamond cuffs around each wrist, and a choker around her slender neck complete the look that I'm a hundred percent sure will send me insane by the end of the night.

Dragging my gaze down her length, I feel my cock harden.

She's fucking phenomenal.

Massimo and Mateo notice too, and a fierce possessiveness blazes through me when they sweep their gazes over her.

"I'm ready," she says.

Tonight, she's wearing her red curls half up, half down, and the urge to wrap strands of it around my wrist as I sink balls deep into her is extreme. I have to fight the groan in my throat.

Massimo doesn't show any restraint. He gives her a wolf whistle. "Goddamn, Bella. You look fucking hot."

She offers him a dazzling smile. "Thank you."

Her sparkling eyes switch to me but her smile slips. She thinks I don't appreciate what I'm looking at because I'm standing frozen to the spot looking as unaffected as always.

But damn, I *am* affected.

I'm so affected I've momentarily lost use of my motor functions.

Her diminishing smile is a kick in the balls and I want to put it back on her face more than I want the goddamn air in my lungs.

I clear my throat and take her by the arm, leaning in so my lips brush her ear. She stiffens at the closeness, goose bumps dancing on her skin beneath my touch. *God, up this close, she smells like heaven.* "You look fucking phenomenal."

She grins at my compliment and the smile on her glossy lips makes me want to taste them.

I think of my demand earlier today when I made her come in the dressing room. *Tonight, don't wear any panties at all.* Now, I'm picturing her completely naked under that dress, and the images in my head are setting small fires all over my body.

I haven't been able to get her out of my mind all fucking day. The way she looked standing in that dressing room wearing that lingerie. The confidence I could see on her face for the first time. It radiated off her, and damn, if it wasn't alluring. Confidence looks good on her.

We take the elevator to the underground parking garage. Massimo and Mateo take the front seats, while Bella and I take the back. As Bella slides into the soft leather seat, her hem rides up her thigh. Only a few more inches and I'll be able to see whether or not she's wearing panties, and for a guy who hasn't had sex in God knows how long and who is suffering the worst case of blue balls known to man, it's almost too much to take.

I force myself to focus on what I'm doing. Stare straight ahead. Breathe. And don't fucking think about the lack of panties beneath that dress.

I'm a man used to being in control, but large cracks are deepening in every one of my walls.

Not helping matters, her scent is teasing me.

It's a warm night, and the twilight air is filled with the heavy scent of roasting chestnuts and the sour bite of Ginkgo trees as we pull up to the nondescript building in Lower Manhattan.

Massimo opens the door, and Bella climbs out. But before I can leave the car, I have to adjust myself because I've been hard the whole drive over here.

She looks up at the dark building. "Are you sure this is the right place? It doesn't look like anyone is here?"

"This is an exclusive club," I explain as I take her elbow and guide her across the street. "We don't advertise, and we keep it discreet. Only members know its location."

"Really? Isn't that bad for business?" she asks.

I grin at her naivety. "I think the best way to answer that is to show you why the exclusivity makes it so popular."

Before we step inside, she looks up at the neon sign over the door.

It's one word glowing in red.

Lair.

26

Bella

Lair is nothing like I've ever seen before. The front entrance is a long, dimly lit corridor that opens into a room where shadows are lit in deep red. There are booths and tables, and a backlit bar that shines like a diamond in the shadowy light.

"What is this place?" I ask. It looks like a club, but there is a strange undercurrent in the air that I can't put my finger on.

"It's where people come to indulge," Nico replies hotly in my ear.

I glance around me, taking in the other patrons. It's a mixed crowd. In the corner, a beautiful redhead dances like she's in a trance, her back pressed against a man who holds her by the hips and sways with her in time to the music, his face buried in her shoulder.

Across from them, sitting at one of the cocktail tables, a young couple leans in close to one another as they have an intense conversation, but the man's hands have slid along her thigh and are moving beneath her barely-there hem. Wait, is he…?

I almost jump when an attractive woman with a pixie cut wraps her arm around my waist as she dances past, her eyes fluttering up at me as she offers me a beaming smile. There's a lot on offer in that smile, and when she dances away, she keeps glancing over her shoulder at me until a gentleman at the bar steals her attention, and I'm forgotten.

It's then I see the cages across the room. Two of them. Where dancers in next-to-nothing gyrate against the steel bars, moving their bodies in time to the throbbing beat of the music.

"Don't look so worried," Nico says with the casual assurance that is both charming and dangerous. "You're quite safe here."

I don't feel safe. But I'm not scared either. Something about the club is fascinating. But I can't explain what it is.

A beautiful woman wearing a cigarette girl uniform approaches us. Her hair is blond and shiny, and carefully coiffed into a 1940s style like an actress from the silver screen. Her ruby lips spread with a dazzling white smile.

"My name is Ginger, and I'll be your server this evening," she says, her eyes twinkling in the dim light. "Your room is ready. Will you please follow me?"

Nico wraps his arm around my waist and leans in. "Are you ready to experience Lair?"

His words are spoken in a low, hoarse voice laced with warning and danger but also with a dark promise of excitement and pleasure.

I nod as if controlled by something else.

Something that's always lived deep inside me, but that I've never uncovered before.

A hint of a smile touches his lips. In this light, the shadows curve his cheekbones deeper into his handsome face, and his eyes are impossibly black. They gleam with predatory heat, and I can't help but feel like I'm a lamb being led to meet an unavoidable fate.

Seductive music throbs around me, tingling against my skin as we make our way down a long hallway toward the back of the club. The deeper we go, the more I feel like I am being pulled into a heady new world.

I can't explain it, but I feel my walls begin to drop with every beat of the music. With every throb of the bass. I feel the fever building inside me and awakening something new and exciting.

We follow Ginger through the shadows toward the rear of the club where the peep rooms are located. Each room is accessed through a glossy red door that leads into the small but comfortable viewing area. It's dark in here, the only light being a small lantern on the table.

In front of us is a window of dark glass. Music filters in through speakers on the walls and in the ceiling, erotic and throbbing with sensual melodies and beats.

Ginger guides us to the small table and runs through the drinks ordering process, which is accessible through a button on the table.

She looks at the iPad in her hand. "I see you've selected a couple for your viewing pleasure."

I have no idea what she's talking about. But Nico nods, so I assume he arranged something earlier.

"Excellent choice," she says, like he's just ordered some

chef special off the menu. "Can I get you some drinks before the show starts?"

"Yes, I'll have Jameson. Bring me the bottle. And...?" He looks at me.

"Champagne," I say. "Please."

"A bottle of *Le Fleur De Tit*." The name rolls off his tongue effortlessly.

Ginger smiles. "I'll bring those right over."

When she disappears, I lean forward. "What exactly is happening?"

"We're in a peep room," he explains casually.

"I know, but what happens in a peep room? Will someone dance for us?"

"Among other things," he says cryptically.

"Like?"

"Whatever turns you on."

My eyes widen. "You mean, like sex?"

He smiles wickedly. "I like that sex was the first place your mind went."

His lack of denial ignites panic in me.

I stand. "I'm not having sex with a stranger."

Nico is unfazed by my explosive reaction and remains casually seated in his chair, his arm slung across the back of the one beside him. "Relax, tonight is about watching."

"Watching what?" My eyes widen as I realize the purpose of this room. *This club.* "You mean people have sex, and we can watch?"

"Yes."

I feel way out of my depth. "People really do that?"

"Are you asking if people like to watch, or if people like being watched as they fuck?"

The way he says *fuck*—it's like he is fucking the word with his own tongue, and it sends a bolt of excitement running up my spine.

"Both," I reply.

"Some people enjoy watching others while some people enjoy being watched. Lair caters to both desires."

I ease back into my chair.

"We're going to watch people have sex?" I ask with a whisper.

"Only if you want to," he says calmly.

His response ignites erotic images in my mind, and I feel the heat of them sing in my blood. I don't know what to expect, but I know I'm intrigued. Voyeurism isn't really my thing.

Well, I don't think it is.

But I'm hardly running for the door.

"You enjoy watching?" I ask, breathlessly.

"When it comes to sex, I enjoy a lot of things, Bella."

The connotation in his voice sends a dark, unfamiliar thrill through me.

Of course this man doesn't do vanilla.

He drips vanilla in century-old scotch and sets light to it.

That primal part of me, the one that knows me better than I know myself, rises to her feet with piqued interest.

Ginger reappears with our drinks, and while she pours my champagne into a crystal flute, Nico fixes himself a scotch.

"Will there be anything else?" she asks him dutifully.

"No, that will be all for now."

She leaves, and I sip my champagne nervously. I want to say something to ease my nerves, but I get distracted by the sudden rave party on my tongue. *The champagne is delicious.* No, it's more than delicious. It's like heaven and sunshine had a baby and called it *La Fleur De Tit.*

A moan escapes my lips before I can stop it, and Nico's eyes dart to mine.

"This is amazing," I say, taking another modest sip. I want to down the whole glass to calm my nerves, but champagne that tastes this good deserves to be savored.

Nico chuckles at my display of appreciation. His smile warm. His body relaxed. His eyes gleaming.

We lock gazes, and something hot and tense tingles in the air.

I can't look away, and I know hell will freeze over before he does.

I open my mouth to say something to ease the strange tension building in the space between us, but the lights go up behind the dark glass and illuminate the couple on the other side.

Wearing nothing but a bra and panties, the woman is bound to the brick wall behind the bed where a headboard should be. Her wrists are encased in steel, her body tense as the man, wearing nothing but tight briefs, circles the bed predatorily. He's holding two blood red silk scarves in one hand and winds them around the other as he stalks the outer edges of the room.

My first instinct is one of fear, and it tells me to look away. But my second instinct comes from some primitive part of me that will not turn away.

He has the kind of body born from long hours in the gym. Thick abs. Strong thighs. A diamond-cut chest. Shoulders as round as boulders. He moves achingly slow as he approaches her, his muscles gleaming in the dull light. When he reaches her, he grabs one of her ankles and secures it to the edge of the bed, repeating it with the other ankle, so her legs are spread wide.

Every move is made with deliberate slowness to increase anticipation.

Lust aches between my thighs as I watch him crawl up the bed, dragging his muscular frame over her petite figure, the thick outline of his erection brushing over her panties.

Without thinking, my thighs part.

After my orgasm in the changing room at the House of Bianchon, I've been riding high all afternoon. It's like a door has opened somewhere inside me and where it leads to is anyone's guess. But that's the exciting part. I've opened myself up to a part of me, and I have a feeling it's capable of anything and everything.

With a growl, the man grabs the woman's chin and kisses her deeply and fiercely. All the while, the music plays, a deep, probing beat that pulses at my core.

"This is turning you on," Nico says beside me in a deep, smooth voice laced with lust.

My entire body ignites with heat. His words and tone are a potent aphrodisiac to my senses.

Keeping my eyes straight ahead, I lick my lips. "I don't know."

But it's a lie, and he knows it.

"There's nothing wrong with enjoying what you enjoy, Bella," he says, his hot gaze fixed to my profile.

I struggle to swallow as the man rips the woman's panties from her body and buries his head between her thighs. Her whimpers echo around us and my pussy throbs hungrily.

I bite down on my lip because I want to feel what she's feeling. A pair of warm lips sucking my clit. A strong tongue stroking my pussy. The ache builds tight inside me until I have to squirm in my seat.

I'm desperate to reach down and touch myself, but I don't dare.

"There is a lot of freedom in letting go," Nico says, his voice like warm honey as he continues to watch me and not them. He leans closer. "Let go with me, and I promise you an unimaginable amount of pleasure."

His words reach my clit like the lick of a velvety tongue.

I try to swallow back the moan, but it escapes anyway.

On the other side of the glass, the woman writhes on the bed, gripping the edge and arching her back, while I'm frozen in my own torturous hell as my body begs for relief.

Oh God, I need to quench the throb between my legs.

I glance at Nico. His face is tight with lust, his eyes hooded and focused on the man and the woman, his legs spread with one hand resting on the bench seat next to him, the other curled into a fist on his thigh.

The woman moans, and the man mutters dirty, filthy words before penetrating her with his tongue once more.

I lick my lips and grip the edge of the seat, clasping so tightly I'm white knuckled.

I imagine how it feels. Being suckled. Being penetrated.

Nico leans closer.

"Do you want to come?"

His voice is ragged and hoarse in my ear.

Desperately, my body screams.

I'm so turned on I feel like I'm going to lose my mind.

I squeeze my eyes closed as if I can shut it all out.

The Devil's Den

This club. Nico. The man and woman fucking in front of us. They're causing a sensory overload, and I'm afraid to give in to my desire because I don't know what I'm capable of if I let it take control.

All I know is I desperately want to.

"Answer me," Nico demands hoarsely. "Do you want to come?"

"Yes," I blurt out.

My eyes are still stuck on the man fucking the woman with his tongue, but I can feel Nico smile beside me.

"I want to watch *you*." His voice is a hoarse whisper. "Show me how you make yourself come when you're alone."

The pulse in my core is sweet agony. Relentless and hungry.

"Let go, Bella," he says roughly. "Touch yourself."

Involuntarily, my legs part farther, and I slide my fingers down my thighs, a tremble rolling through me when I reach that sweet spot. My clit aches for friction, and the moment my fingers slide over the slippery nub, I let out a groan.

"That's it," Nico rasps beside me. "Make yourself feel good."

He ignores the man and woman in the peep room, and it occurs to me that I'm giving him his own voyeuristic show, which turns me on even more.

Beside me, he is calm and collected. But the energy radiating off him is that of need.

I quicken my pace, not too fast, just the perfect amount of friction and tempo to send streams of pleasure funneling through my veins. I sink my teeth into my lip and moan as the wave builds higher and higher inside me. My legs grow restless, and my breathing accelerates, my heart pounding because not only am I about to come but I am making myself come in front of the man I hate. Somehow that makes it so much hotter and exciting.

And forbidden.

"Such a good fucking girl," Nico groans in my ear.

The girl on the bed lets out a cry as she comes, and my head drops back as my own orgasm crashes through every wall and every self-conscious doubt I've ever had about this situation, and spreads through me in a warm, sweet wave.

The cry that leaves me is almost alien as I'm swept away by a current of pleasure.

"Fuck," Nico growls and slumps back against the velvet backrest. "You're so fucking hot."

Panting and high, I start to laugh.

But as I come back to reality, my laughter fades, and my half-lidded gaze falls to the peep show once again.

The man sits in the chair now, his large erection leaning against his belly as the girl kneels between his parted legs and slowly drags her tongue along his thigh. As she nears his groin, he takes his cock in his hand and begins to slowly stroke it, groaning as her tongue finds the soft skin of his balls.

A new wave of need pulses at my core. A need that has been growing since Nico burst into the changing room today.

I glance beside me. His legs are parted, his collar is open, and his hand is carved through his hair. My gaze drops to his erection straining against his zipper.

Seeing him as turned on as I am, a new urge takes over my common sense.

I stand and turn to face him. Fixing my gaze to his, I

remove my dress and discard it, revealing my nakedness underneath. No bra. No panties. Only me in my birthday suit and a wicked pair of knee-high boots.

His eyebrows shoot up, and his throat works as he swallows, those dark eyes glued to mine, watching every move I make.

"Unzip your pants," I demand.

He doesn't question me. He unbuckles his belt and lowers the zipper.

"Take out your cock, Nico."

He reaches into his briefs and pulls out his massive cock. Seeing the thick column of flesh in his big hand makes my mouth water and my body warm. He's so virile. So fucking hard and ready.

Knowing I'm beyond the point of no return and no longer thinking about consequences, I look over my shoulder. Behind me, the woman sinks onto the man's cock and begins to ride him.

Intoxicated with lust, I climb onto Nico's lap and slide my thighs on either side of his hips, absorbing his scent and the heat of his body as I straddle him.

"I'm done with watching," I whisper. "I want control."

His dark eyes tell me there is no chance. He'll relinquish control when aliens land.

But I'm determined. "You have me cornered, Nico. At least let me have this."

The muscles in his jaw work, but he says nothing and reluctantly relinquishes control, dropping his arms to the side.

"Good. Now no touching until I say you can," I say, and his eyes flare with warning.

He hates giving up control.

But it's a delicious hate because he knows he'll be rewarded.

He trembles as I take him in my hand and slide the thick head through my wet folds.

"Goddammit…" He hisses with pleasure as I brush the engorged head of his cock back and forth over my aching clit.

His breathing becomes labored, and his body grows restless. He's dying to take control, *to take me.*

He begins to pant, and his fingers curl restlessly into the edge of the seat.

In one smooth move, I sink onto his rigid cock, and his eyes roll into the back of his head. A gasp escapes my parted lips, and I squeeze my eyes shut at the sensation of his cock filling me.

God, he's so fucking big.

Impaled, I don't move. Instead, I meet his gaze and find his eyes filled with heat and darkness. And need. *So much need.*

Not moving is sweet torture for both of us. But I know the reward will be mind-blowing.

My greedy hands stumble over the buttons of his shirt, and in my desperation to feel his flesh, I rip it open, sending buttons popping and revealing a chest colored with tattoos.

Without thought, my lips trail kisses across his inked skin, and Nico draws in a rough breath.

He tastes clean and warm, his golden skin hot to the touch. Groaning, I know I want more than just a taste.

I straighten, and Nico's gaze sears heat across my flesh, his lips wet, his eyes dark and possessive.

"You can touch me now," I whisper hoarsely.

Not waiting, he takes one nipple into his mouth and softly sucks until I'm clenching his cock with pleasure. Groaning, he does the same to the other nipple, torturing it with velvety strokes of his tongue.

Needing to move, I begin to rock against him and am instantly rewarded with streams of pending bliss rising in my core.

"Fuck, Bella," Nico growls and grabs my face, pulling me down for a rough, searing kiss. His tongue thrusts into my mouth as his strangled groan falls between us. He digs his fingers through my hair and grips the roots, sending a tight sting across my scalp. "Ride my cock, baby. That's it, nice and slow. Christ, I'm going to come so hard if you keep doing this."

I groan and bite his lower lip, relishing in the sting of his grip in my hair and the desperate need in his voice.

Mindlessly, I ride him, and a ragged sound jerks out of him.

Desperate for the friction, I increase my tempo, feeling full and stretched and desperate to bring relief to my aching clit.

"I'm going to come," he pants.

His hands find my hips and take command, pulling me back and forward over his cock.

I lean forward, deepening his length into me. "Come inside me."

With a growl, he bucks upward, his cock thrusting in and out with an urgent tempo until his eyes lose focus, and he jerks to a stop. A primal growl roars out of him, unchecked and raw. His thick length pulses and throbs against my walls as he comes, jetting his seed powerfully into the deepest parts of me.

Feeling him come throws me over the edge, and I follow just as fiercely, gripping his broad shoulders and not giving a damn as I come apart on his lap.

He might be the enemy, but it's the furthest thing from my mind as my body gives in to the hazy pleasure of my orgasm.

"Nico..." His name drops from my lips as I disappear under a wave of ecstasy.

I collapse against him. I feel shaken and spun in circles, my breathing slowly evening out as the impact of what we've just done hangs in the air around us.

Still inside me, he reaches for my chin and brings his lips to mine, his kiss easing us both back into the present.

I groan against his lips. "That was..."

"Fucking incredible." He slaps my ass and then squeezes it.

Still trying to catch my breath, I lift off his wet cock, my thighs sticky with a mix of me and him.

With heated dark eyes, he puts his cock away and watches me slip into my dress.

He reaches for the bottle of Jameson on the table, and I slide into the seat beside him, wondering what the protocol is here.

Do we pretend it never happened and keep watching the show?

But my uncertainty is short-lived. When I glance at Nico, the look on his face tells me he hasn't finished with me yet ...

And that I won't be getting any sleep before the sun rises.

27

Nico

The sudden explosion of sunlight assaults my eyes as I leave the underground parking garage and ease onto the busy street. Pulling on my sunglasses, I suck in the pretzel-scented air of a late New York morning and head to my office.

I'm already late, which I don't tolerate from anyone. Staff, soldiers, associates. *Me.* But this morning, I don't care about breaking my own rule. I'm hungover as fuck and exhausted from lack of sleep.

But for good reasons.

Last night, I repeatedly fucked my bride-to-be until we were both too exhausted to come anymore. With her walls down, my little hellcat wasn't shy in taking what she needed from me, and her tantalizing body writhed beneath me as she came over and over again.

When we finally collapsed from exhaustion and drifted

into a heavy sleep, the sun was breaking on the horizon. There had been no time to consider the consequences of what we'd just done. Her letting her walls down and me drinking from the poisoned chalice to only want more.

It was a surprise to wake up beside her this morning and not feel the usual next-day regret as I have in the past if ever I've mistakenly fallen asleep in my companion's bed. It's only happened twice in ten years, and each time was just as awkward and stomach-churning as the other.

In fact, if I'm really honest, waking up with Bella was as far from awkward as possible. Instead, it felt... *almost fucking normal.* As if waking up still high on the numerous orgasms from the night before is something we do every day.

Driving through heavy New York traffic, I harden at the memory and have to adjust myself as a renewed need gathers inside me. A need to ravish her body with the same savagery we both enjoyed last night, so I can wake up beside her and see that delicious sleepy smile on her plush lips again.

The memory sends a kick to my heart.

Feeling soft and warm in bed beside her, I had wanted to kiss that smile from her lips and sink into her warm body and somehow satiate this need she's awoken in me. But she'd kiboshed that thought with a dark look and a raised eyebrow.

"Hold your horses, sex fiend. This body isn't a theme park ride you can climb on whenever you want a good time." She sat up, her glorious curls cascading over her naked shoulders. "Just because you made me come a couple of times—"

"I believe it was more than a couple," I said lightly.

"—doesn't mean I'm open for business at your beck and call."

"What if that beck and call promises immense sexual satisfaction with unlimited orgasms?"

Her eyes had flared, and I had watched the war take place behind them as she did what any smart Mafia princess would do. Weigh her options.

Suddenly, she was open to negotiation.

And if I'm good at anything, it's negotiating something until I get what I want.

When my hands slid between her thighs, the hiss on her lips and the way she parted her legs were the end of her argument. She gave in to her desires, and we spent our morning doing the more pleasurable things two naked people can do in bed.

I grin to myself, ignoring the blare of car horns as I overtake cars and zoom into the parking garage beneath my office above the cocktail den.

I pull out my phone and send her a message.

> I was wrong. You're not going to kill me. My hangover is.

Three dots appear immediately. Then a picture of a boob shows on my screen.

A delicious boob with a taut pink nipple that screams to be sucked and licked and teased with my tongue.

I quickly text back.

> I stand corrected.

Riding the elevator, I remember the little whimpers she

made when I bent her over the balustrade, and a wave of lust kicks my hangover in the balls. I smile and remember how her knees went weak when my cock slid into her from behind, and the moan on her lips as I conjured her orgasm from her with slow, torturous strokes.

I don't doubt she still hates me. But now that I know she wants me, the potential for pleasure is boundless.

"Nico!" Anastacia's worried voice greets me the moment I step out through the door and into the reception area. "I've tried calling you all morning."

"And I've ignored every single one of them," I say as I keep walking, disregarding her look of indignation. "Cancel any appointments I have today and reschedule them for tomorrow."

She trots after me. "But tomorrow is your wedding day!"

I open my door. "Then reschedule them for the day after."

Not waiting for a reply, I close the door, my hangover throbbing in my skull. Now that the party is over, and my dopamine levels are slipping, my headache is gaining power.

"Well, well, well, someone looks like he had a good time last night."

I groan when I see my brother sitting on one of the couches by the window. He's helped himself to an espresso and sips it from a small white cup.

"I'm hungover as fuck. What do you want?" I growl, fixing myself a coffee.

"Is that what we're calling this?" he says, gesturing with his hand to point out my unshaven face, disheveled hair, and tired eyes. "Looks like someone didn't get much sleep."

He wiggles his eyebrows, and I groan, rubbing my temples as my coffee drips from the machine.

He chuckles. "I'd ask if you had a good time last night, but I'm pretty sure I already know the answer."

"Get to the reason you're here."

He rises to his feet. "I've just come from our father's house."

"And?" I drag the cup to my lips and almost die from pleasure as the first mouthful of coffee hits my tastebuds. The nectar is a much-needed elixir to the violence occurring against my brain as we speak.

Massimo puts down his cup and comes to stand in front of me. "Thought you might like to know how his cruise went."

I don't. But my pounding headache hasn't sent me blind. I can see my brother is up to something.

"*And?*"

He grins. "The old bastard got married."

"He fucking did what?"

Massimo can't contain his laughter. "He brought home a new bride."

"Fuck." I drain my cup and immediately make another.

It's too early, and I'm too dusty for this shit.

Since stepping down as a don, our father has become impulsive.

A trait he could never flex as the head of the Mafia unless he wanted to die.

Now he does whatever he wants, when he wants.

A trip to Vegas here.

Buying a Learjet there.

"*Boys, I'm taking a three-month cruise around the world.*"

Now, he's gone and gotten himself hitched.

To a stranger.

I swear, my father is as reckless as he is impulsive.

Unless his new bride is involved in our world, she'll either run when she finds out or become a liability.

And guess who will have to clean up the mess?

Massimo pushes an invite into my chest.

"Here's your invitation to the wedding reception he's throwing her tonight."

"He's aware I'm getting married in the morning?"

"Don't worry, Sleeping Beauty. It's an early dinner. Plenty of time for you to get your beauty sleep before your big day."

28

Bella

I know something is up the moment he gets home. As soon as he walks through the elevator doors, he heads straight to the cellarette to poor himself a scotch.

With his back to me, he growls, "My father got married."

"Married?" I exclaim from the couch where I'm drinking a glass of wine and scrolling Instagram.

"Funny, that's exactly what I said," he mutters before taking a mouthful of scotch.

Agitation rises off him like steam.

"Have you met her?" I ask.

"No, we'll meet her tonight," he says gruffly, shaking off his jacket and throwing it on the couch. "He's throwing a wedding reception for his bride at Zanzibar."

Zanzibar is a restaurant in the Lower West Side.

My brow lifts. "But tomorrow is our wedding day? I was going to spend the night with Imogen. She's booked a room for us at The Plaza. We're going to drink mocktails and talk about all the different ways you can hide a body. You know, stuff I might need to know in the near future."

He throws me a dark look. "Plans change."

I sit up straighter. "Are you telling me the wedding has been called off because Daddy has come back to town with a new wife?"

My upbeat tone seems to irritate him further. "No."

I sigh, disappointed. "Are you sure? I mean, I'm happy to wait."

He stalks off, muttering, "You need to get dressed. They're expecting us at six."

"So that's it?" I jump off the couch to follow him to the bedroom. "I'm expected to cancel my plans with my bridesmaid on the night before my wedding?"

He throws his shirt and tie on the bed. "Yes."

My mood plummets. "I don't remember agreeing to be at your beck and call when I agreed to this arrangement."

"It was implied."

"Hardly an argument that would stack up in court."

He stops by me on his way to the bathroom. "So sue me."

He stands shirtless in front of the sink and begins to shave.

I feel positively combative as I stand in the doorway watching him. The injustice of everything that is my current life seems almost too overwhelming to make sense of right now.

And now we've gone and thrown sex into the chaotic mix.

I think about all the sex we've had in the past twenty-four hours, and my body flushes from my head to my toes.

We haven't had time to discuss what it means to our fake relationship.

If it means anything at all.

"Why are you so upset by your father remarrying?" I ask.

Nico continues to shave as he says, "Because it's reckless and impulsive. We don't know who she is or who she might be associated with."

"So vet her."

"You say that like I haven't spent the entire day doing exactly that."

"And what did you find? Is she associated with anyone?"

"No," he says in a low, angry voice. "But the searches aren't finished. Besides, that's not the point."

"Then explain it to me."

He rinses his razor under the faucet before shaking it off and sliding it across his skin with cutthroat precision.

"The older he gets, the more unpredictable he gets, which is a giant pain in my ass. He would never have done this as don. It opens the family up to too many threats. Yet here he is living like a man who doesn't have a closet full of skeletons." He cleans the shaving cream off his blade again and resumes shaving. "When it all falls to shit, I will be the one who has to clean it up."

"There's one thing you haven't considered," I say. "What if it doesn't fall to shit? What if they find their happily ever after?"

He pauses to give me a doubtful look. "We're De Kysa men, we don't have luck with love. It's something I accepted a long time ago."

And there it is.

The giant elephant in the room that has always been

with us but we've chosen to ignore—why Nico never came to find me on our eighteenth birthday.

And why he hates me so much.

But Nico's current mood is so volatile that bringing up past hurts will only be as helpful as turning on gas near a naked flame.

Which isn't the deterrent it should be.

I cross my arms and lean against the doorframe. "Is that why you didn't come for me on my eighteenth birthday?"

Nico stops shaving but doesn't look at me. He braces against the sides of the sink, and I feel his mood darken even further. Tension tightens in his broad, muscular shoulders. He drags in a deep breath to steady his temper.

Then wordlessly, he picks up his razor and continues shaving.

Which pisses me off even more.

"Don't you think I deserve some answers?" I demand. "It's the very least you could do."

The sound of the razor dropping against the porcelain basin clangs around the room and makes me jump.

He looks like a wild storm about to hit an unprepared coastline, brewing in the distance and pregnant with chaos. A promise of destruction ahead.

Yet he remains silent.

And the silence is deafening.

God, it's like I'm not even here.

He picks up a towel from the countertop to wipe his face.

Fed up, I throw my arms in the air. "Jesus, Nico—why was it so easy for you to forget me?" I cry.

Without warning, he moves at the speed of a tornado.

Grabbing me by the throat, he forces me backward until my shoulders hit the wall behind me.

It's like a bomb has gone off in the bathroom.

All bright light and white heat.

He brings his face close to mine, and the possessive fury in his expression is frightening.

"You think I didn't lie awake every night after you left remembering every tiny detail about you? Your smile. Your hair. Your eyes. Your body. You think I didn't remember how your lips tasted?" He moves his hand to my jaw and squeezes. "Or how it felt to be inside you? How hard you made me. How I died with pleasure every time you came on my cock."

I grit out, "Stop."

But he has no intention of stopping.

"Do you know what it was like for me when you left? The crushing ache I felt for you. The need to touch you. The desperate longing. Do you have any idea what it did to me remembering those whimpers you made every time I slid my cock inside you and know I'd never hear them again?" His black eyes burn with raging fire. "And the way you'd cry out and scream my name when I made you come *over and over and over* again."

I clench my teeth. "I said stop."

"I remembered *everything*, Bella. The way you moved. The way you felt. The way you tasted. The way you told me how much you loved me."

I try to swallow, but the pressure of his fingers around my jaw makes it impossible.

"But you know what I remember the most? I remember how I wanted you so desperately that I was ready to go against my father's wishes and betray my family for you." His teeth glint in the dimly lit room. "How I was prepared to defy him and run away to find you, only to have you replace me the moment you left. So don't talk to me like I was the one who forgot a goddamn thing."

He releases me, and I sag against the wall, and my hands go to my jaw. "I didn't forget anything." I study him as I rub my jaw. "Arianna told me you came looking for me. But I never saw you."

Nico moves away from me, his muscular frame tense. "I'm not doing this right now. Go get changed. We have a dinner to get to."

Apparently, the conversation is over. But I'm not ready for it to be over, so I step in front of him. "No, I want to know what you mean when you say that I replaced you?"

His jaw clenches. "Move out of my way, Bella."

When he tries to move around me, I push my palm into his chest to stop him. "You started it, and now we're going to finish it. I never replaced you."

He looks at my hand in the center of his chest, then slowly raises his stormy eyes to me. I imagine it is very intimidating when he does this to his rivals. And I'm no different. The cold fury in his gaze is a stark warning that this man is dangerous.

"You don't want to do this now," he growls. "It's not going to improve my mood, and you don't know what I am capable of doing when I lose my temper."

"Okay, *Dr. Banner*, but I'm beyond caring right now. You can turn green and grow an extra set of muscles, I don't give a goddamn. But at least do me the courtesy of answering my question. How did I replace you?"

The Devil's Den

He raises an eyebrow. "Are you denying that you did?"

I open my mouth to deny it but close it when a long-forgotten memory falls into place, and I remember David.

A boy I tried to move on with.

And so everything falls into place.

My hand drops to my side.

"So you came to America and saw me with a boy," I say with the sudden knowledge.

The stony silence from Nico tells me I'm right.

"But you didn't just see me with a boy, you saw me kiss a boy."

Nico's voice is low and dangerous as it cuts into the silence. "Yes."

I nod, feeling the regret of a sixteen-year-old girl who made the mistake and tried to move on when everyone told her to. "It's not what you think," I say.

"You mean it wasn't you on a date with another boy?" He moves as if suddenly coming to life and takes a predatory step forward. "It wasn't you kissing him in the doorway of your father's apartment building? It wasn't him putting his hands on you as that kiss turned into something much, much more than a simple kiss good night?"

"You were watching—"

"Yes, I was goddamn watching," he barks. "I was watching as my entire fucking life came crashing down around me. I had run away to find you. To disappear with you. To be with you. Only to find you with him..." His eyes blaze, his jaw ticks. "It was like being struck by fucking lightning. In a split second, everything changed."

"What you saw... it was only a small fragment of what my life was like when I first came to America."

"It didn't feel fucking small to me."

"You have to understand the upheaval I'd just gone through."

"My mother had just died, and my girlfriend was three thousand miles away. Don't talk to me about upheaval."

I draw in a deep breath to steady my nerves. There is so much I need to say, but the mood in the room is tense and volatile, so I need to choose my words wisely.

"When I arrived in America, my father told me I had to move on. I was only sixteen years old, and the separation from you became more and more difficult to live with. I made friends, I started hanging out. They saw how miserable I was missing you and encouraged me to move on. Just like my father told me to do. I couldn't bear the idea, but eventually, I couldn't take the loneliness anymore. It fucked with my head. It was either fit in or fall apart. You seemed so far away, and I got confused. So I agreed to go on a date with David. I tried to forget you, tried to move on just like everyone told me to. I was too young, too naive to realize what a mistake I was making."

I remember the crushing loneliness like it was yesterday. How foreign everything was and how desperately I wanted to feel normal again.

When you're sixteen, everything seems so much bigger and more tragic.

"But when I went on dates with him, when I kissed him, it didn't feel right. It was a big mistake, and I realized very quickly that hanging out with a new boy and kissing him wasn't going to make me love you any less, so I broke up with him."

The Devil's Den

When he says nothing, I huff out a breath. "I made a mistake. Haven't you ever made one of those?"

His jaw ticks. "I don't make mistakes."

Of course, he doesn't.

"We were teenagers, Nico."

"Don't you think I know that? I would've gotten over it. Moved on. But I didn't get the chance. Because when I came home, my father told me how my mother killed herself because of your father, and my heartbreak morphed into something more than just a broken teenage heart. It became something much darker."

My eyes widen. "Why would your mother kill herself because of my—"

"They were having an affair, Bella."

His words catch me off guard. Not to mention harpoon me in the heart.

I take a step back. "You're lying."

"After your mama and brothers died, they started an affair."

"Don't say that," I warn.

A warning he chooses to ignore.

"When she learned of your father's plans to move to the States, she begged him to take her with him. But he refused. So she killed herself in front of the two men who'd let her down the most in her life. A final fuck you for the sad, loveless marriage she'd endured with my father and the disappointing end to a passionate love affair she had with yours."

"I don't believe you," I whisper.

"It's true, Bella. Ask your father."

I grit my teeth so hard my jaw spasms. "I will, and then

you'll owe me a big fucking apology when we find out it was a lie."

"You're right. We'll talk to him about it. And then you'll know the truth."

I glare at him. But his stormy eyes tell me he couldn't care less.

Exhausted, I let out a heavy breath.

I finally have the answers my broken teenage heart had longed for—answers I will process alone. But it seems obvious to me. Fate had been against us from the very start. "After the wedding, we will talk with my father. Until then, I don't want to hear anything more about it."

He nods. He seems calmer, his head slightly bowed, but his body is still taut and tense and braced for battle.

I reach for him and cup his strong face in my hands. "I'm sorry for my mistake, but I will not apologize again for it. I'm sorry our parents let us down and betrayed friendships. I'm sorry for all of it. The wars. The bloodshed. The death. But we can't change what happened. We can either move forward and make things right or live in the past with all our demons."

I feel the tension in his body ease slightly as another brick tumbles from the wall around his black heart.

I rise on my tiptoes to press my forehead to his. "I have agreed to marry you. I will live with you. I will play the role of your wife in public as I am expected to. I will respect and honor our agreement. But if you ever put your hands on me again, Don De Kysa, then as your queen, I will destroy you."

29

Nico

My mood thaws during the car ride to the reception dinner.

Beside me, Bella stares silently out the window while I stare out the other.

I'm trying to put a name to the strange feeling lodged in my chest.

The one that tells me I might be losing control of the situation.

I never expected any of this.

Truth be told, I was so consumed by my need for revenge I didn't form any expectations of what *we* would be together.

Oh, I knew Bella would fight me. But I never thought she'd play along, let alone rise up like a queen.

If you ever put your hands on me again, Don De Kysa, then as your queen, I will destroy you.

And the feeling it stirs in my blood makes me wonder what the hell is happening to me.

With no warning, a tight knot has lodged in my chest when I think about my bride, and it's not a knot of panic or fear or irritation.

It's a knot of longing.

Somewhere along the way, I've started to enjoy her company.

And somehow, I've started to consider her feelings more and more.

Like right now, when I realize this dinner will be the first time she's seen my father since Italy. Back when he was the giant asshole of the family.

The crown he has since passed down to me.

I take a glance at her. Her pulse thumps against her slender throat, and she silently bites down on her bottom lip. It's a nervous tic that makes my lust ignite and my cock hard. I turn away before I give in to my urges and hate fuck her against the back seat.

She's probably petrified.

I steal another glance.

No, she's not petrified. But she's nervous.

And she has every reason to be.

Gio De Kysa is a mean, impulsive son of a bitch who still hasn't forgiven her father for what happened that night.

He also mopped up the tears of his brokenhearted teenage son when he returned home after running away to the US to find his girl.

So much has changed since then.

Without speaking, I reach over and take Bella's hand in mine, and I hold it tight all the way to the restaurant.

It's like a De Kysa family reunion.

After word spread of my father's spontaneous nuptials, all the De Kysas in the US have descended on the restaurant where the wedding celebration is being held. Uncles. Cousins. Distant relatives. Somehow they've hauled ass to make it on short notice.

When Bella and I walk in, we make a beeline for the bar. My father's new wife, Juliet, descends on us like a shooting star crashing to earth.

"Domenico, it's so lovely to meet you." A plume of Chanel No.5 engulfs me at the same time a pair of bedazzled arms wrap themselves around me. "I've heard so much about you. I heard you were handsome, but your reputation doesn't do you justice. Look at that thick head of hair and those cheekbones. My lord, you look like your father. Have you met my daughter, Eve, yet? She's a little peculiar, but you'll get used to her."

My father's new wife is like a cannonball erupting out of a cannon at full speed. High energy and explosive.

And she likes to talk.

A lot.

She loops her arm through mine. "I do hope we can spend some time together and get to know each other. You must visit us at the house. I'll fix you my shrimp and grits, it's to die for, and you can get to know your stepsister a bit better. We're family now. Perhaps we can visit the Low Country as a family. Good Lord, look at your wife. She's beautiful. Look at that hair." She sighs as she looks at Bella. "I have to pay for that color, but you are a natural beauty."

Bella chuckles politely. "Thank you."

I observe the new Mrs. Gio De Kysa.

The willowy redhead from South Carolina is nothing like the women my father has dated in the past. She looks like she fell into a vat of glitter and sparkles in her short skirt and tight jacket covered in pink and white sequins. Even her high heels sparkle. Thick makeup does nothing to hide the years she has on my father. If I were a betting man, I'd put her somewhere in her early sixties.

My old man nabbed himself a cougar.

First impressions are good. She seems genuine in her feelings for him.

My stepsister, Eve, on the other hand, is a precocious wild child with untrusting eyes and an obstreperous attitude. She's somewhere in her late teens, and her deep frown and crossed arms tell me she'd rather be anywhere but here.

I feel her suspicious gaze fix on me from across the room as Bella and I talk with her mom.

When I look and nod at her, she rolls her eyes and looks away. Only to glance back and scowl at me again.

Juliet continues to talk Bella's ear off.

"We must get together for some girl talk. Let's do a spa day, a couple of De Kysa gals getting their mani-pedis," she says, full of bubbly excitement. "Oh look, there's my uncle Emmett raiding the dessert bar. Best I distract him before he eats all the cake."

Bella chuckles as we watch Juliet sweep across the room to stop her elderly relative from stealing four slices of wedding cake. "She's not what I expected," Bella whispers. "I really like her."

The fact that my father chose a wife who is talkative and loud, and nothing like the well-put-together dolls he usually lures into his bed, tells me he's getting more sentimental in his old age.

Not that being in his late fifties is what I'd call old.

"What do you think he sees in her?" I ask Bella.

"She's fun."

"Fun?"

"I know that's a novel concept to you, Don De Kysa," she whispers, amusement glinting in her eyes, "but some people actually enjoy letting their hair down and having some fun."

I scoff. "I know how to have fun."

"I mean real fun, Nico. Not *your* type of fun."

"*My* type of fun?"

"Yeah, waving your gun around and dreaming up your next evil plan."

"Exactly what do you think I do all day? Sit in my office and stick pins in voodoo dolls of my rivals while thinking about different ways to take them out?"

"Pretty much."

I shoot her a pointed look. "I know how to have fun, Bella."

"Sure," she says, looking around the room.

"That sounds like a challenge."

Her beautiful gaze comes back to me. "Is that a fact?"

I stand and take her hand. "Challenge accepted."

Her eyes gleam as she accepts it. "Do your worst, villain."

As I take her hand and lead her to the dance floor, the DJ decides to play a golden oldie. "Machine Gun" by the Commodores. A throwback to the disco era.

I grab my bride-to-be, crush her to my body, and slide my fingers into hers.

As a rule, I'm not a dancer. Sure, I'll dance at my engagement party. Hell, I'll dance at my wedding. But for fun? No fucking way. I'm way too tense to enjoy it. But with Bella in my arms, anything is possible. And right now, every inch of me loves her luscious curves grinding against mine as we move around the dance floor.

I spin her and she laughs, and before I can stop myself, I'm smiling and laughing too.

I yank her back to me and hold her against my body. "Let's blow this party and go home."

"We've been here five minutes," she says, winding her arms around my neck.

"Which is five minutes too long." My palms glide over her juicy ass. "And I can think of better ways to spend the eve of my wedding."

"I had plans too, remember? But you made me come to this instead."

"Let me make it up to you?"

"And how do you plan to do that?"

I cup her ass and pull her against my erection.

"You know I don't like you, right?" she says with an arched eyebrow.

"Like has nothing to do with it," I whisper in her ear. "I think we've both learned that hate fucking can be a lot of fun."

Her cheeks flush. "I still haven't forgiven you for any of this, just so you know."

"Good. You can take it out on me in bed."

Lust glimmers in her eyes although she fights it. "You're a rapacious sex fiend."

"I don't hear you complaining when I'm making you come."

The Devil's Den

She bites down on her lip. She's hot and bothered. I press my lips to her throat and feel her racing pulse. "Don't fight *it*, fight *me*. In bed. All night long. You know you'll enjoy it."

She pulls in a shaky breath. "That's not going to happen."

I chuckle. "You'll have to say it with more confidence than that, Bella."

I'll have her coming before the clock strikes midnight.

She pushes her palms into my chest. "I'm not a sure thing, Don De Kysa."

My eyes lock to hers. "But I am, my love. We both know my name will be on your lips tonight."

Her eyes flare. "Yes, when I call 911 to tell them I've murdered my fiancé."

Amusement twitches on my lips.

I could volley with her all night, but the song finishes, and she leads me over to our table, where she downs a glass of water and fans herself with the menu. "I need the bathroom. But your new stepsister is coming over. Promise me you'll behave."

"I'm not the one who's been shooting death cannons from my eyes all night," I mutter as Eve makes her way through the crowd toward us.

"She's young, and you're ferocious. Be nice."

"Like an angel," I mutter.

"That's what I'm afraid of, *Lucifer*."

Bella leaves, and my new stepsister flops into the seat next to me.

"Your wife is hot," she says, taking a sip of champagne.

"Thank you, I think so too."

"But then, I expect nothing less from the don of the De Kysa Mafia."

I have to hand it to the kid. Not too many people can catch me off guard, but her comment just did.

I chuckle before I can stop myself and gesture toward the glass of champagne in her hands.

"I think all those bubbles have gone to your head. Are you sure you're old enough to drink?"

"Relax, gangster. I'm nineteen and can handle a glass of bubbly. Besides, take a look around the room. I think underage drinking is the last thing the authorities would be interested in, given the guests in attendance. It's like a *made men* museum in here."

"Made men?"

She nods. "You know, the Mafia. The mafioso. *Goodfellas. I'm going to make him an offer he can't refuse.*"

I almost choke on my mouthful of scotch at her attempt to impersonate Don Vito Corleone. "I believe that particular quote was from *The Godfather*, not *Goodfellas*," I point out.

She shrugs. "Whatever. You get the point."

"Not really. Other than you're good with impersonations. Can you do others?"

"Not nearly as well as you can change a subject." She takes another sip of champagne. "You're not worried about our parents tying the knot after knowing each other for a mere five minutes?"

"They're adults."

"Not to mention reckless." Her gaze shifts to our parents dancing cheek to cheek on the dance floor. Admittedly, they look very happy. Especially my father.

"They call you the Heartless King from the North," Eve

states randomly. I get the feeling she's been itching to bring it up since I walked in. "They also say you're equally revered as you are feared."

"You seem to know a lot about me," I say.

She lifts her glass. "Google is a fabulous thing."

"And so reliable," I deadpan.

Her expression tightens. "Listen, my mom is a good woman."

"I'm sure she is."

Her face softens as she gnaws the inside of her mouth. "You seem like an alright guy. Please don't let anything happen to her."

It's fleeting, but I don't miss the flash of vulnerability in her eyes.

"Why would anything happen to her?" I ask.

"I don't know. But when this all falls apart because they've only known each other for a couple of months, what happens to her then? She'll be privy to all your Mafia secrets."

For all her googling, Eve really doesn't know how this works at all.

Juliet will never know any secrets.

It takes years for a bride to become privy to anything that happens within the inner sanctum of our family business.

Eve pleads, "Promise me nothing will happen to her."

"What exactly do you think I'd do to her?"

"I don't know, a pair of concrete shoes or something?"

I can't stop the chuckle that escapes me. "You've been watching too many organized crime shows."

We don't bother with concrete shoes anymore.

We've developed more creative ways of disposing of our enemies.

Not that any De Kysa bride has ever been on the receiving end of something so heinous.

"I like your mom," I say.

"You do?" She looks surprised.

"You're not bad either. For a brat stepsister."

Her eyes widen, telling me she likes the comment. Then her gleaming eyes narrow. "You're not nearly as scary as I thought you'd be. You know, for a Mafia madman."

I clink her champagne glass with my scotch tumbler. "Oh, I'm scary. I'm just on my best behavior tonight."

30

Bella

It's *a business deal.*

I remind myself as I stand in front of the full-length mirror wearing my wedding dress.

Then why does it feel like my heart is about to be nailed to the wall?

Because you can't help but hope that somewhere inside the man you're about to marry is the boy you used to love.

Which is pointless, I know.

But the heart can't help but want what it wants.

Frowning, I refocus my attention on my wedding dress.

Magda Bianchon has done an incredible job. It's simple and classy, with twenty-five thousand dollars' worth of elegance thrown in. It's rare Italian silk in the purest of whites, with spaghetti straps and a plunging back. Every inch clings to my curves until it reaches my toes where it fans into a sweeping train.

Today, my unruly red-gold curls are pulled tight off my face and secured into a taut bun at my nape. I reach up and touch my veil, which is yards of the silkiest tulle trailing to the floor in soft white waves.

I draw in an unsteady breath and then release it shakily.

I miss my mama, and her absence weighs heavy in my heart.

As does the loss of my wedding day. *My real wedding day.* The one I'm supposed to share with a man I am giddy in love with, not the man I can barely stand the sight of... even if it is hard to keep my hands off him sometimes.

My cheeks grow hot when I think about just how often that is.

"You look stunning," Imogen says, picking up the bridal bouquet off the table. "No, you look more than stunning. You look *phenomenal*." She grins cheekily. "Nico is going to pop something when he sees you walk down that aisle."

I haven't told Imogen about the sex with Nico. I guess it's because the situation is already complicated enough without involving someone else. And until I know what any of it really means, it's best to keep my mouth shut.

"He's too grumpy to pop anything," I say.

"Well, that ends today. If that boy doesn't cry when he sees you, then he's a robot."

"He *is* a robot. A grumpy robot monster with no feelings."

She smiles wickedly. "I think you're wrong. Under all that stony facade and alpha male manliness is a man smoldering with feelings and lust and needs." She sighs. "If you weren't already marrying him, I'd offer myself to him on a platter."

I hold out my bridal bouquet to her. "Great, you meet him at the end of the aisle, then."

She gives me a pointed look. She doesn't really want Nico. This is her way of telling me I'm going to be okay. *Hey, if it was me, I would jump.*

Her expression grows serious. "I'm pretty sure there's only one girl he wants to see at the end of that aisle when the music starts." It's not often my flighty best friend gets sentimental, but I hear it in her tone as she says, "He's a very lucky man, I want you to remember that." Tears well in her eyes, then she adds, "And if he hurts you, then I'm going staple his balls to my car's bumper and drive around the block. It'll just take one phone call from my best friend, you got it?"

I laugh and pull her in for a hug. "Got it."

No matter what happens, I know I have Imogen in my corner.

"Are you ready to do this?" she asks, stepping back.

I let out another shaky breath, my pulse racing.

It's a business deal.

"Might as well jump in feet first," I say. Taking the bouquet from Imogen, I give my best friend a nervous smile. "Let's do this."

～

As far as weddings go, mine is as chilly as the North Pole in a blizzard.

The tension in the air is palpable, the temperature cold and hard.

The threat of danger simmers beneath the surface.

The ceremony takes place on the terrace of the Stone Mill in the New York Botanical Gardens.

A blue carpet serves as an aisle that leads me away from my old life and toward my husband to be.

On one side are the Isle Ciccula and their soldiers.

On the other are the De Kysa and their soldiers.

Walking down the aisle with my father, it feels as safe as swimming in a pool of great white sharks.

I know my father is wearing Kevlar beneath his suit jacket, and it wouldn't surprise me if Gio De Kysa is too.

Nico, however, seems cool and calm as he waits for me at the end of the aisle. I know for a fact he isn't wearing anything under that custom suit and crisp white shirt of his, because it is tailored to perfection against his powerful body and leaves no room for armor.

When the marriage celebrant asks *who gives this bride*, my father bristles and murders Nico with his eyes. A warning of what will come if anything should happen to me, forcing me to squeeze his hand reassuringly to let him know it is okay.

I'm in safe hands.

I think.

Nico's gaze sweeps over me with approval and lust-soaked eyes. "You look stunning."

"Thank you."

A smile tugs on his full lips. "This is where you say I look stunning too."

I raise an eyebrow and shrug. "I mean, you look okay."

I'm downplaying it because he looks fucking gorgeous.

Slicked-back hair. Trimmed beard. Sharp jaw. Long lashes.

The Devil's Den

One perfect dark brow pops up. "Just okay? I'm fucking hot, and you know it."

He grins. Sometimes I think he says things because he knows I'll fight him, and he gets off on my retorts. But I don't. Instead, I look away because the twinkle in his eyes makes me nervous, and I look back at the crowd, and the sea of Mafia faces sends a new wave of anxiety through me.

Nico takes my hands in his, and I'm startled by the strength I feel in them. It's then I realize that mine are shaking.

I take another nervous glance over my shoulder at the two rivals continuing to glare at one another across the aisle.

"Don't look at them, look at me," Nico says with a kindness in his voice. "Today, they don't matter. Today is about you and me."

"It doesn't look that way." I lean in and whisper, "I feel like we're going to be this evening's headline when the massacre breaks out."

"Oh, we're definitely this evening's headline. Can't you hear the choppers circling above?"

He's not wrong. The beautiful stone building provides us with enough protection from the media, but beyond that, it's chaotic with press and news crews eager to report on New York's most eligible bachelor getting hitched.

A thousand cameras went crazy when I arrived.

I huff out a nervous breath, knowing I won't ever be comfortable with that level of attention again.

Nico's eyes are warm when he chuckles. "Relax, Bella."

"Easy for you to say. You're not marrying a—"

"Psychotic piranha."

My eyes round, and I glare at him.

The only person I've ever said that to was Imogen.

On a phone call.

In my bedroom.

Weeks ago.

It doesn't take a genius to work out how he knows. "You bugged my room?"

"You're surprised?" He whispers as he leans closer, "I'm a bad man, remember?"

He smirks, and I'd give anything to be able to wipe it off his face.

But as usual, he has the upper hand.

"At least you're honest," I grumble.

Beside us, the marriage celebrant clears his throat, reminding us that he is waiting to marry us.

I can tell he's nervous. I get the feeling he's waiting for the tension to ignite too.

But then he begins the ceremony, and slowly, the stormy weather system eases from the atmosphere.

Not that I hear anything he says. All I'm aware of is Nico's hot gaze warming my skin and the way it hasn't left me since he took my hands in his.

I don't look at him because I know what will come over me when I do. It will be the same tightening in my stomach and relentless pulsating throb between my legs I felt when I saw him waiting for me at the end of the aisle, looking all delicious and dangerously hot.

We fuck a lot because of that tightening and throbbing sensation.

It comes over me and all rhyme and reason leave me, resulting in lots of sweaty, uninhibited sex.

And neither of us seems to be tiring of it.

The Devil's Den

For me, it feels safe. Like I know where I sit with him.

For him... who knows? We don't talk about it. And the only words he says to me during sex are filthy and depraved, and deliciously carnal.

Like this morning, when I kneeled in front of him, and he fucked my mouth with his engorged cock and told me my juicy lips were made for sucking cock. *His cock.* "Suck me harder, baby. Make me come with that greedy little mouth of yours."

I did, and he came in hot spurts down my throat until he was milked of every last drop.

Then he returned the favor until I was a writhing mess on the bed with his head between my parted thighs and his name on my kiss-drunk lips.

I blush, suddenly remembering where I am.

I glance at Nico, and the amused smile on his filthy mouth tells me he knows exactly what I was thinking about. My cheeks get hot. It's like he can read my mind, which knowing my luck, he probably can.

Before I know it, we're reciting vows.

Then the marriage celebrant announces us man and wife, and Nico reaches for me.

He takes my face in his big hands and kisses me, and just like that, we're married.

∼

I'm Bella De Kysa.

Wife to don Nico De Kysa.

The words seem to be on repeat in my head during the reception being held inside the Stone Mill.

Music plays. Champagne flows. Gourmet food is ferried from the kitchen to the tables where Mafia dons and their soldiers and families eat heartily, one hand on their glasses, the other on their guns.

Gio De Kysa and my father stare at one another across the room, but neither makes a move toward the other. They might be an alliance in marriage, but the old rivals are not ready to forgive and forget.

At least they're not shooting each other, I think as I watch them from the bridal table.

My father leaves after the speeches, and Gio De Kysa does the same not long after.

Nico leans over to me. "It's time for us to leave."

"Now?" I look around the room full of guests. Granted, I don't know a lot of them, but still, it feels rude to leave them so early.

Nico's fingers trail down the bare skin on my back. "I want to fuck you in that dress, Bella. I have ever since I saw you walk down the aisle, and I can't wait any longer."

His black eyes sweep over my face, igniting a throb at my core.

We take a limousine back to his apartment. In the back seat, he pulls me onto his lap and begins kissing me deep and hard.

His big hands roam my body while I enjoy the hardness of his erection between the cheeks of my ass. If I wasn't bound by my dress, I would straddle him, sink onto his glorious cock, and ride him all the way home to Manhattan. Instead, I gently rock against him, knowing the friction drives him wild. I feel it in his kiss. In the way his fingers grip my arms. In the growl he unleashes.

"Bella..." His voice is rough. "You'll make me come."

"And the problem with that is...?"

He rasps, "I want to come inside you when I do."

I reach between us and massage the thick outline of his cock.

"I mean it," he growls. "Unless you want me to rip open your dress and fuck you senseless right now, you need to stop."

I don't want my dress ruined, so I stop torturing him and settle for kissing him instead.

Soft, gentle kisses. The kind you do when you feel something so deeply for someone.

I frown and break it off, unnerved by the thought.

But eye to eye, something passes between us in the confined space, something that unnerves us both in the silence. If I were to slide out of my dress and sink onto him, it wouldn't be fucking. It would be making love.

"Champagne?" he offers, reaching for the bottle in the door caddy.

"Yes, please." I move to climb off him, but his strong arm holds me in place.

"You're not going anywhere, Mrs. De Kysa."

I remain on his lap as he opens the bottle of Dom Perignon.

He doesn't bother with glasses. Instead, he raises the bottle to my lips and gently tips the delicious champagne into my mouth.

When I slide my lips from the tip of the bottle, he pulls my mouth to his and kisses the champagne from my lips.

By the time we reach Manhattan, the bottle is half gone, and I'm feeling light-headed and excited. Anticipation fizzes through me as we pull up to the apartment block, knowing what's going to happen once we get inside.

Nico slides me off him so he can open the door and climb out. We're in the private alleyway at the back of the building, only accessible by a key card, to avoid the paparazzi waiting out the front.

Clutching the bottle in one hand and steadying myself against the door with the other, I follow my husband out of the limo and through the back entrance.

"Home sweet home," he says, punching the elevator button.

Once inside, he kisses me up against the wall, groaning when it goes deeper.

"Put down the champagne bottle, Bella," he says, caging me in his arms.

"Why?"

"So I can carry you over the threshold."

With a head full of bubbles, I put down the bottle and then throw my arms around his neck. Our lips crash together as the elevator doors open.

Kissing me fiercely, he accidentally stands on my dress, and we tumble over the threshold and into the penthouse.

"You're supposed to carry me over the threshold, not throw me." I laugh, splayed across the marble floor in a twenty-five-thousand-dollar Magda Bianchon.

He crawls over me, and all I can do is gaze up at the smoldering heat on his face as he stares down at me.

"Did you wear the La Perla?" he drawls, his gaze raking over my breasts which are barely covered by my dress.

"Have you seen this dress? There isn't a lot of room for

underwear." I give him a wicked smile and whisper, "I'm practically naked underneath."

Lust flares in his dark eyes. "Naked, huh?"

"Apart from a teeny tiny thong, yeah." I give him a little shrug. "It was my something blue."

He reaches between us and gathers the hem of my dress. I gasp when his fingers brush across the satiny front of my thong and whisper across my clit. Hooking his finger, he tugs on the soft panties, rolling onto his side so he can slide them down my leg.

He holds up the icy-blue thong. "It is indeed teeny tiny."

I chuckle, but it fades as I lift an eyebrow and say, "Now *I am* naked underneath this dress. Any idea what you might like to do about that?"

Nico discards the thong and unbuckles his belt. Unzipping his dress pants, he crawls over me. "I'm going to fuck you for the first time as my wife."

"Right here on the floor?"

"Do you have a problem with that?" he growls, lowering himself between my legs.

I raise an eyebrow. "What do you think?"

Reaching between us, he springs himself free. With one smooth push, he slides his beautiful thick cock into me, and my back arches with pleasure.

"Admit it, you've wanted this since you saw me waiting for you at the end of the aisle," he rasps, his eyes hooded.

"Murder was out of the question, so I figured this was the next best thing." He thrusts in deeper, making me cry out. I dig my nails into his arm. "You savage."

He growls with appreciation. "Keep digging your claws in, hellcat, and I'll show you how savage I can be."

Another deep thrust kisses the back of my womb.

"Do your worst, demon."

My wrists slap the floor above my head as he pins them to the floor and drives his cock into me. He wants to come. I can see it on his face. He's fighting it. But he won't let himself. Not until I do.

Which won't take long.

He grinds his pelvis into me, setting light to every raw nerve ending in my clit.

God, why does this feel so good when it's so very wrong?

"I hate you," I whisper as if I need to remind myself.

"Don't lie, you fucking love me," he rasps, stroking his cock thick and hard into me.

I clench around his cock, close to coming. "I don't love you. I like *fucking* you. That is all."

He responds by thrusting deeper and harder, his balls slapping my pussy and detonating my orgasm as he growls, "That's good enough for now."

31

Nico

"Call Cian the Violent and organize a meeting," I growl from behind my desk in my office.

It's the day after my wedding, and instead of lying on some beach somewhere, fucking my bride until we're too weak to walk, I'm here, dealing with this shit.

While I was busy getting married, the Irish decided to decimate one of our warehouses on the waterfront. They blew it sky high like it was the Fourth of July.

It was a message. *Pay attention.*

"You're going to sit down with that crazy son of a bitch?" Massimo frowns.

"The Irish are moving in, and the Russians aren't far behind them. I need this sorted out now. No more fucking around."

"Cian the Violent can't be trusted," Mateo says.

"He's going to have to show some trustworthiness

because my patience is running out. He either sits down with me, and we work something out, or he dies. I'm feeling generous, so I'm giving him the choice. Meet me or don't meet me. The former would bode better for him."

"You're seeking a truce?" Massimo sounds incredulous.

"I'm seeking a business arrangement," I say calmly. "The Irish want in—they can have in. *For a price.* Let's reach out to the Russians as well. Call Vicktor Voltan and invite him to the meeting. It's time to spread the love."

"I will get the messages out," Mateo says, rising to his feet. "When do you want to meet with them?"

"Sooner rather than later."

"The Restaurant?" he asks.

The Restaurant is an abandoned café on the waterfront and is considered neutral territory between all rival crime syndicates. As a matter of honor, no blood is to be spilled there. Breaking the sanctity would mean death for everyone involved.

Mateo nods and leaves the room, leaving me alone with my brother.

"Married two minutes and you're throwing offers of truce around like candy," he mutters.

"Marriage has nothing to do with it. This is business. And moving forward, this is the *only* way."

"How is Bella, by the way?" He picks up a bronze paperweight from my desk and begins studying it.

"Probably at home planning my murder because I'm here and not there," I reply, taking it from him and putting it back where he found it.

"No honeymoon?"

"We're flying to London tomorrow to pack up her old life and bring her belongings back home."

The sooner we can put that chapter behind us, the better. I know Bella still harbors some insecurity because of that ridiculous idiot Simon. Let her forget that part of her life and grow stronger at my side.

"Sounds romantic," Massimo deadpans.

"It's not supposed to be. It's pragmatic. Now that she's my wife, it's time she moves her life back to the US for good."

"But you're developing feelings for her," he states, matter-of-factly.

"She's the bane of my existence," I say dryly.

"That you have feelings for."

"I wouldn't call not wanting to tape her mouth closed with electrical tape and locking her in a room every time she opens her mouth *developing feelings for her*," I say flatly. "I barely tolerate her."

If my brother was the eye-rolling type, he'd be doing it now. But he isn't. He simply gives me one of those pointed looks that makes me feel like *I'm* the younger brother who has much to learn.

"She's getting to you," he says, knowingly.

Of course she is. I can't seem to keep my hands off her.

"Yes, she's getting on my nerves on a daily basis," I lament. "Can we forget about Bella and talk about this meeting with the Irish and the Russians?"

"Ah yes, the meeting. Two months ago, you would have declared war on both factions, and now you're offering to buy them lunch."

"Now that we're aligned with the Isle Ciccula, they know trying for the East Coast would be a foolish move. They won't win, and their camps would be decimated in the process. Last night's attack was the death rattle. Their final show of power fizzled like a dead skyrocket at launch." Leaning my elbows on my desk, I rub my temples. "Me offering them a small piece of the pie is the cherry on top to ensure they don't try again and waste all of our time."

"So you'd rather make love not war? Christ, being married really has gone to your head."

"I don't look at it as making love. I look at it as making money." I fix my brother with a sharp look. "I'd rather be a rich man with a pulse than a dead man in the ground, and this deal improves the odds."

Massimo lifts his brow. "So that's it, we're all just friends now?"

"Not friends. Not even alliances. Just business partners. You know the old saying, keep your friends close but your enemies closer."

My brother stands. "Just remember, Cian the Violent isn't just an enemy. He's a snake in the grass and can't be trusted."

"And I have a bullet with his name on it if he tries to strike." I stand and walk around to face him, leaning against my desk in front of him. "I know what I'm doing, brother."

"I hope so," he says. "Because I'm still not convinced all the blood hasn't left the head on your shoulders to fund the permanent hard-on you have in your pants for your new wife. You can lie to me all you want, Don De Kysa, but she's having an effect on you whether you like it or not." He grins, and it's laced with mischief. "Me personally, I'm kinda digging it. You're not nearly the asshole you usually are."

When I finally get my annoying younger brother to

leave, I put some focus on our legit business interests and send off a couple of emails that have been pressing me for my attention before I leave the office.

It's dusk by the time I find myself riding the elevator to our apartment.

The door opens, and I find my wife waiting for me on the edge of the sofa wearing a pair of black Louboutins.

And *only* a pair of black Louboutins.

She parts her tantalizing thighs a little wider when I step out of the elevator.

"Welcome home, husband."

I know it's probably a trap.

Bella should come with a warning.

She probably has plans to distract me with sex so she can plunge a knife into my back.

But damn if I care.

I rip off my tie and discard it as I let the doors close behind me. "Hello, wife."

32

Bella

I wake up to the sound of Anastacia's voice in the lounge room. I open my eyes and stretch my limbs and yawn, feeling more relaxed than I ever have in my entire life. Which is surprising, given the lack of sleep I got last night. A thrill runs up the length of my spine when I remember how creative Nico got with his tongue in the early hours of this morning.

The things he did to me might actually be considered depraved, I think as a wicked smile slides across my face. *But very, very welcomed.*

I sit up and hold the sheet to my naked chest when Anastacia breezes into the bedroom.

She gives me a look that says she'd rather give herself a lobotomy with a spoon than deal with me today.

"Good morning." I smile brightly, determined to win her over.

"And look, she's still in bed," she says, yanking open the curtains.

Outside, the city is covered in whispery gray clouds as rain drops pelt the buildings below. Rainwater falls in shimmery rivulets down the glass, like tears down a cheek.

The perfect day to stay in bed and fuck your man until you can't walk.

Those were the words I said to Nico this morning as we lay satiated in our bed, our bodies still humming from our early morning lovemaking. But he was needed at the office and very reluctantly climbed out of bed, whispering to me, "Tonight, I will fuck you until you can no longer move."

I don't doubt it. The man has stamina.

"So how are you this morning?" I ask Anastacia. I knew she was coming over. Today, some fancy-pants fashion stylist is coming over with some clothes for me to try on.

"Busy," she drawls as she takes my robe off the wall and hands it to me. "You need to take a shower before the stylist gets here. You have half an hour."

"You don't like me very much, do you?" I say lightly as I put the robe on.

"It's not my job to like or dislike you."

"I know, but unless you're a robot you must have feelings." I tie the robe at my waist. "I think we got off on the wrong foot, and I'm sorry. The day we met—"

"And you went off like a bull in a china shop looking for Nico?"

Ah, there it is.

"I'm sorry about that," I say truthfully.

"I take my job very seriously, Bella. I work very hard to

make sure everything is organized and in its place. What you did that day made me look like a fool in front of Nico."

I give her a remorseful nod. "It wasn't my intention, I assure you. I was... *emotional* about the—"

"Arrangement," she says with a raised eyebrow.

Her use of the word reminds me of how much has changed since then. A month ago, I would never have dreamed I'd be warming Nico's bed. *And coming over and over again with his name on my lips.*

"Yes, it was all a bit overwhelming, and I'm sorry if I upset you."

She stiffens and looks indignant, not meeting my eyes. But I get the feeling this is her accepting my apology.

"Like I said, the stylist will be here. Best you take a shower." She turns to walk out but stops at the door. She doesn't fully turn back to look at me but offers me her profile. "You like your coffee black with no sugar, right?"

I smile. Anastacia's arctic frost is beginning to thaw. "Yes."

She gives me a short, curt nod and leaves the room.

～

"Well, if my eyes don't betray me!" I exclaim when I see the stylist walking into Nico's large lounge room. "LaLa La Trobe!"

I leap off the couch to hug my old friend.

"The one and only," he replies, his deep, smoky voice full of affection as he wraps his arms around me. I squeeze my arms around his large frame, happy to see him.

We break our embrace, and he holds me at arm's length

so he can get a good look at me. "Bella Isle Ciccula, always the belle of the ball. You look stunning as always."

I've known LaLa since I was in college, and he was an up-and-coming stylist working as a performer at Buster's. The colorful club was in West Village, and Ari and I used to visit it every Saturday night. We met LaLa and quickly became friends with the six-foot glamour. When Imogen wasn't on a date, she'd join us, and our little foursome had some wild, wonderful nights forged in cocktails, laughing, and dancing.

Unfortunately, we lost touch when I moved to London.

"You're the fancy-pants stylist who will make me look like a million bucks?" I beam happily.

"Baby Belle, ain't nothing I can put you in to make you look a million bucks that you ain't already doing with that natural beauty of yours."

LaLa is from Southern Georgia, and I could listen to the sing-song cadence of his deep velvety voice for hours.

I swat him playfully. "There's the LaLa I know and love. You always were such a charmer. I can't believe you're really here."

"And I still can't believe you're the famous Mrs. De Kysa everyone is talking about. When I first heard you'd married that delectable billionaire with those smoldering good looks and all that facial hair, I thought well done, Baby Belle, well done. You married the king."

Anastacia visibly balks at the reference, which LaLa notices and does a double take.

I hook my arm through his. "Ignore her, she hates me."

He gasps theatrically. "How could anyone hate my sweet-as-pie Italian cannoli?"

"Poor taste, I guess." I grin at Anastacia. "But I'm wearing her down."

This time, she dramatically rolls her eyes at me.

"So what have you brought me today?" I ask, excited because LaLa *gets* me. He won't have brought anything vanilla or stuffy with him. It will be colorful and fun.

"Are you ready to be dazzled?" he asks with a mischievous grin.

I clap my hands with excitement. "Yes!"

"Well then, sit down, my sweet cannoli, and let the show begin."

Grinning from ear to ear, I take a seat next to Anastacia, and when LaLa snaps his fingers, the elevator doors open, and three assistants wheel in clothing racks loaded with outfits of all colors and styles. Behind them, four models strut in, ready to work the imaginary runway in Nico's living room. Somewhere, music starts playing, and the fun fashion show begins.

Each model parades a new outfit in front of me, twisting and twirling so I can see every detail of the outfit. While LaLa explains in great detail everything about the outfit, from the designer who created it and the fabric used, to what event it should be paired with.

Beside me, Anastacia takes notes, scribbling in her planner.

One model comes out in a long gown with a halter neck and covered in tiny black Swarovski crystals. It's stunning and makes me think about the black-tie charity auction we're attending at the Savoy in London tomorrow night. A dress like that would definitely earn me brownie points with my husband.

As if reading my mind, Anastacia leans closer to whisper,

The Devil's Den

"That would be perfect for London."

"I was just thinking the same thing," I reply. "But it looks very expensive. What's the budget?"

She looks at me like I spoke to her in Martian and not English. "There is no budget."

"No budget?"

"No. Budget."

LaLa leans into my other side. "You married a billionaire, honey."

When the show is over, I'm surprised to see it's been going on for more than an hour.

With a clap of his hands, LaLa dismisses the models, and they leave quietly.

He turns to me and holds his hands wide and asks, "What do you think, Baby Belle?"

"I think you have very good taste."

An hour later, I've selected eight outfits, including the black crystal dress, some incredible shoes and accessories, and managed to spend almost twenty thousand dollars.

When everyone leaves, including Anastacia who seems convinced I'm going to somehow make us miss our flight to London in the morning, I stand in front of the massive mirror and admire the new clothes I'm wearing.

I'm wearing a short skirt with a black jacket and heels when the elevator door opens, and Nico appears.

Butterflies take flight in my stomach.

Because seeing him in a suit never gets old.

His heated gaze sweeps over me, lingering on my legs and high heels.

And within seconds, my new outfit is discarded on the floor.

33

Nico

We fly into London the next day.

The charity auction we're expected to attend is being held in the Lancaster Ballroom of the Savoy London.

I'm expected to attend because it is one of those networking events imperative to the De Kysa stronghold in Europe.

I can't afford to be out of sight, out of mind. People need to see the face they're allied with.

But my real reason for coming to London is to tie up loose ends and bring all of Bella back to the States with me.

After arriving by Learjet in the morning, we take a black cab through the rain-soaked streets to Bella's old apartment in Kensington.

I know the address because six months ago, I spent a great deal of time standing in the shadows in front of it, watching and waiting, planning how to lure her back into my world to serve a purpose that almost feels vile now.

A fact I've yet to divulge to my new wife.

Oh, she knows I watched her. *Stalked* her. Just not to the depth that she would find palatable.

I figure I will come clean about it one day.

Just not on my honeymoon.

Because she'll go straight for my balls when she finds out my stalking had no bounds. That watching her come and go from this very address became just as addictive as it was necessary.

"Do you miss it?" I ask as we pull up to the curb.

She steps out of the cab and looks up at the apartment block, then turns to look back at me. "No." Her face is tight. Her eyes sad. This place doesn't hold the fond memories she thought it did.

The look on her face guts me. I want to take every ounce of pain from her and make her happy.

Thankfully, it only takes an hour to pack up her belongings and organize shipping back to the US. But afterward, in our room at the Ritz, she is quiet and withdrawn. So I fuck her hard and fast in the shower because I want to fuck whatever has caused her to be sad and withdrawn out of her mind.

She responds with fevered need, her body undulating against mine as I make her come.

But the weird feeling lingers.

"You're different," I say later, as she sits at the dresser and applies red lipstick.

She looks stunning in a black halter dress covered in shimmering crystals.

She lifts an eyebrow at me in the mirror. "How?"

"You're quiet." The corner of my lips tug. "And we both know, you usually have so much to say."

She turns around.

"It feels strange being back in this town. I'm not the same person I was when I lived here." She pauses, then adds. "Being with you is confusing. I thought I knew what I wanted. That living in London was it. But I was wrong, I'm happier now... because of you."

Unexpected emotion hits me in the chest. Something close to love.

"But don't let that go to your head." A small smile plays on her lips. "God knows that's big enough as it is."

"Too late."

She turns back to look in the mirror and sighs.

"It's been a long time since I've cared what people think about me," she says. "But tonight, I do."

"Because you're in love with me," I say matter-of-factly, sliding on my jacket.

She rolls her eyes. "No. But I am your wife, and these are your people."

"I assure you, these are not my people."

"Then why go?"

"It's business."

She looks down. "Will Amélie be there?"

The hint of jealousy in her voice is unmistakable.

"I'm not privy to Amélie's comings and goings."

"I get the feeling she's privy to yours," she mutters.

I like the jealousy.

"She means nothing to me," I say.

Because it means Bella's walls are crumbling.

She thinks for a moment, then nods. "I'm just nervous, I guess."

I drop a kiss on her shoulder. "Everyone is going to love you." My eyes linger on her face in the mirror. "Just not as much as I do."

Her shoulders tense.

"Are you saying you love me?" Her eyes narrow. "Like a child loves a puppy and the desert loves the rain?"

I pull her to her feet. "I don't have a word for how I feel about you, wife. But whatever it is, it's fucking potent and addictive, and I can't get enough of it."

I wrap my arms around my bride.

And for the first time since we arrived in the country, Bella's beautiful lips break into a dazzling, wicked smile.

～

An hour later, we arrive at the Savoy.

The event is one of those ridiculously priced black-tie galas where rich people rub shoulders with other rich people while trying to outdo one another with how awesome they are. They're stuffy and vapid, and full of rich, entitled socialites.

As we walk in, all eyes are on us. On Bella. *The new De Kysa bride.*

I feel her stiffen beside me, so I take her hand and hold it tight in mine.

A passing server stops and offers us champagne, which Bella accepts readily.

"There is no need to be nervous," I whisper as we move away from the crowd. "You look stunning."

And she is. The black halter dress fits her luscious curves like a glove, falling over her perfect body in waves of shimmering black and showing off her slender arms and neck.

She whispers back, "They're all looking at me."

"Because you're beautiful."

She glances at me, and the vulnerability in her eyes eases.

A smile plays on her ruby-red lips. "Does anything make you nervous, Don De Kysa?"

"No."

"Nothing?"

"No." I want to tell her that the worst has already happened to me, so I have nothing left to fear. That losing her was the darkest feeling I'd ever known. Even now, after all the bloodshed and violent business undertakings where people have attempted to take my life, losing her was the worst.

But I don't tell her.

Instead, I brush a stray curl off her face and say, "And now that you are with me, you don't have anything to fear either. I will protect you."

The twinkle in her eyes and the soft smile on her lips kicks something to life in my heart. Lifting her face, she brushes her lips across mine. "You might drive me crazy, but I kinda like you."

"No, you don't. You love me. Admit it."

"Never." She sweeps her tongue into my mouth, and I'm seconds away from taking her hand and leading her out of

The Devil's Den

the event so I can fuck her all night in our hotel room. But she pulls away.

"Sex fiend," she whispers.

I lean in. "I'm going to punish you for this." I grab her hand and subtly hold it against my crotch so she can feel how hard she's made me.

The mischievous gleam in her eye tells me her punishment will be her pleasure, and the idea of my little hellcat purring as I fuck her rough and hard excites me even more.

She brushes her lips to my ear. "I'm not wearing any panties under this dress."

I groan.

"Careful, Bella," I warn. "There is only so much a man can take."

"What are you going to do, take me in front of all the people in this room?"

"You don't think I could make you come in a room full of these people?"

"I'd like to see you try."

I think this is the moment I realize I'm truly in love with her.

I down my champagne.

Pull her close.

Crush her against my erection.

My breath brushes against her cheek. "I'm going to sit down at one of those tables, and you are going to sit next to me."

"And?"

"And I am going to slide my hand beneath that dress."

"And..." She squirms against me, and I know she's already wet for me.

"And I'm going to fuck you with my fingers until you come." I'm so fucking hard at the idea of fucking my bride in this room full of people I can feel the precum leak from my cock.

I take her hand to lead her to an empty table, but on the way, we are stopped by a business associate who manages to successfully cock block me.

By the time I untangle myself from him, the moment with Bella has passed.

"Shall we?" I gesture to the table.

She shakes her head. Her arousal cooled. "I'm not letting you finger bang me in a room full of people."

"What about the bathroom?"

"What about we wait?"

I pull her to me. "See, that's the problem. I don't like waiting."

She laughs. "I can see the headlines now. De Kysa Billionaire Finger Bangs Panty-less Wife at High-Class Event."

"Your point?" I grab another glass of champagne from a passing server.

"My point is... let's get this over with so you can take me back to the hotel and make me come."

Fuck. Just when I think she's putting out the fire, she tips gasoline all over it.

"I have one thing to take care of and then we're leaving," I say, deciding to speed up the events I have planned for tonight.

As if on cue, my eyes land on Bella's ex-boyfriend. *Simon.* The one Bella and Imogen nicknamed the Earl of Ego because the asshole has one as big as a solar system.

Yeah, yeah, I have one just as big.

But at least I have the big fucking balls to back it.

His gaze finds Bella, and immediately, my insides tense. Not just because he once had the honor of knowing her intimately but because he's an asshole who should never have been given the privilege.

When I began watching her in London, I witnessed his bad behavior too many times. The way he would talk down to her as if she were a child. The way he would dismiss the things she said as if they were unimportant or unintelligent.

In order of his priorities, she came second to his desire for adulation from his blue blood peers.

He's old money. Was born with a name and title.

Has a big-as-fuck house on land to the north.

But he's stone-cold broke and can't afford the upkeep.

He's also painfully unaware of how much of a dick he is. He had no idea who he had on his arm and how fucking amazing she was.

Stalking them, I couldn't hear a lot of what was said, but his body language told me exactly what I needed to know.

Simon, the Earl of Ego, was toxic for Bella.

One day, I observed them inside a coffee shop together. I saw him hand her a folded piece of paper and cross his legs as he watched her read it. Across the room, I observed them —watched as her brows pulled in and her expression filled with hurt.

I didn't know it at the time, but in her hand was a list of things he wanted her to change about herself.

When I saw her emotional reaction, I was overcome with a surprising need to wipe the floor with his face.

And if it hadn't been imperative that my reconnaissance

remain undetected, I might have done that, just for taking away her sunshine and making it rain.

At the time, I told myself it had nothing to do with her and everything to do with me not tolerating assholes.

But now I can see I was lying.

Now I can see, my need to protect her never left me. No matter how hard I tried to hate her.

Luckily for him, she dumped him after reading the list. She tore it up and threw it at him in the crowded coffee shop, so I no longer needed to worry about the asshole.

Beside me, Bella stiffens, and I know she's seen him too.

"What the hell is he doing here?" she mutters.

She tries to move in the opposite direction, but I stop her by taking her by the elbow. "If you don't face him now, a part of you will always hurt because of him."

"What are you saying?"

"I'm saying it's time to take back that part of your heart that still hurts because of his cruelty."

She looks up at me, horrified. "I'm not speaking to that jerk."

I gaze at her beautiful face and run my knuckles across the smooth planes of her cheek.

I hate that the little shit attempted to diminish her shine by putting her down. He never saw her as an equal. Never saw her as the queen she is.

To move forward, she needs to put all those little moments of his nit-picking into a hypothetical paperback and set it on fire, so his memory drifts into the dark recesses of her mind and makes room for better memories.

"No, I don't mean speak to him. But let him see you and what he fucking lost."

She looks up at me, and without a word, I place my lips against hers. At first, I think she's going to pull her face away, but instead, her lips part, and we kiss slowly. A tender kiss. To let her know that she has nothing to fear and no reason to slip into the crowd unnoticed.

It catches Simon's attention, as it should. Let him know that the woman who wasn't good enough for him is more than perfect for Don De Kysa.

Our eyes meet across the room, and he sees it as an invitation to introduce himself. He moves through the crowd, looking smug and confident, with the air of someone who thinks they're important and influential.

He thinks he belongs in this room full of powerful people. But he's wrong. He's not even a blip on the radar.

Beside me, Bella's soft curves tense, and I feel her begin to panic, and it pisses me off how the mere presence of this bozo can strip her of her confidence.

It makes me want to shake Simon by the ankles over the balcony before I drop him to the concrete below.

Instead, I thread my fingers through hers. She steals a glance at me, and I wink at her, which makes her smile and then relax a little.

When Simon reaches us, he attempts to greet Bella with a kiss, but I step between them.

He doesn't get to touch my queen ever again.

"Domenico De Kysa," he says, oblivious to the situation he's just landed in.

He offers me a hand but for a moment I resist accepting it. I'd rather cut it off before I offered it to him. But that won't serve my plans in the long run, so I accept it and shake it, squeezing it to a point of his discomfort while offering him a dark smile.

"I don't believe we've met," I say.

He grimaces, tries to hide it, but fails.

"Simon Worthington, the Earl of Eastwood," he says with a wince as I release his hand. "I'm the owner of the Spirrier Art Gallery in London."

He speaks with a superior clip to his voice.

As if I am beneath him.

What the hell did Bella see in this guy?

Granted, he's good looking— I'm sure those blue eyes make panties drop all over the countryside—but no amount of handsomeness can make up for the absence of personality.

Clearly, my wife's tastes have improved.

Even if they did need a little convincing in the beginning.

"Spirrier." I give him a blank look. "The name isn't familiar."

"I assure you, in art circles, it's renowned." He glances at Bella. "Hello, Bella. It's been a while."

When he says her name, I want to cut his tongue out just so he can't ever say it again.

She nods. "Simon."

Again, when he attempts to greet her with a kiss, I block it, and he looks unsure of what's going on.

He finally reads the room right.

That I have a problem with him.

A big fucking problem.

He sighs, as if it's something that happens to him every day because he is so eclipsing and above everyone.

"I see what's happening. You're the jealous husband." He

waves it off. "Yes, Bella and I dated, but it's okay, you have nothing to fear. Bella and I weren't a right fit. I'm no threat to you, so there's no need to feel intimidated."

Which is not the right thing to say to a Mafia don simmering with anger.

I fix him with a look that should tell him to stop talking. "I assure you, nothing about you intimidates me."

His eyes gleam with amusement, which tells me either this guy has a death wish, or he has his head stuck so far up his ass, he can't see the danger.

"I mean no disrespect, of course." It's a lie. He does. He can't help himself. "I simply don't want you thinking there was more to our relationship than there was. It was a *convenience* more than anything."

Bella leans toward me while keeping her eyes on her ex. A second ago, she'd looked uncertain about what was unfolding. She was scared for Simon. Now, her uncertainty is gone and replaced with something stoic. *Retribution.* He's pissed her off.

"Simon is right, baby. He wasn't anything worth mentioning really. Gave me a bit of art talk and boring vanilla sex." She looks at me. "He doesn't know how to fuck like a don knows how to fuck."

I can't help but grin.

God, I love my wife.

"There is no need to be so vulgar," Simon chides her.

I've never wanted to shoot someone in the face as much as I want to shoot this guy.

Which is saying something.

Bella tilts her head. "Not vulgar. Just honest."

His face pinches. "I can see perhaps now is not the time or place to talk."

"I happen to disagree," I say. "Now is the perfect time and place to talk."

I pull out my phone. Ready to tie up tonight's loose ends.

I came prepared because I knew he would be here despite the ten-thousand-dollar entry. For a pompous jerk like Simon, it's important to keep up appearances when the opinions of your peers mean everything, even if it means selling your family estate for way less than it is worth to an overseas investor so you can maintain a lifestyle that says you have a lot more money than you actually do.

If anyone knew he'd sold his family's legacy to the highest bidder, he'd be ostracized by the blue bloods and social elite.

I hold up my phone so he can see the screen clearly, and press play.

The image on the screen is of him and a young woman whose face we can't see. The footage is shot from across the room. A hidden camera. Like a predator.

"You're not filming us, are you?" the young woman says.

"Of course not," Simon lies.

The woman sounds nervous. *"I probably shouldn't be here. I should go."*

When she turns to leave, Simon yanks her back to him. *"Not before we have some fun."*

The woman struggles. *"This is making me uncomfortable."*

"What are you talking about? You've wanted this all night. Following me around. Making eyes at me. Don't be a cock tease."

He kisses her, but the woman whimpers and pushes him away. *"Please, stop."*

But Simon ignores her and shoves her to her knees. He unbuckles his belt. "Stop fucking complaining and suck my cock, you bitch."

I stop the video.

Simon looks furious. "You stole that from me."

I lift an eyebrow. "You filmed this without her knowledge."

"It was consensual."

"Didn't look fucking consensual to me." I lean close. "You know what I hate more than an asshole who hands a beautiful woman a list of twenty-eight things he wants her to change about herself? It's a raping son of a bitch."

Simon's lips twist with indignation. "She wanted it."

"Shall I hit play again so we can see how she says no, but you don't listen?"

His mind races behind pale-blue eyes. "It was a game we played."

"Role-play? That's seriously how you want to spin it?"

His eyes narrow. "You have no proof it wasn't."

"Yeah, I do, because you filmed it all, asshole."

His throat bobs as he struggles to swallow. "You son of a bitch, how dare you do this to me. You broke into my house."

"Not me. An associate of mine. He's really good at finding out secrets. In your case, a drawer full of flash drives with some very dubious content on them."

"You asshole," he seethes.

"No, I'm the Don De Kysa, and you will do well to remember that."

Balking, he darts his eyes to Bella. "You're involved with this?"

He looks at her with such disgust that my hand itches for my gun.

"Don't you look at her until I say you can look at her," I growl.

He wants to fight me but knows it's not in his best interest.

"Let's get one thing straight. From this moment forward, you will do exactly what I say or face the consequences. First, you're going to apologize to my wife for being an undeserving pig who doesn't know how to treat women. Then I will give you the flash drives."

Simon's eyes round. "All of this because I didn't think she was good enough for me?"

I take an intimidating step toward him. The room is still noisy, but some people nearby stop talking to watch.

My voice is low and dangerous. "She's the only reason you are still breathing, do you understand? The only reason you aren't worm food is because I know she wouldn't want me to hurt you. So I'd start hedging your bets, you dumb fuck, and start showing her the respect she deserves. Now, apologize to her before I forget what my wife wants and make you eat my fucking gun."

"Fine, you son of a bitch." He glares at me, but he's trembling as he narrows his eyes to Bella. "I'm sorry." He looks back at me. "There, are you satisfied?"

Yeah, this guy has a death wish.

"I'm pretty sure I could shoot you in front of everyone here and none of them would give a goddamn. Now, apologize again, but this time with more feeling,"

He glares at me. There is only one way out, and he knows it.

The Devil's Den

He looks at Bella. "I'm sorry. I was a jerk. I should've treated you better."

I look at my queen. Gone is the uncertainty on her face. "Satisfied?" I ask her.

She narrows her eyes as she looks at Simon. "No, I don't think he really means it."

Simon makes the supreme mistake of rolling his eyes.

Bella folds her arms. "Perhaps if he were on his knees."

"You're right." I agree. "Get on your knees and apologize."

"On my knees? I won't get on—"

I open my jacket so he can see my gun. "When I tell you to do something, you fucking do it. Now, for the last fucking time, get on your fucking knees and apologize to Bella."

Rage tightens his expression. But fear forces him to his knees.

"I'm sorry, okay? I'm sorry."

Around us, more and more people start to pay attention, and it's humiliating for him.

I glance at my wife who stares at the man on his knees in front of her. "Happy, my love?"

She smiles and winks at me. "Very."

Still on his knees, Simon looks up at me with pleading eyes. "I did what you wanted. Now give me the flash drive."

I throw it at him.

He thinks he's in the clear.

But tomorrow the police will pay him a visit.

Humiliated, he glances at all the people now watching and whispering.

I shoot the pathetic asshole a dark look. "Tearing down someone and blowing holes in their confidence makes you an asshole. Doing it to Bella—it was a big fucking mistake."

I lean down.

"By the way, I bought that run-down festering pit of a house of yours. Tomorrow, the bulldozers move in. Feel free to go and watch."

It's the final blow.

He drops his head to his hands.

34

Bella

We escape the party and run through the rain to an awaiting limousine and slide into the back seat.

As far as ex-boyfriends go, Simon was as much fun as running barefoot across a field of rusty nails.

As far as husbands go, I won the lottery with Nico.

In the back seat of the limousine, I flick my husband a wicked look, the corners of my lips curved with a devilish grin. I lift my foot and brush it against his groin.

He raises his brow, and his lips respond in kind with the same devilish grin.

On repeat in my head is the way he annihilated Simon. Proof that my husband doesn't need a gun or chaos to bring retribution to his rivals.

I'd be lying if I said it didn't turn me on.

It does.

Big time.

My whole body is lit with tiny little fires waiting to ignite into one giant wildfire.

I slide to my knees in front of him and unbuckle his belt.

He gives me a heated look. "What are you up to, hellcat?"

"Showing my husband some appreciation," I say, watching the desire shimmer in his expression as I lower the zipper and reach inside.

His cock is thick and aroused, and I feel the tremor roll through him as I bend my head and slide my flattened tongue over the wide, plush head.

"I think crushing the ego of socially inept prats has just become my new favorite thing if this is the response it gets," he says, hissing in a breath and dropping the back of his head to the headrest. "Goddamn, I love your tongue."

I reward his praise with a long, torturous glide up the thick column of flesh.

He rasps in a deep breath, then groans. "Fuck, yes. You make me so fucking hard, Bella. You and that perfect tongue of yours."

Again, I reward his praise with a slow, vacuumed glide of my mouth down his long, swollen length. His hands grip the bench seat, and his low, shaky moan fills the car.

He thickens in my mouth, and I gag as the engorged head hits the back of my throat.

He chuckles and carves his fingers into my hair. "Such a greedy little mouth."

While my mouth fucks him, my hands massage his balls, earning me another generous moan. His fingers tighten in my hair, sending a delicious sting across my scalp.

Outside, the hotel comes into view. Any second, the

driver will pull up to the curb. But Nico notices too and knocks on the glass, telling him to keep driving. His driver knows. Of course, he knows. And for some reason, that excites me even more.

"Fuck, Bella." Nico's voice is ragged. His eyes glazed. I love these brief moments when he loses control, and it thrills me to know I take him there. "You're going to make me come..."

I increase my speed, my mouth and lips and tongue licking, sucking and gliding, while one hand pumps at the base of his cock. Nico rocks his hips, driving deeper into my mouth.

With a shudder, he stills, and a salty warmth hits the back of my throat. But I don't stop. I keep sucking. Keep pumping. Keep taking everything he gives as the tension builds between my thighs.

When I sit back, his hand is carved through his hair and his eyes blaze down at me like glowing embers.

He gently glides his thumb along my bottom lip. "This perfect mouth belongs to me."

The look on his face and the purr in his voice send my stomach crazy.

Looking up at him through my lashes, I nod, and the scorching heat in his eyes makes me shiver. *Yes, it does.*

Which is insane, considering I wanted to write his obituary mere days ago.

But now here I am, kneeling at his feet, worshipping his cock, knowing I don't want any other.

Offering me his hand, he guides me off the limousine floor and pulls me onto his lap. Without a word, he slants his mouth over mine and kisses me deeply, stroking his glorious tongue into my mouth with delicious appreciation. I succumb to the strength of his arms around me and melt into his muscular form, knowing there is nowhere I'd rather be than right here, in the back seat of a limousine, in the strong arms of my man.

When we finally pull up in front of the hotel again, Nico lets me go long enough to climb out but then takes my hand as we run through the rain and into the hotel. We cross the sea of marble floor and run straight into the open elevator.

Once the doors close and the elevator moves, Nico grabs my wrist and spins me around to face the mirror, and he is behind me.

Our eyes lock in the mirror. Scorching heat blazes at me from the glass.

Surprising me, he slams on the emergency button, and the elevator car jolts to a stop.

"What are you doing?" I ask.

"I want you right now." His eyes trail across my shoulders, down my spine, and over my ass.

In the mirror, his face tightens with lust and desire, and all the things he wants to do to me.

"Two minutes and we'll be in our room," I remind him.

But he's already made up his mind.

"When I want something, I tend to take it, Bella," he rasps, and a tiny thrill zips along my spine. "And I want you, right now."

With a yank, he shreds my dress open at the side seams, exposing each thigh. He pushes the fabric over my hips, and his large palms glide over my ass. He lets out an appreciative groan as he continues to study my flesh with his big hands.

He presses me against the railing.

Nudges my feet apart.

Lifts my hips higher.

Lowers his zipper.

It always amazes me how quickly he can recover from one orgasm and be ready for the next.

He takes his length in his hand. Spreads my ass with the other. Impales me with his insatiable cock.

I gasp and close my eyes, his fingers finding my jaw. "Open your eyes, Bella. Watch me fuck you."

I lift my lashes. Watch us in the mirror. Watch him thrust his cock in and out of me. Lose myself in the rhythm of every stroke into my body.

"Good girl," he rasps.

I bite down on my lip. His cock surges deeper into me. He reaches around and finds my clit with his fingers.

"Oh God..." I moan, clamping my hand around the railing to steady myself. My eyelids flutter.

He holds my hips, rocks deeper,

"Look at us, Bella. Look at how perfect we are together."

For some reason, tears spring to my eyes.

It's all too much.

Feelings come from nowhere.

A tear breaks loose to slide down my cheek.

I don't know why I'm crying. But I suspect it's the old me stepping aside so the new me can take the reins.

Behind me, Nico growls. His fingers circle my clit while his cock pumps into me.

"Nico..." I cry, gripping the railing harder, certain my legs are going to give way.

A broken moan falls from my lips and I come, falling hard and fast.

Nico follows, stroking hard until he jerks to a stop and shudders, jetting deep into my body.

He relaxes against me, panting.

Another loose tear escapes, followed by another.

When Nico sees them, he pulls out, turns me around, and takes me in his arms.

He searches my face, then silently leans down and kisses the tears from my skin.

"Did I hurt you?" The concern in his voice warms my heart. The part that has been dead to him for a long time.

I shake my head.

"Then why are you crying?" The back of his fingers are gentle on my cheek, as is the look in his eyes. In his voice, I hear *how do I fix this?*

It's then I realize I'm afraid.

Afraid of these feelings for him.

Knowing he could break them apart and destroy me.

"Am I enough?" I ask.

His brows draw in. "What do you mean, are you enough? Bella, you are every-fucking-thing."

I smile, hoping he will kiss the stupid off my lips.

But because I am married to a Mafia kingpin, he spins me back to look at us in the mirror.

He grips my jaw with strong fingers but gentle enough that it's welcomed, and holds my face in place, making me look at myself.

"Look at her... she's a queen." His words brush the soft shell of my ear in a low, luring rumble. *"She's my queen."*

I bite down on my lip.

He rasps, "Now let me hear you say it."

The Devil's Den

I stare at the woman in the mirror and feel my strength rise and move through me.
"Say it," he commands.
I meet his eyes in the mirror.
A renewed strength comes over me.
"I'm a motherfucking queen."

35

Bella

After returning to New York two days later, I receive a summons from my father to attend a formal brunch at his house.

We arrive just as Sophia, who is now in her late seventies and won't retire, is removing a homemade parmigiana di melanzane from the oven.

"That smells divine," I say as we enter the spacious chef's kitchen.

Her eyes light up when she sees me. "My Bella."

She hurries over to me and kisses me on each cheek.

When she sees Mr. Tall, Dark, and Dangerous next to me, her eyes soften.

"Domenico... what a handsome man you are." She reaches up and pulls him into her arms. "It's good to see you, it's been too long." Their embrace is warm and long, and when he straightens, Nico's jaw ticks with emotion.

The Devil's Den

"It's good to see you too, Sophia," he says, his voice thick.

When we were young, we used to spend hours in Sophia's kitchen watching her bake and cook. She'd fix us whatever we wanted, which was always spaghetti, and she'd fuss over us with all the affection of a grandmother even though she wasn't related. She was the grandmother neither of us had.

She returns her attention to me, her bony hand reaching up to swipe a curl from in front of my eyes. "You look good. You're glowing." A gleam shines in her old eyes. "Almost like you're with child."

I laugh. "No, Sophia, I'm not pregnant."

She smiles knowingly. "Given time, you will be."

Beside me, Nico coughs.

She looks at him and smiles. "Looks like marriage suits you both, Domenico. But marriage is hard work, and you must both put in the effort to make it survive. Don't lose what you have when you reach your first hurdle."

She has no idea the marriage is fake and will be over in twelve months.

Which doesn't excite me as much as it used to because we've entered confusing territory. What started as an arrangement has grown into something a lot more.

I glance at my husband, wondering if he's thinking the same thing. But he remains expressionless, and my gut tightens because I want to know how he feels.

Sometimes I think I'm breaking down his walls. Other times, I feel like he's already breaking my heart. Like I'm falling toward something that isn't really there, and I can't break my fall.

My father appears in the doorway dressed in a suit and tie, looking every inch the successful businessman.

He cuts an imposing presence. But there is an even bigger presence in the kitchen—my husband—and the two are about to collide.

All morning I've been on edge about having them in the same room. I'm not sure how this meeting will end and what fires I might have to put out.

He greets me with a kiss on the cheek. "Bella, my beautiful daughter."

When it comes to greeting Nico, my father stops in front of him. The two men lock eyes. Tension tightens around us. My breath hitches. But my father surprises me when he offers his hand to Nico. "Welcome to my home."

Nico's back stiffens, but he accepts his hand. "*Grazie*."

I let out the breath I was holding. But I still feel uneasy.

"Come, follow me into my den," my father says. "Sophia will call us when brunch is ready."

We leave the delicious smells of baking frittata, percolating coffee, and the freshly baked parmigiana behind us and follow my father through the alfresco tiled foyer and into his office. The impressive room, with its wood paneling and million-dollar paintings, smells of leather and cigar smoke with a hint of something sweet.

"I suppose you want to know why I invited you here today," he says, walking to his desk and taking a seat.

"The thought had crossed my mind," Nico replies, the dark tones in his voice unmistakable.

My father gestures for him to sit, but he declines, and I remain standing beside him.

"Twelve months is a long time." My father removes a

cigar from a box on his desk. He offers one to Nico, who declines, then lights it. "I think we need to find common ground while you are wedded to my daughter. I invited you both here to work out how we make that happen. We may be rivals, Don De Kysa, and I may not have forgiven you for this, but you are family... for the next twelve months, at least. Let's lay our cards on the table and find a truce so this arrangement works instead of blowing up in all our faces."

Nico remains rigid. "I'm listening."

"Perhaps we can try to trust one another."

Nico scoffs. "Just like that?"

"I have nothing to hide. How can I prove that to you?"

Nico looks completely calm, but his voice is threaded with dark danger as he says, "You can start by telling me how you were involved in my mother's suicide."

Fear flushes heat across my skin. Any second now, my father is going to pull out a gun and shoot him.

Or vice versa.

But I'm wrong.

Unfazed, my father leans back in his chair and puffs out a mouthful of cigar smoke. "You're misinformed, Nico. Your mother didn't commit suicide. Your father murdered her."

36

Nico

Your father murdered her.

Vincent's words spin in circles in my brain, and my immediate urge is to put a bullet in him for such a lie.

But Bella would never forgive me.

And truth be told, a little part of me knows there could be some truth to it.

When my father was don, he was capable of anything. I saw him cut off a man's hand for repeatedly touching my mother while she flirted with him. Their marriage was an unhappy one. Mamma hated him and resented us kids. Did the old man finally tire of her stony looks and frosty words?

My jaw stiffens. "You're lying."

"No, son, I'm not."

I have to give it to the old fuck. His expression of remorse looks genuine.

He folds his hands in front of him on his desk.

The Devil's Den

"The night she died, Marianne called me frantically. She said that Gio knew about the affair but worse—" He pauses, choosing his next words carefully, and I feel a sense of foreboding tighten in my stomach. "He knew she was working with the feds."

The moment the words drop from his lips, my fingers itch to reach for my gun.

The lying fuck.

First, he accuses my father of killing my mom.

Now he accuses her of working with the fucking feds.

"No fucking De Kysa would ever work with the feds," I growl.

"But she wasn't a De Kysa, was she? She was a Draconi."

That's it. I rip out my gun and point it at Vincent.

Beside me, Bella gasps. "Nico, no!"

Vincent waves his hand to tell her it's okay.

But it's not okay.

I'm two seconds away from unloading my clip into him.

"Your mother was born Marianne Draconi. She was Michele Draconi's youngest daughter. Your father met her when she was just sixteen and forced the marriage by brokering a deal with Michele. His daughter in exchange for no war. Gio had Michele over a barrel. He had no choice... sound familiar?"

My father did to my mother exactly what I did to Bella.

I tighten my grip on my gun.

The asshole is lying.

This is Vincent trying to mess with my head.

Surely, I would know if my mother was a Draconi. *Our sworn enemy.*

As if Vincent can read my mind, he says, "Your father

was careful to hide her true identity. He didn't want people to know she was a Draconi. He told people she was a Sorbello, a prestigious family from the South. Of course, there were rumors because Michele Draconi made a big deal that a De Kysa had stolen his daughter, but Gio said they were the ravings of a crazy man. He was the mighty Gio De Kysa, so no one would believe Michele over him. And of course, he made it clear to your mother that if she told anyone who she was, then she would pay with her life." He sighs. "Soon, everyone believed the lie."

"The Draconi are rivals. He hates them. Why would my father want a Draconi wife who would bear him children with Draconi blood?"

"Because the moment he saw your mother, he wanted her." He drills me with a look of resentment. "And what better way to hurt your rival than taking the daughter he loves?"

The truth scrapes along the nerves of my spine.

Is my father's venom so infectious that it's turned me into him?

I refocus my gun on Vincent. "What happened the night she died?"

"Your mama called me and told me Gio knew everything. She was terrified for her life."

"Get to the bit about the feds," I growl.

"Your mother wanted out, Domenico, and the feds were the only way. After she found your father with one of the maids, they fought, and he gave her a beating. She'd had enough. She made contact with the feds. Offered Gio on a platter if they would help her escape to America. They said they would put her in Wit Pro if she gathered information on her husband."

"How do you know all of this?"

"Because my wife and sons died, and in the weeks following, I was in so much pain, and so was Marianne. Kitty was her only friend. The grief brought us together, and before we could stop it, we were having an affair. A few weeks into it, she confided in me."

"Why the fuck would she do that? You were my father's best friend and business partner."

He takes a deep breath and levels me with a look. "Because I told her I wanted out."

Vincent's admission rattles around the room.

I frown, trying to work out how all the pieces fit. "Go on."

"I was tired of the life. Of the war. Of the bloodshed. I'd lost my wife and sons, and for what? There was no honor in what we were doing, and no amount of money in the world was worth looking over your shoulder every single second of every day."

I hate it, but what he says is true. Power comes with a price. Like always looking over your shoulder or checking the shadows for someone with a gun. In this business, lots of people want to kill you, and it's fucking exhausting.

I think of Bella and what I'd do if anything happened to her.

I'd fucking die if anything happened to her.

I relax my arm and return my gun to my waistband. Beside me, Bella lets out a relieved breath.

"So you're telling me you were working with the feds too?" I ask, disgust coating every word. In this world, working with the feds is the biggest betrayal.

"It was the only way out. You know no one leaves this business alive. If I'd tried to leave the syndicate and move Bella to the US, they would've come after us. They don't let you leave because you know too much, and you become a liability. You know that."

I do.

That's why I resigned myself to the darkness early on. There was no other way. I had to embrace this life with all its ugliness and pain to survive.

"So you sold my father out to the feds," I snarl.

"No, I never met with the feds. Your mother was to arrange a meeting with her contact, but she died before she could speak to him."

"What happened after her phone call that night?"

"Alberto and I sped to your place. I knew I had to get your mother out of there. When we arrived, there was a gunshot. We heard it as we entered the home. In your father's den, she was dead on the floor, and your father stood over her with a gun in his hand."

He pauses.

"Keep going," I demand.

"All guns were drawn. Your father said he knew everything. The affair. The feds. He said I would be dead by dawn. We argued. He knew he couldn't explain a dead wife *and* a dead best friend. He knew the heat it would bring. I mean, your father was a creative man when it came to disposing of his victims, but as much as he wanted me dead, he knew I wasn't worth the risk. Now that he knew the feds were sniffing around, he had to rein in the body count. Your mother's death was impulsive. His emotions got the better of him, and he made her pay. He had time to think about me and the blowback my death would cause." He sits back in his big leather chair. "Your father's last words to me were, *you leave for America tonight and I never see or hear of you again.* It was a trade-off. A new life for me in America if I kept my silence about what had happened."

I think back to that night. About seeing my mother being loaded into the back of an ambulance, and the grief I felt as a seventeen-year-old boy comes surging back.

"Did he ask you why?" My voice is hoarse. This life has taken so much from everyone. "Did he want to know why you planned to rat him out?"

"Weeks earlier, I told him about my plans to move Bella to the US. I'd already lost two children, and I didn't want to lose her. He resisted it. Said I was needed there. I was his lieutenant. But he had a change of heart about a move to America after he saw the potential in expanding operations on American soil, and he agreed to let us relocate."

"But remain in the De Kysa Mafia?"

"Unfortunately, he wasn't going to let me leave the organization. Then your mother mentioned the feds to me—"

"And you saw your way out."

He nods and exhales deeply. "Standing in that room with our guns drawn, it was easier for your father to kick me out of the family than to dispose of me. But I knew he would come looking one day."

Me. The sudden knowledge echoes in my head.

My father did go looking for Vincent. But he sent *me* to do his bidding.

A new reality begins to emerge. If what Vincent says is true, then my father stoked the fire in me with all his lies, knowing I would exact my revenge on him somehow.

I look at Vincent. "Did you love her?"

"No."

"Did she love you?"

"No." He pauses, then adds, "But for a moment there, we were each other's only sunlight."

I feel sick under the weight of my father's legacy. He gave me this. The venom polluting my veins. But I embraced it. Because I was a seventeen-year-old boy fighting a broken heart.

And in the end, I did exactly as he did.

Steal a wife. Force her into a life she did not want.

A real chip off the old block.

My gaze shifts to Bella.

How the fuck am I going to make it up to her?

She reaches for me. Her touch soft on my arm. Her eyes gentle. She gives me a kind of strength I didn't know I needed. But I need it now.

I also need the truth.

And I mean, the *real* truth. Not the recollection of an old man who was one of the three people in the room. Sorry, the three *alive* people in the room.

Let's not forget that this happened as they stood over my mother's body.

"I'm going to talk to my father," I say, then abruptly turn and leave the room.

I'm almost at my car when Bella's voice calls out to me. "Nico."

I look up at my wife standing at her father's front door.

"You're not going to kill him, are you?"

Despite my dark mood and the burning itch to find out

the truth, I can't help but chuckle. That's what I love about my wife.

She knows me so well.

"Never say never," I grumble, climbing into my car and driving away.

37

Nico

"I hate you. Why are you trying to ruin my life?" My new stepsister's voice floats through the open front door as I climb out of my car and walk to their stoop.

"I'm not the one ruining anything!" her mother replies, strained.

They must be in separate rooms because they're yelling back and forth like a tennis volley.

"Oh, so now *I'm* ruining *your* life? That's rich. I'm not the one who married into fucking Mafia royalty."

"Stop being so dramatic. Honestly, where do you get these ridiculous ideas from?"

"Are you blind? His whole family is neck deep in Mafia murdered corpses."

Amusement tugs at my lips. I have to give it to my stepsister, she's creative.

"Why don't you put those crazy ideas to good use and write a damn book or something," Juliet yells back.

"Oh, so now I'm *crazy*?" she yells.

"Again, with the theatrics, Eve." Juliet sounds weary.

"If that's what you think of me, then I'm leaving—" Eve stops yelling when she appears in the doorway and finds me standing on the step. Her eyes widen for just a split second, then narrow. "Hello, gangster. Been lurking on the doorstep long?"

"Long enough," I say smugly.

She shrugs. "Have you come here to clean house or is this a friendly visit?"

"Clean house? Exactly what do you think I do?"

She avoids answering by asking another question. "Do you have a gun?"

"I do."

She leans her hip against the doorframe and folds her arms. "Have you come to use it?"

"Do I need to?"

She leans forward and whispers, "I know your secrets."

I lean forward and whisper, "Have you been googling me again?"

Because her threat failed to get the reaction she was aiming for, she yells over her shoulder. "Mom, one of my annoying new stepbrothers is here."

"Your stepbrother?" Juliet shouts back. "Which one?"

Eve's eyes twinkle across at me as she yells back, "The scary-looking one."

I lift my brow. I'll take the compliment.

Even if it wasn't meant as one.

Turning her attention back to me, she says, "If you've come to murder me, I was just leaving."

"Now why would I want to hurt my delightful new stepsister?"

"I don't know. Because you're a Mafia don, and that's what you do when people know your secrets."

I have to hand it to her. She has balls. Not that she knows anything. My father keeps his secrets locked up tighter than the crown jewels.

But I like this kid's spark.

I struggle to keep the smile from my lips. "Hmm, is that so? I'll have to keep that in mind."

She sighs. As if *I'm* the exasperating one. "Well, if murder is off the table, why are you here? Shouldn't you be out doing gangsterish things with your gangsterish friends?"

"Like?"

"I don't know, like hanging out in questionable places and stealing from the rich."

"You're confusing me with Robin Hood. I assure you, I'm not that predictable."

That piques her interest. I see the delight stir in her eyes.

My stepsister is attracted to the dark side.

Which is fortunate, given her circumstance.

"I was just leaving," she says.

"So I heard." I step out of her way. "By all means, don't let me keep you from storming out of the house."

She smiles even though she doesn't really want to and steps past me.

Curious, I ask as she passes me, "If I'm the scary-looking one, what is Massimo?"

She gives me a wicked look over her shoulder, her eyes

sparkling. "He's the good-looking one. Have a nice day, gangster."

I watch her walk away. "Hey," I call out, and she turns around again. "Do me a favor and don't tell him that. His head is already big enough."

Another wicked grin spreads her ruby-red lips. "I've already speed-dialed his number."

Grinning, she disappears down the driveway and vanishes from view.

"Nico." Juliet appears at the front door looking battle weary after arguing with her teenage daughter. "What a delight. I'm sorry you had to hear that. Eve can be a little trying sometimes."

"I imagine she is," I say. "Is my father home?"

"Yes, he's in his office." She steps aside to let me inside. "Can I offer you a coffee or a wine? I'm having wine. A nice pinot noir." When I look at my watch and see it's only eleven o'clock, she adds, "Don't judge me until you're the mother of a teenage daughter with enough sass to drown in."

Fair enough.

I offer her a small smile. "I'm fine. But enjoy your glass of wine."

She pats my arm and gives me a wink. "Oh darling, I'm drinking the entire bottle."

We part ways, and I head to my father's office, where I find him behind his large desk. He looks up when I walk in.

"Domenico! My son!" He rises and walks around his desk to greet me. With arms outstretched, he embraces me warmly, thumping my shoulders and hugging me tight. "You look well. Marriage suits you."

I'm waiting for a sly comment about Bella being an Isle

Ciccula, but when it doesn't come, I remember I'm dealing with the alien version of my father who returned home from a three-month cruise with a new bride on his arm and a new one-eighty view of life.

"As it does you," I say.

He gestures toward a chair. "Please, sit. Tell me how you are. Are you happy?"

I look at him like he's just spoken to me in Klingon and realize just how much my father has changed.

I don't think he has ever asked me if I'm happy.

Or to tell him how I am.

I relax into my chair and study the man who used to terrify me. Who would pound his fist against the top of his desk and bellow threats when things didn't go his way.

He's nothing like he used to be. Brows pulled in. A scowl marring his features. The weight of the world on his shoulders. An aura of tension and danger.

Because he is no longer the don.

You are.

Is it really possible that he's changed that much?

Looking at him now, he's relaxed. Happy.

Fuck, am I jealous?

Then I remember why I'm here.

Tension tightens in my shoulders, and I lock my gaze to his as I ask, "Did you kill my mother?"

My question takes him by surprise. His eyebrows snap together, and his eyes narrow. Silence stretches between us as he mentally tries to put the pieces together. Why am I asking? Who told me? What are the consequences of answering with the truth?

The Devil's Den

He begins to nod slowly, his expression resigned. Almost as if the above questions don't even matter to him anymore.

"You've been speaking to your new father-in-law, I take it," he says.

It's not a question. It's a statement.

"It doesn't matter who I've been talking to." My tone is as sharp as a knife. "Answer the question. And I want the goddamn truth."

He sighs as if he always knew we'd be having this conversation one day.

"Your mother was a thorn in my side, that is the truth," he says. "But I didn't kill her."

I tilt my head. "Vincent Isle Ciccula was lying?"

"Not exactly." He opens his hands on the desk. "What he thought he saw and what actually happened aren't exactly the same thing."

"Mama wasn't working for the feds?"

"Oh, she was working for the feds, but I didn't kill her."

"I find it hard to believe. A rat is a rat."

"No, not in this case. I loved your mother. Even after I discovered the truth about the affair and her running to the feds. I wasn't the one who brought the gun to the conversation that night."

"Then tell me how the fuck she ended up dead on the carpet."

For a moment, I think he's going to shift the blame to Vincent Isle Ciccula. Claim he came in and shot my mother.

But he doesn't.

"The person with the gun was your mother."

I frown. My mother hated guns. As much as she hated the Mafia life. "You're lying."

"No, son, I'm not." His remorse looks genuine, I'll give him that. "She knew I'd discovered the affair she was having with Vincent. I assume he told you about that too?"

"I'm aware that they had an affair."

"I also knew about her involvement with the feds, thanks to one of my informants. Your mother overheard me talking with this informant. She was terrified and instead of waiting for retribution, she decided to confront me."

What he says aligns with what Vincent said about her frantic phone call to him that night.

"She came into my den with a gun in her hand and her arm raised. Told me she was leaving. Told me I could have you kids because she was starting a new life in America."

The pain of having an absent mother renews in my gut.

I always felt her disconnection from her children. The lack of cuddles. The absence of a soothing word. The nonexistent smiles and praise I so desperately craved from her.

I thought I had made peace with it. But learning she was going to give us up to start a new life only reinforces how much she didn't want us, and even as a grown man, it fucking hurts.

"We fought. We struggled. The gun went off."

That would be the gunshot Vincent and Alberto heard.

"When Vincent arrived, he found me standing over her body."

"Why didn't you tell them what happened? Why make them believe a lie?"

"Because my best friend fucking betrayed me. If I could've killed him and got away with it, I would have. I could pass your mother's death off as a suicide. But disposing of Vincent and Alberto was a little more than I was willing to take on at that moment." He shakes his head. "I let him go."

"And Mama? If the gun hadn't gone off, would you have killed her?"

"Back then?" My father fixes me with apathetic, hooded eyes. "Without a fucking doubt."

"And now?"

He thinks for a moment. "I wouldn't touch a hair on her head."

"Why?" I ask, still struggling to understand this new version of the once ruthless Don De Kysa who knew no mercy.

"Because I am not the same man I was back then, Domenico." He looks at the photo of his new wife in a frame on his desk, then lifts his gaze back to me. "And I thank the Lord for that every single damn day."

∼

After leaving my father's house, I lose hours in my office trying to work, but I'm too distracted.

I need to make sense of the situation, but I can't.

Well, that's not exactly true.

I can make sense of it, but I don't want to admit it. Because every time I try to untangle the facts, they always lead me back to the same conclusion.

I was wrong.

But admitting I was wrong leaves me with a fuck load of mess to clean up.

By the time I leave the office, it's late, and the sky is bruised with storm clouds. Having sent Mateo home for the night, I drive through the streets as raindrops hit the windshield and lightning bolts hit the city. I have no real destination in mind. I just need to drive and untangle the mess in my head.

Bella is already in bed when I let myself into the penthouse. I strip out of my clothes and step into the shower, taking my time to wash the sins of the day off my body. But no matter how hard I soap up my skin, the stench of truth doesn't leave me.

My quest for vengeance has been time misspent.

Out of the shower, I dry off and climb into bed naked, seeking the warmth of my wife's body for comfort.

I pull her closer.

Her lips are gentle against mine as she kisses me sleepily.

Another truth I realized today.

My wife is an angel.

If only she'd never married the devil.

38

Bella

The next day, I meet Imogen for lunch at a luxurious restaurant in Manhattan called the Bird Cage, known around the world for its elegant high tea and exceptional fine dining.

Her eyes light up when she sees me walk into the crowded restaurant wearing a short skirt and fitted jacket, matched with a pair of limited-edition Louboutin heels. "Wowza, Bella." Her gaze does another pass over my outfit. "You look sensational."

I beam a smile her way. "You like?"

"Oh, I like... I like very much. You always had a cool bohemian style going on, but this is something else." She stands up and makes me turn around. "Boy, I wanna be you when I grow up."

Once we're settled at the table, Imogen gives me a warm, genuine smile. "You really do look good, Bella. I haven't seen you this happy in a long time. I was kinda worried you'd struggle with it, but marriage to Nico clearly suits you."

I look at her over my menu. "Well, I haven't murdered him yet, so that's a good start."

She gives me a suspicious smile. "I bet you're having lots of yummy sex."

"We fight more than anything."

"Okay, lots of yummy makeup sex, then." She sighs. "Next, you'll be popping out the most beautiful babies."

The sudden thought of giving Nico a baby sends butterflies loose in my stomach. But the excitement dampens just as quickly because how could I bring a child into this life of continual surveillance and potential danger? As if drawn there by instinct, my gaze shifts to James across the restaurant, his back rigid, his shoulders square. Every inch of him on alert and ready to protect me from Nico's enemies.

It's one thing for me to be swept up in the glamour and excitement of the Mafia world, but to raise a child with possible threats hiding in every shadowy corner is another.

Not to mention that this is a business deal only.

Okay, business with benefits.

Okay, business with lots of really good benefits.

But that's as far as it goes.

Although, we haven't exactly been smart with protection. I'm on the pill, but I've missed a few days here and there.

Maybe he's already planted the seed.

My stomach tightens.

Could I already be pregnant?

An excited tingle snaps and crackles at the base of my spine like popping candy. But I ignore it. Best not to get excited about things that can never happen.

The Devil's Den

"No, babies are not a part of this contract," I say, pouring us both a glass of water.

She pouts. "Pity. You two would make deliciously beautiful babies."

And there I go again, getting excited about being pregnant with Nico's baby.

I clear my throat as I push the ridiculous notion to the back of my mind.

That's when I hear a familiar shrill across the restaurant.

"Bella—Bella Isle Ciccula, is that you?"

Amélie appears at our table in a cloud of expensive perfume and floaty red Valentino. Immediately, the hairs on the back of my neck stand on end.

"It's Bella De Kysa now," I correct her.

Her smile tips just a little. "Of course, congratulations on your nuptials. They were quite the affair. I was surprised I didn't receive an invitation, but I suppose it's understandable, really, given the type of relationship we used to have."

Imogen's expression darkens while mine remains unaffected by Amélie's dig.

I plaster a smile on my face. "I'm glad you didn't take offense."

She laughs and waves it off.

"I'm so pleased I ran into you today," she says, sitting down uninvited.

Imogen and I glance at one another.

No, please, take a seat.

Amélie is fully aware that she's intruding but doesn't care.

"I receive so many questions about you at every single function I attend, or so it seems, so it only makes sense that we should get to know one another. I can be very useful in social situations. I know everyone. Best of all, I know everyone's secrets." Her eyes twinkle with malice. She's hinting at something.

Does she know that my marriage to Nico was arranged?

No, there is no way... Nico stressed the importance of no one knowing about the arrangement.

Unless he told her after he fucked her, the nasty voice of doubt whispers in my ear.

I quickly push it away.

Nico assured me it was over with her.

Instead, I think about the way he fucked me against the mirrored walls of the elevator the other night, and again this morning as he moaned my name over and over again when he was buried deep inside me.

Amélie might've had him in bed, but I'm confident she never got the side of Nico where his sexual creativity meets his emotions.

She smooths down the front of her dress, her jeweled fingers gleaming with diamonds and rubies. "So tell me honestly, what's it like being the wife of the most sought-after man in New York?"

Imogen looks at me, and I smile, turning my attention solely on Amélie.

"You really want to know?"

"Like my life depends on it." She smiles, but it's empty.

I lean forward and whisper, "It's full of lots and lots of hot sex and dirty talk. I mean, my husband fucks me so hard with that giant cock every morning and every night, I'm surprised I can even walk most days."

The Devil's Den

Imogen's ruby-red lips drop open in a gasp and then spread into a smile. "You dirty little whore, I knew it."

But Amélie's eyes flare with something nasty before she gets ahold of her feelings and offers me a big fake smile. "Well, I can attest that he certainly knows how to use it."

I raise an eyebrow, hating that Nico used to fuck this woman who feels it is quite appropriate to hijack a lunch between two friends simply to flex her *I used to fuck your husband* muscle in an attempt to intimidate me.

"Ah yes, he did use to fuck you," I say, not seeing any point in holding back. If the witch wants to flex, I'm going to flex right back. "But he grew tired of it and came looking for me."

Her jaw visibly tenses, and she looks down her nose at me, her arrogant eyes hard and full of spite. But then a smirk tugs at her bloodred lips in an attempt to rattle me. To make me doubt whether that is true or not.

"You say that with confidence," she says.

"Because I know it's true."

"Because he said so?" She scoffs and leans forward. "You shouldn't believe everything he tells you. Men lie."

"So do women."

"Yes, but he has more to lose than I do."

I raise an eyebrow. "What are you trying to imply?"

She sighs. "I'm not the enemy. I'm just looking out for you."

"No, you're not. You're angry and resentful because he picked me and not you."

Beside me, Imogen chokes on her wine.

While Amélie's mouth tightens.

"You may think you won him," she says cooly. "But it

won't be long before he moves on to something that requires less effort."

"Like you, maybe?" I tilt my head.

"We have a bond."

In your dreams. "No, you don't."

"How can you be so sure?" she asks smugly.

I lean forward and whisper, "Because I'm his motherfucking queen."

Our eyes lock, but I will die of old age before I let her win.

Finally, she stands. "May the better woman win."

I lean back in my chair like I don't have a care in the world. "She already has."

Amélie walks off in a huff, her chin raised but her pride wounded. She failed to rattle my cage as she'd intended.

"Good riddance." Imogen leans forward. "You are my hero, Bella De Kysa. You just slayed that evil witch and blew her ashes into the wind."

"Hold that thought," I say, standing. "I need to use the bathroom real quick. But when I come back, we're going to get messy drunk on cocktails because after that, I need a stiff drink."

Imogen holds her hands out to the side. "And what kind of best friend would I be if I didn't support you in messy drinking?"

I leave the table. James tries to follow me, but I stop him.

"It's okay, I'm just heading to the ladies' room," I say, wondering if I'll ever get used to being shadowed again.

I make my way through the crowded restaurant, taking a left at the massive water fountain and turning down the hallway toward the restrooms.

Inside the bathroom, I take a breath at the sink, splashing cool water on the nape of my neck and breathing in the subtle scent of vanilla and cherry blossom as I try to calm my heart. Around me, gold gleams in the dimly lit room.

I don't enjoy being in competition with another woman. Usually, I'm Team Women United. But when a bitch throws the towel in the ring, I need to step up if I am to survive in this world.

There will be more Amélies in our future. But let word get out that I won't suffer them very well.

Resting my clutch on the vanity, I remove my lipstick and touch up my lips, then smile at my reflection in the dimly lit bathroom. Two months ago, I would never have stuck up for myself. I would've taken Amélie's assault on my confidence on the chin and let Amélie get it out of her system. But my days of being anyone's doormat are done.

I tuck my lipstick into my tote bag and cross the Italian tiles to the door.

But the moment I step out of the bathroom, something hits me in the head, and my world fades to black.

Blackness.

I only become aware of the nothingness as I slowly rise out of its murky depths.

Feeling foggy, I open my eyes and blink, and my blurry vision begins to sharpen.

I'm sitting in a chair, my hands tied behind my back, my shoes and jacket gone.

A man steps in front of me. "Welcome back, sleepyhead."

I glance around. We're in some sort of warehouse. It's dimly lit, and the musty stench of mildew is in the air.

"Do you know who I am?" he asks.

"A kidnapping asshole?" I manage.

He leans down and scoffs. "You always were too feisty for your own good." He stands. "My name is Luca Bamcorda. You will have heard of me."

"Don't flatter yourself."

Of course, I know who he is.

But I won't give him the satisfaction of admitting to it.

"My family was once aligned with the mighty De Kysa. When your father and Gio De Kysa became rivals, it was the Bamcordas who stepped in and formed an alliance with Gio. An alliance forged in honor and respect... both of which have been spat on by this truce. Nico had no business offering peace. And your father had no business accepting it."

"You've done this because the De Kysa and Isle Cicculas are no longer rivals?" I pull a sad face. "Aw, are you sad because no one wants to play with you, Timmy?"

My mockery earns me a swift smack across the cheek.

"You really aren't in a position to disrespect me," he growls.

I glare up at him, my skin stinging.

"You've kidnapped me to get to my husband?" I taste blood, and it sends anger up my spine.

"Good to see that little bump on your head hasn't affected you."

I swallow thickly. Behind my back, I'm furiously working on the knots binding my wrists together.

The Devil's Den

"You stand to gain nothing from doing this," I say.

"Oh, but that's where you're wrong. There is nothing like the sweet taste of revenge." He smiles evilly. "Kill you, and I destroy your father, *and* I let your husband know what happens to people who decide to betray me."

I narrow my eyes, my head hurting like a son of a bitch. "They will find you."

"Oh, I don't doubt that. In fact, I'm counting on it. You see, I'm a proactive man, Bella. I like to be the one to draw first blood and declare war. And that is exactly what I plan to do. But by then, it will be too late for you." He reaches for his belt buckle. "Now, I'm not normally a taking man, Bella, but I want your husband and father to know exactly what I did to you."

He crouches before me and yanks my knees apart and runs his hands up my thighs.

I growl and push them closed, but he laughs. He stands, and his eyes gleam menacingly as he unzips his pants. "You might want to make your peace with it now, Bella Isle Ciccula, because the next hour is going to be hell for you."

I look up at him and smile. Something he wasn't expecting.

"You're in so much trouble," I say.

"Ah, yes, your husband. What will he do when they pull his beautiful wife's lifeless body out of the Hudson?" he taunts.

I shake my head. Blood drips from my nose onto my swollen lips.

"No, it's not him you should be afraid of right now," I warn.

"No?" He mocks surprise. "Who then?"

My eyes zone in on his. "Me."

Before he can reply, I'm out of that chair so damn fast he doesn't have time to react. I get him first in his stomach which bends him over, allowing me to get him in the eyes with my fingers, and his balls with my foot.

He fights back, but I've done enough Krav Maga that it's hardwired into my instincts.

When he goes down, his weapon spins across the floor, and I grab it before fleeing out a door and down a set of stairs.

I'm still inside the warehouse but I can hear traffic nearby.

At the bottom of the stairs I run into a bodyguard. But before he can reach for his gun, I have mine pressed into his forehead. He steps back, and I run... I run so fucking fast my lungs feel like they're on fire.

I'm woozy and out of sorts, but there's nothing like a threat to your life to get you moving.

I expect more resistance. More bodyguards. More something. But Luca Bamcorda has clearly underestimated me, bringing minimal manpower with him to the warehouse where he planned to rape and murder me.

I see a door and sprint toward it, knowing my path to freedom is on the other side of it.

Flinging it open, I run straight into a bulldozer of a man who raises his gun above his head and strikes me viciously on the side of the head. Pain shoots into my brain and engulfs me, sending me falling back into the blackness once again.

39

Nico

"Why did you apply for this position?" I ask the good-looking couple sitting across the desk from me.

"We like sex," the man says.

"And we like people watching us have sex," the woman adds.

Somewhere in their late twenties, they exude sex and confidence.

She pushes her long dark hair over her shoulder. "We figured why not get paid to do it."

"And you're aware some people will offer extra to participate?" I ask.

She grins. "We hope they do. Getting someone all worked up and wanting to join in is half the fun."

"My wife and I enjoy group scenarios," the man says.

"We're more than happy to show you if you'd like," she

adds eagerly, undoing the top button of her see-through blouse.

My phone rings, but it's a number I don't recognize, so I ignore it.

"That won't be necessary," I say, cursing Massimo for landing me with this interview. This is his area, not mine. But this morning, he called me to tell me he's been held up with something that requires his immediate attention.

"The Irish and Russians are closing in, and you want me to drop everything to interview a couple about banging in front of people at the club?" I'd asked.

Massimo had sighed dramatically. "I know you're a big don and everything, but this is our business, brother. I don't trust anyone else to do this."

I agreed only because my marriage is turning me into a more agreeable person, or so Massimo likes to tell me. Which I'm not sure he meant as a compliment or an insult.

Either way, he has a point. Being with Bella has put me in a permanent good mood, and I can't say I hate it.

"All performers require the necessary health checks, as do the participants," I say, declining another call on my phone.

"Of course, we are happy to comply with the conditions," the woman says, her eyes drifting over my face with obvious interest. She bites her lip and looks up at me through long lashes. "And anything else you might want from us."

Her invitation is clear. But like my ringing phone, I ignore it.

"When can you start?" I ask them.

"Right now, if you'd like," the man says.

I smile because I admire his enthusiasm.

"We're at full capacity tonight. But Massimo will work you into next week's schedule. His assistant will call you with the details."

After the couple leaves, I begin to work through a couple of emails that have been demanding my attention for some time.

When my phone lights up with a message, I decide to ignore it, but a quick glance tells me it is a photo.

A photo of...

I grab it.

What the fuck?

The picture is of an unconscious Bella, strung up by her wrists.

My vision becomes a hazy shade of red.

The screen lights up with a text message.

> If you don't answer my call the next time your phone fucking rings, I'll fucking chop her goddamn hands off.

~

My phone rings.

"I will find you, and I will kill you the slowest way possible. Do you hear me?" I seethe into the phone the second I answer it.

My threat is met with laughter on the other end of the line.

"Your anger is admirable, Don De Kysa, but is poor use of your energy," Luca Bamcorda says with his usual condescension.

A condescension I intend to burn off his face and rip out of his larynx the moment I get my hands on him.

"You should never have disrespected me," he snarls. "But the ball is in my court now. This is my game."

"No," I grit out. "This isn't your game, you old fuck. This is your *mistake*."

With one hand, I hold the phone to my ear. The other is reaching for extra fire power, taking a second Ruger from the top drawer of my desk and shoving it into the back of my dress pants.

I know where he's holding her. The Bamcorda have a warehouse down at the docks. I recognize the familiar brickwork that is common in the area because we have warehouses that look the same.

It's a trap. I didn't get this far as don by not recognizing an ambush coming a mile away.

Luca Bamcorda wants me to show up and save Bella.

He's trying to distract me with my own emotions. He wants me wild and half-cocked with emotion so I might fuck up.

Not the calm, calculated man he knows I am because he knows that version of me is capable of anything.

What he didn't count on was me being in love with my forced bride.

That she is the air that I fucking breathe.

That needing her more than I need my own heartbeat has made me even more ruthless, even more capable of raining down fire and brimstone and all that hell can bring, more so than usual.

"What do you want?" I growl.

"I want you to know what happens to people who disrespect me and my family."

"You need to tread very carefully, Luca. If you hurt Bella, you cannot imagine the things I will do to you and every single asshole bearing the Bamcorda name."

He chuckles. "Come find your bride, *stronzo,* and we'll talk."

40

Bella

This time when I wake up, my arms are stretched above my head and my wrists are tied to a bolt in the ceiling. I can stand, but my legs are weak, and my body aches with exhaustion.

It takes me a second to realize I'm being slapped on the face to wake up.

When I open my eyes, they land on Luca Bamcorda's smug smile. "Ah, the princess is finally awake."

Blood trickles down my temple and through my eyebrow, dripping onto my cheek and lips. I taste the metallic tang of it as I look at the man who has me bound as his prisoner.

"My husband is going to kill you for this... slowly."

My voice is hoarse, my throat swollen and sore, and I wonder exactly what they did to me while I was unconscious. My clothes are still intact, and I don't feel any pain that might suggest sexual assault, so I don't think I've been violated in that way. Besides, Luca Bamcorda is such an evil narcissist I'm pretty sure he would want me awake for anything like that.

Going by the stinging pain in my scalp and the tightness in my neck, I think they dragged me by the hair and held me up by the throat as they bound my wrists and secured me to the ceiling.

A new smile spreads across Luca's spongy lips. "You think I care about Domenico De Kysa? I just care about being the one to cut up his bride."

His words send a sharp shiver through me, like a blade of a knife running down my spine.

"You see, your husband has a lot of enemies. It's nothing personal. It simply comes with the role." He steps closer, his forehead beaded with sweat and gleaming in the dull light. "But with me, it is very, very personal. He disrespected me, and he disrespected my daughter. And now, the only way he can pay for this scourge is with your life."

When I see the knife, I whimper, and my pulse pounds against my throat.

I'm going to die, but I won't go down without a fight. I lash out at him with my legs.

It catches him off guard, and he stumbles but quickly rights himself, and all I've done is made him mad.

He punches me so hard in the cheek I see stars, leaving me docile and nauseous as I watch my fate unfold before me.

He leans closer, and I'm engulfed in the stench of tobacco and garlicky sweat as he brings his mouth to my ear. "If it wasn't me, Bella Isle Ciccula, it would be someone else."

I squeeze my eyes close and wait for the pain.

But it doesn't come.

Instead, gunfire and men yelling in the distance breaks into the silence and tells me things are about to change.

Nico.

But Luca doesn't appear worried. In fact, he smiles and says, "Showtime."

More gunfire rings out. More yelling as Bamcorda soldiers try to stop the moving war machine that is my husband.

The noise comes closer until the door bursts open, and Nico appears like a dark demon in the doorway. Black suit. A gun in each hand. A face wild with determination to make Luca pay.

Behind him lay the bodies of the men who tried to stop him from getting to me.

Luca moves behind me and brings the blade to my throat.

Nico's dead eyes burn holes into Luca's face. "You don't want her. You want me. Let her go, and you can take me."

Luca's words have a smile in them. "Think I'm fine where I am."

The wrath radiating off Nico is like a raging inferno.

"You wanted me here." He holds out his arms. "Well, here I am."

"Well armed, too." He gestures with his head. "Put the guns down or your bride dies."

"I told you, you can take me. That's who you really want."

Luca scoffs. "You're trading your life for hers. How sweet. But the moment I let her go, you'll put two bullets into me."

He jams the knife into my skin, not deep, but enough to draw blood. I wince, terrified.

"Fine!" Nico says quickly. He puts his two guns down on the ground. "Satisfied?"

"No, Domenico, no, I'm not satisfied. But spilling the blood of a De Kysa bride will fix that."

"You know this is a declaration of war," Nico growls. "The De Kysa will decimate the Bamcorda for good. I'll make it my life's mission to fuck up every single one of you."

"You think I'm going to let you walk out of here after I kill her?" Luca laughs coldly. "Son, your bride is just the beginning. Once I gut her, I'll take pleasure in killing you too."

Nico snickers. "That's the thing about us De Kysas. You cut off one head and another one will grow. You kill me and my brother will come looking for revenge. And he might be the funny one, but his temper is just as dark and just as creative as mine. To put it plainly, you're fucked."

The blade slides into my skin, but quicker than a blink, Nico rips the gun from his waistband and fires.

I feel the whoosh and crackle of the bullet as it strikes Luca right in the middle of his face and blows out the back of his skull.

With a thud, the old gangster falls to the floor.

Nico storms over and puts another one in his chest. Then thinking better of it, he fires a third and says to the corpse, "No one touches my wife."

He quickly unties the binds holding me to the ceiling, and when I crumple to the floor, he catches me in his strong arms.

He presses a kiss onto my lips and carries me out of the

warehouse, stepping over the bodies of Luca Bamcorda's men.

"You're safe," he says, holding me tight.

But I don't feel safe.

And I don't think I will ever feel safe again.

41

Nico

I carry her to the car and climb in, but I don't let her go. I hold her in my arms during the entire drive back to my apartment. She wraps her arms around my neck and buries her face into my shoulder, as if letting me go would mean sure death.

"I've got you, baby," I assure her as my hatred for Luca Bamcorda collides in my chest with the fierce love I feel for my bride.

She nods against my shoulder, a small whimper escaping her slightly parted lips, and I hold her closer, knowing I will do whatever it takes to keep her safe.

The city is a blur as it rolls past the window because all I can see, think, and feel is the need to protect my queen from further harm.

A soft rain begins to fall as we pull into the underground garage, and Mateo parks the car in our usual spot.

"Call Dr. Sage," I instruct him as I carry Bella to the elevator.

"No," she murmurs, her lips brushing against my neck. "I don't want to see anyone."

"You need medical attention," I say.

"What I need is my husband." She lifts her head. "And only my husband."

Her big eyes are soft and pleading, and how the fuck am I supposed to say no to that?

I look at Mateo. "I'll call the doctor later myself. Until then, I need to be alone with my wife."

Mateo nods. "I'll wait for further instructions from you."

The elevator door closes, and we ride to the penthouse alone.

Bella's salty tears pool on my skin, and I can feel the thud of her heartbeat as if it is syncopated with my own. My arms are beginning to get tired, but I'll let them fall off before I let her go.

Once inside my apartment, I carry her to the bedroom and set her on the end of the bed. "I'm going to run you a bath, okay?"

She nods, shivering, and I take another look at the bruises on her arms and can almost make out a handprint. Flames heat every inch of my body, knowing it is Luca's handiwork, and my hands fist at my side.

Keep focused. Bella needs all of you right now.

I stalk to the bathroom and run the bath, waiting for it to fill with warm water before adding the perfumed bubble bath I know she loves. When it's ready, I stand and take a steady breath, trying to calm the anger that I know will only be dampened by the flames of violence.

Not tonight.

Tonight is all about Bella.

She's where I left her on the side of the bed, her hands gripping the edge and her hair hanging limply past her shoulders as she stares with unfocused eyes at a spot on the carpet.

Crouching before her, I reach for her bruised face. She flinches and closes her eyes. "I'm so fucking sorry, Bella."

Tears spill down her cheeks.

I take her hands. "I'm going to undress you, and then I'm going to help you into the bath. Is that okay?"

I don't think I've ever asked anyone for any kind of permission, ever. When you're the don of one of the most powerful families in the world, you don't need to. People trip over themselves to offer you everything, and soldiers do as they are instructed or face losing their place at the table for lack of loyalty. But my heart has been flayed open by what has happened to my queen, and I need to ease her pain, and I need to know that she is okay with me doing this.

Wordlessly, she nods, and when I see her eyes soaked with tears, I feel the crushing weight on my chest.

It's not sexual as I slowly peel the ripped and stained bra and panties off her. It's a transfer of strength. *I've got you. I will look after you.* And once she's naked, I gather her in my arms again and carry her to the bathroom, savoring the knowledge she is safe.

I ease her into the warm, soapy water that smells like ocean and wild lilies, and she hisses as the water licks at her wounds.

"Fuck—" I say, ready to hoist her out of the water.

"It's okay," she croaks. "They're nothing, really."

She looks up at me and a small smile teases her lips. "I'm going to be okay, Nico."

They're words of strength, but her expression is anything but strong.

Again, that crushing weight sinks in my chest.

I've done this to her.

In the ginormous bath, she looks small and wounded, and I can't stand it. Kicking off my shoes, I strip out of my clothes and step into the porcelain tub and gather her in my arms.

I hold her to my chest, and she melts against me and begins to sob.

Tremors wrack her body, and her tears coat my skin.

Guilt crashes through me, colliding with the simmering rage boiling in my blood.

Killing Luca a thousand times over couldn't make this up to her.

Eventually, she stops shaking, and her tears ease. But we don't speak. I know she is listening to the thud of my heart as it bashes against my ribs, and I pray she knows that it beats for her.

When she is calm, she pulls away from me, and the sadness in her eyes strikes a match to a terrible sense of foreboding lingering in the pit of my stomach.

Irreparable damage has been done.

It's in the silence. In the stiffness of her shoulders. In the way she can't look me in the eyes when I tell her that she is safe now.

I turn her around so her back is to me and reach for the shampoo on the bath caddy, squirting a pool of the golden liquid into my hand. I run my fingers through her hair, lathering the shampoo through the long, wet strands. She moans and leans into my fingers as I massage her scalp.

I rinse the shampoo away with the handheld showerhead, then repeat the head massage with a palm full of conditioner, relishing her moans and the peaceful sag of her shoulders as she relaxes beneath my touch.

When we're done, I turn her around to face me. The bruise on her cheek where Luca punched her sends a new wave of anger through me, and it's an anger I don't know how to deal with.

"Tell me how to make this right," I say.

For the first time in my adult life, I don't have the answers.

"I don't know," she croaks, and the tremble on her lips lands a new blow to my gut.

"I will do whatever it takes," I say, reaching for her wet hands.

"Even if it means letting me go?"

I didn't see her question coming, and it hits me with the force of a sledgehammer. My body tenses, every muscle balling up tightly at the thought of losing her.

"Is that what you want?" I can barely move my jaw to speak. And it's damn impossible to keep the edge from my voice.

She sighs. "I'm tired, and I need to sleep. Can we talk about this in the morning?"

My heart beats rapidly in my chest. I want to take her thoughts of leaving me and machine gun them to pieces.

I was angry and tight with fury for what happened to my queen, now I can add anxiety to the mix. I'd rather fucking die than lose her.

But I respect her wishes and remain quiet. In the morning, when she wakes up rested, we can talk.

We leave the bath and dry off in silence, each of us lost in our own thoughts. I can't shake the persistent scratch in the back of my mind that everything is about to fall apart.

Once we're dry, she lies on the bed, and I protectively lie behind her, wrapping my arms around her and holding her close.

"No one will ever hurt you again," I say, knowing without a doubt that I will do whatever it takes to keep her safe. I'm already going to hell, so if it means burning down the world, I will.

She relaxes against me, and I press a kiss into her hair.

"I love you," I whisper.

But she doesn't respond, and in minutes, she is asleep.

42

Bella

The next hour is going to be hell for you, the monster says.

I can't see him, but I can feel him, smell his sweat and rotten breath. My hands are tied, my body aching. I can't move, and I'm afraid. Then she appears, the witch in the red dress, her long nails curled around Nico's thick bicep as her bloodred lips pull back maniacally with laughter.

"Men lie, Bella," she says, followed by another bellowing laugh. "You'll never know what it's like to feel safe again."

Nico tilts his head. His face marred by evil. "If it wasn't me, Bella, it was going to be someone else."

Gasping for breath, I wake up drenched in sweat and gripping the bed sheet beneath me. I sit up abruptly and gulp in the cool air, waiting for the nightmare to recede. Darkness and shadows fill the bedroom, but enough moonlight streams in through the parted curtains for me to see where I am.

The apartment is still. The red blinking light of the alarm across the room tells me no one unwanted is in our home.

I exhale heavily and push my hair out of my face. Beside me, Nico is lost in heavy sleep.

I want to sleep but I can't because I've been woken by demons, so I reach for my own monster to chase them away.

I slide my thighs on either side of him and lean down to kiss him. He stirs, his big hands reaching for me in the silvery light.

My kiss becomes needy, my tongue exploring his mouth as my hands reach for his cock.

He hesitates, his voice thick with sleep. "Bella—"

But I kiss him to shut him up. "I need you."

I don't need his concern or judgment. I just need him to fuck the past twenty-four hours out of my mind.

"Please," I beg against his lips. "Fuck me and make me forget."

He responds with a growl and flips me onto my back so he is on top and in control.

Sleepily, he pushes my arms above my head and threads his fingers through mine as he slowly but strongly slides into me. I moan and arch my neck as his cock surges deep and hard, stretching and filling me, bringing to life the pleasure unfurling at my core.

I wrap my legs around his hips, pulling him deeper, and he groans into my shoulder.

"Nothing feels as good as this," he moans, his breath ragged and hoarse. "And nothing in this world tastes as good as my queen."

He takes my mouth again with a strong, restless kiss, his

body flexing and his hips rolling with expert precision as he plunges deeper and deeper.

Pleasure sweeps through me, a building tension I start to chase. I rock underneath him, raising my hips to meet every stroke of his cock, desperate to feel something other than the fear nipping at my heels.

"Nico." I barely breathe his name.

"You're so perfect... so fucking perfect," he rasps.

His pace quickens.

"I love you," he mutters desperately. "I goddamn love you so much."

His words send me over the edge, and my orgasm hits with the power of a nuclear bomb going off in the room.

His follows quickly with a ferocious force, a primal cry stealing past his lips and roaring into the room.

My emotions get away from me, and tears slide down my cheeks as I come in waves of unchecked pleasure. I hate this life. I hate the fear and the unease that shadows me because of it. I hate that Luca Bamcorda thought he could hurt me. I hate that Nico had to save me. I hate that I crave this man so much but can't stand his world.

But worst of all, I hate that I love him just as he loves me, but I can't say it because then it will be real, and when something is real, there is too much to lose.

His world isn't made for love.

It is only made for pain.

Lying in his arms, I pray I will wake up the next day and not feel this way.

Because if I do, I know I'll have to leave.

In the morning, I still feel the same.

I wake up with the weight of what I have to do sitting on my heart.

Beside me, Nico sleeps soundly, his beautiful, golden body relaxed among the white sheets. I take a moment to study him. The long lashes fanned against his cheek. The sharp contours of his face. The scruff of hair along his jaw. Lips I could live a hundred lives over and never get tired of kissing.

I resist the urge to touch them. He doesn't need to watch me walk out the door.

My bag is already packed and sitting by the bedroom door. Last night, after making love, I packed while he slept, moving quietly in the shadows of our bedroom to gather my belongings.

Now, it's time to go.

I dress quickly and brush my teeth quietly in the bathroom, pausing to take in a deep breath.

This is the right thing to do.

Leaving the bathroom, I avoid looking at the bed, knowing it will only make it harder to see him one last time.

But his voice stops me. "Bella."

Reluctantly, I turn around. He's standing by the bed, every glorious inch of him gleaming with perfection in the early morning light. He's pulled on his dress pants and belt, but he's shirtless.

My nerves rattle inside me.

"Where are you going?" His voice is low but filled with something dark.

"I'm leaving." My gaze meets his, and I pray my words

don't fail me now. "I never wanted this life, Nico. But I wanted you, so I tried. But it doesn't work."

"It does work," he says with that same dark edge to his words.

"No." I shake my head. "We're like fire and ice. Made to destroy each other."

Nico's expression darkens.

"You're wrong, Bella. We're both fire. And fire on fire builds an inferno and that is what we are. An unstoppable inferno." His jaw tightens. "You're not leaving me."

I stand my ground. "You don't get to ask me to stay."

"I'm not asking," he growls. "I'm telling you."

Something in me snaps.

He doesn't get to control me anymore.

Not after yesterday.

I storm over to him and shove him in the chest. "I almost died because of you."

I throw my fists into his bare chest, but it's like hitting a brick wall.

He grabs my wrists and yanks me to him. "And I would die a thousand times for you."

I struggle in his arms. "You want this life. I don't."

"I have no choice."

"But I do, and I'm making it."

Darkness sweeps through his expression like a storm cloud. "So that's it. You think you can just leave me?"

"You might not have a choice to leave this life, but I do," I yell, pushing against him. "Now, let me go."

"Not until you've calmed down and are ready to talk."

"I don't want to talk about it. I don't want this life, and

yesterday, Luca Bamcorda obliterated any capability I had to compromise."

"I told you nothing like that will ever happen again."

"But you can't guarantee it. For every enemy you destroy, another one appears."

His tone drips with venom. "And I will destroy them too while protecting my wife."

"But I don't want to be your wife!" I yell.

Stunned by my outburst, his grip on me loosens, and I make a break for it.

But he catches me, and I thrash wildly in his arms until he throws me on the bed. Before I can move, he crawls over me like a panther stalking its prey before it strikes.

Black eyes burn down at me. "You *are* my wife, and until I say otherwise, that fact isn't going to change."

Imprisoned by his powerful body and big arms, I know there is no way out for me but with words.

I look up at him. He is beautiful. Even in this dark moment quilted in pain and fear, he is the most beautiful man I have ever seen.

"Please let me go?" My voice is small. "Please don't do this to me anymore. I'm no Mafia queen."

Something ripples in his dark expression. Something unguarded and gentle. "You're *my* queen."

A tear slides down my cheek and slips onto the pillow behind me. "No, Nico. I'm not."

With a growl, Nico recoils and leaves the bed and moves to stand at the window, his broad back to me.

The silence is loud until he speaks.

"I'm in love with you." His voice is strong, but pain curls around the edges of each word. "Does that mean anything?"

The Devil's Den

I sit up and scoot to the end of the bed. Tears stream down my cheeks. *He loves me.* But it's not enough.

My throat closes around the lump in my throat, and when I don't respond, his defenses go up as if they were physical things.

Hurt and anger hang heavily in the room.

Finally, he says, "If you're going to leave, then go."

My heart breaks open in my chest. He's giving me what I want. He's letting me go.

Why does it hurt so much?

Leaving the bed, I pick up my bag but falter at the door because walking away from him will be the hardest thing I've ever done.

He doesn't bother to turn around. And I don't say goodbye.

I leave the access card and my wedding rings on the kitchen counter before I step into the elevator and let the doors close behind me. *On our marriage.*

Despite my pedigree, I'm not cut out for this life.

And Nico needs to find another queen to rule by his side.

43

Nico

Three weeks later.

"Good riddance," I say as I pour whisky into the glass tumbler. It's my second glass in the twenty minutes Massimo has been in my office busting my balls over everything.

Now he's just brought up the topic he's been dancing around. *Bella.* Just the sound of her name is enough to drive me to drink.

Her being gone is a good thing. I was insane to think this could work.

Now I can get back to doing what I do best without the distraction.

"You don't mean that," Massimo says.

"I've never meant anything more in my entire life." I take

a mouthful of scotch and swallow, savoring the burn searing a path through my chest. "I've moved on."

"You don't act like a man who's moved on."

"How so?"

"Avoiding social events and refusing to accept any invitations to things that would help alliances. Like locking yourself in this office with a case of scotch and not resurfacing for three days." He crosses his legs and looks amused.

"So the fuck what? It had nothing to do with her and everything to do with me needing some time out. Even the king needs a break every now and again."

"But I've never seen you take a break."

"I thought now was a good time to start."

"And now that this break is over, what are your plans?"

"I get back to ruling my fucking kingdom."

He watches me drain the glass. "And you plan on ruling your kingdom drunk?"

"If that's what it takes."

"To what, forget about her?"

"To refocus and get shit done."

Massimo sighs like a parent who is fed up arguing with their kid. "So you're letting her go just like that?"

"Just like that." I snap my fingers. "She was too much of a distraction. Too much hard work."

"What did you expect when you force someone to marry you? You have to expect a little pushback." He folds his arms. "But it wasn't like that in the end, was it?"

I actively ignore him and pour a third scotch. I don't need to think about how it was in the end.

"You still have eyes on her?" he asks.

"Of course. Until the fallout from Luca Bamcorda's death is handled, she's still a target."

So far, the consequences of taking out my rival have been minimal. But when it comes to Bella's safety, I'm not taking any chances.

"Does she know?" Massimo asks.

"They're very discreet."

"And they report back to you daily, no doubt."

I know what he's getting at. That I'm using the bodyguards to spy on her. But I'm not. I don't need to know what she's up to, or if she's missing me, or if she's as miserable as I am when the sun goes down and our bed is empty.

"You want to know what I think?" Massimo asks, his dark eyes watching my every move.

"Do I have a choice?"

He ignores me. "I think you love her, and that scares you."

The mouthful of whisky I've just taken turns into razorblades going down my throat. "I thought I did, but I was wrong."

"No, you weren't wrong. You love her. I'd bet my balls on it, and you know I'm fond of my balls."

"What I feel for her now is far from fucking love," I mutter.

But Massimo is not convinced.

"That pain in your gut, that knot in your chest, that's called longing, and longing is a byproduct of love. You're drinking that scotch to anesthetize them, but it won't work."

I scoff. The pain in my gut and the knot in my chest is agitation from this conversation—not because I can't stand her being so far away from me. Or because I hate waking up without her warm body lying next to me. Or because I've had to jerk off more times than I can count because her smell lingers in my sheets, and I wake up with a determined hard-on that won't quit because of it.

"What happens when she starts dating other men?" He asks.

My eyes dart to him. "Why the fuck would you ask me that?"

"I'm curious."

"I'm curious to see if you float, but I restrain myself from finding out." I grip the tumbler in my hand a little too tight because my brother has the ability to push every single one of my buttons. But I compose myself. "That's not my concern."

"Good, because you've let her go, and now she's free to do as she pleases. Surely you don't expect her to remain single for the rest of her life."

The glass in my hand shatters and sends shards of crystal into my fingers. Scotch mixes with blood. The sting is nothing compared to the frisson of agitation and anger in my gut. "Fuck."

I grab a tea towel from the bar and wrap it around my hand. Blood seeps into the cotton fabric.

"You just let a beautiful woman go into the wild, and it won't be long before someone else snatches her up."

I tie the tea towel around my hand. "Don't you have something better to do than sit here and break my balls?"

Massimo stands and holds his hands up in surrender. But his smile is wicked because he's loving this.

"If you leave it much longer, you might miss your chance at real happiness. It's already been weeks."

I feel my chest constrict.

"I did what she asked. I let her go."

"But she's worth chasing, no?"

"Of course she is," I reply before I can stop myself.

"Then why the fuck haven't you?"

"Because it fucking killed me to let her go to begin with," I snap.

Massimo nods and moves to stand in front of me.

"If you love her, go and get her. Get on your knees. Beg her to come back."

I raise an eyebrow at him. "I don't beg. And I certainly don't get on my knees for anyone."

Massimo puts his big hand on my shoulders and gives me a pointed look. "Then be prepared to lose her for good."

He leaves, and as he closes the door behind him, a prickly sensation crawls up my spine and spreads through my chest.

I hate how this feels.

Fuck.

44

Bella

"So you're really heading back to London?" Imogen pulls a sad face.

"The car is on its way." I zip my suitcase closed. "My flight leaves at six."

"But why? There's nothing left for you there since you lost your job. And why now? You haven't seen Nico in three weeks."

Hurt twists in my stomach.

She's right. I haven't seen or heard anything from him since I left.

I ran away.

But he didn't try to stop me.

Not that I wanted him to.

Well, maybe a small part of me had hoped he would.

But it's better that he didn't.

Because now I can put it all behind me.

The Mafia.

The danger.

The great fucking sex.

Imogen chews on a twisted piece of red licorice. "They say you shouldn't make huge decisions when you're emotional."

"I'm not emotional."

"That's what scares me." She sits cross-legged on my bed. "You haven't cried."

Because if I start, I won't fucking stop.

I yank my suitcase off the bed and sit down. "He said he loved me."

Imogen's eyes go round, and the red licorice twist is paused midair. "When?"

"The night before and the day I left."

"And what did you say?"

"Nothing."

Imogen looks at me like I just confessed to murder. "Oh, Bella."

"Don't *oh, Bella* me!" I stand up, hating that I feel this way. Hating that I miss him. Hating that I wish I was still living in his penthouse and pretending to hate him every day while we enjoy toe-curling, scream-inducing sex every night. "How was this going to work? He's married to a life of crime, and I'm—"

"Lying your ass off to your best friend right now." She stands and cups my shoulders. "Look me in the eye and tell me you don't love him."

I can't say I don't.

Because I do.

"He's a don," I whisper, as if whispering those words will make them less frightening.

"You were raised in the life."

"Which cost me my mom and brothers."

"Yes, that is why you have to be honest with yourself when you make this decision, and I don't think you have been. Not truly. You won't tell him you love him because you're afraid of what loving him means. *Fear. The Mafia. Always having a shadow.* But Bella, just because you don't say it, doesn't mean you don't feel it. Am I right?"

I nod, fighting tears.

I am smack bang in the middle of a love storm for Nico De Kysa.

I'm so crazy for him I can't go a single minute without thinking about him.

But I need space from his eclipsing presence. And I can't get my head straight while I'm in this city.

Everywhere I go, I'm reminded of what I have walked away from.

I made a good life for myself in London once before, maybe I can do it again.

Imogen gives me an empathetic look. "You have to decide which is more important, loving him and living with fear, or leaving him and living without love."

She's right.

Either way, there is a consequence.

And right now, I'm not sure which one is the fry pan and which one is the fire.

I pick up my bag. "Once I've taken care of some loose ends in London, I'll reevaluate things."

"I thought you packed up everything when you went back with Nico."

"Yes, but I still have the apartment in London, and I figure staying there for a while will help me clear my head."

"You're running away," she says flatly.

"Probably, but it feels right."

The buzzer tells me my ride is here.

"I'll come back," I reassure her when she pouts. "When my head is clearer."

With a reluctant look on her face, she pulls me in for a hug and squeezes tight. "You'd better. Or I'm coming over there and dragging you back by the thong."

When I giggle, she kisses my cheek and releases me.

It's not until I'm in the back of the car that the sadness descends to the deepest part of my soul, and I feel the loss of Nico in every cell of my body.

This is the right thing to do, I keep telling myself, despite my heart protesting with every mile that takes me farther and farther away from him.

My flight to London is on a private Learjet. My father organized me hitching a ride with one of his billionaire friends who happened to be flying there for business.

The car takes me to the Westchester Airport, and twenty minutes later, I'm boarding a sleek black Learjet sitting on the tarmac.

Drew Mott is an oil billionaire. A huge Texan with a larger-than-life personality. He greets me with a bear hug that almost knocks the air from my lungs. The only other people on the flight are his father, another bear of a man with white hair and a white moustache, and Drew's assistant, a wiry-looking guy in his twenties called Jethro.

The Devil's Den

They sit at the front of the plane with a pack of cards and crystal tumblers already filled with amber liquid.

"You like poker, Bella? Want us to cut you in?" Drew asks.

"Are you kidding? I'd be broke by the time we landed in London," I say with a wink. "If you don't mind, I was going to try and get some shut-eye during the flight. Is that okay?"

"Of course! My plane is your plane."

I settle in a seat in the back row and buckle in.

The door to the plane closes, and the engines begin to turn, gaining momentum.

Any second, the plane will begin to move, and we'll be on our way.

Except it doesn't

Instead, the engines wind down and stop.

My spine tingles.

I look around the cabin of the plane.

The door opens.

And in steps Nico.

45

Nico

"What the actual fuck?" Drew Mott barks at me when I board his plane. Six-foot-five, the eclipsing Texan towers above me. But he backs away when I throw him a warning look and walk down the aisle toward my bride.

Bella's beautiful eyes harden when they focus on me. "What are you doing here, Nico?"

"I thought it was obvious. I'm stopping you from leaving."

"Why?"

"Because you don't want to leave."

She scoffs and shakes her head. "Your arrogance is astonishing."

"Thank you."

"It wasn't a compliment."

I can't help but smile. She looks beautiful today. Oversized button-up shirt. Short skirt. Curls untamed and loose around her perfect face.

I was crazy to think I could let her go.

"You and me... we're not over," I say adamantly.

"Is that right?"

"We'll never be over."

"Do I get a say in it?" She fires back.

"No."

My simple answer annoys her.

She shakes her head. "It won't work, Nico."

"That's where you're wrong. The only reason you're leaving is because you don't feel safe. But I'm here now telling you that I'll do whatever it takes to make you feel safe, Bella. I'll fucking burn down the goddamn world if I have to."

She turns her face to the window. "You're crazy."

"Maybe. *Probably*. But it serves me well."

Her beautiful face is tight. Her fear runs deep, and my chest constricts with the need to ease her suffering.

I soften my voice. "I'm sorry you got hurt. And I'm sorry you're scared. But nothing like that will ever happen again, you have my word. You're safe. Let me prove it to you."

She shifts restlessly in the chair.

I'm getting to her.

"You can't go around stopping planes," she say as the last of her resolve crashes around her.

"I think you'll find I just did."

She sucks in a deep breath. "You're delusional."

"No, I'm fucking in love with you and am willing to do anything to keep you by my side."

Her beautiful face softens. "It's been weeks."

"I would've come sooner, my love, but my stubbornness is as impenetrable as yours. But I'm here now, and this is me getting on my knees and begging you to return."

"Is that so?" She folds her arms across her chest. "See, I might actually need to see that."

"You want me to get on my knees and beg you to come back to me?" I ask. "Saving you from vicious killers isn't enough?"

"It's a good start."

I step closer. "I made them pay for what they did to you."

She presses her hand into my chest. "Do I need to point out that this happened because you forced me to marry you?"

"I think we can both agree that our marriage has been somewhat satisfying."

Heat flickers across her face. But she won't give in to it. "They came after me because of you."

"And they have paid with their lives."

She says nothing, which, in this case, is a good thing.

"I stopped the plane," I add. "Surely that earns me some brownie points."

The fact that I just used the words *brownie points* shows me just how much this woman has changed me.

"Maybe." Her face softens, but she side-eyes me. "But you let me go."

"Which was a big mistake on my part."

I take her hand in mine.

And then surprising us both, I lower my knee to the ground.

46

Bella

Hell has officially frozen over.

Domenico De Kysa, the Heartless King from the North, is on his knees.

Something I never thought I'd ever see in this lifetime.

But before I can revel in it, he takes my hand and pulls me down until we're eye level. "Let me show you how good our life will be."

"How do you plan to do that?"

"Starting with this." He wraps his hand around the nape of my neck and crashes his lips to mine.

I've been aching for his kiss for weeks. And because I'm already high from the insanity unfolding around me, I give in to the deliciousness of his lips and the delightful sensation of his tongue stroking into my mouth.

I don't want to be a slave to this man's kisses. I don't want to crave his touch. But I do. Because I'm in love with him.

Just as Imogen said, I have to make the choice.

Live with the fear so I can love him.

Or live without the fear but lose him.

As he takes the kiss deeper, whatever resistance I feel gives way, and I know exactly which one I'll choose.

I choose him.

I will always choose him.

With a moan, he breaks the kiss and presses his forehead to mine. Tenderly, his thumbs brush my jaw. "I'm in love with you, Bella. I need you to trust me when I say I will move heaven and Earth to protect you from my rivals. You don't need to run away from me. I will keep you safe."

I nod, and his lips cover mine again, and I get lost in the passion between us as he takes it deeper.

After weeks of heartache, my heart feels giddy with happiness.

And after months of confusion, I finally have clarity.

I'm in love with this monstrous Mafia king.

Without breaking the kiss, he pulls us both to our feet, his commanding lips moving with fierce control and expertise over mine, speaking the truth that he loves me.

"Come with me," he says, breaking it off. "I have something to show you."

My brow lifts. "If you say your cock, then I will probably shoot you with your own gun."

His smile is devastatingly handsome. "I like how you think, baby. But I have a surprise for you first."

"A surprise?" I ask as he pulls out a blindfold from his jacket pocket. "Wait, are you kidnapping me again?"

"That might be our thing," he says, turning me around so he can tie the blindfold over my eyes.

"Perhaps we should try for a song or a movie or cute nicknames instead of a felony crime as our thing. It works for other couples."

His breath brushes the outer shell of my ear as he leans in. "We're nothing like other couples."

"How true," I reply as he gently guides me down the plane aisle. "But nicknames could be fun."

"I agree. You can start calling me master from now on."

"Hmm, I think Satan is more fitting."

"Feel free to call me Gigantor, then."

"Or not," I reply.

I don't see him, but I feel us pass Drew Mott at the cabin door.

"Sorry, Drew," I say.

Although, I am kind of questioning why he didn't try to save me from Nico.

But then again, Nico is kind of unstoppable when he wants something.

And he wants me.

My heart sings.

Because I want him just as badly.

Nico guides me off the plane, and as we walk away, I hear him call out to Drew, "You can have your plane back now."

~

He doesn't take my blindfold off until the car pulls up to the curb. He reaches over and unties it, and I'm surprised to see that during the car ride into the city, the sky has turned a deep shade of blue, and New York is lit up in all its starlight.

I'm further surprised to see we're sitting out the front of

the Landau Gallery, a privately owned and very prestigious gallery in Manhattan.

"What are you up to?" I ask suspiciously as he leads me out of the car and up the stairs to the front of the gallery. "This place is closed after seven o'clock."

"Not for us," he says with a smile. "I know—"

"The owner?" I grin. "Of course, you do."

A security guard meets us at the door. "Mr. De Kysa." He gives him a nod as he lets us into the gallery. "Please come in."

Immediately, my heart begins to sing. I've spent hours in this gallery getting lost in the vibrant color, creativity, and feelings conjured by each piece of art. It was always a dream of mine to be good enough to show something here. But surrounded by such talent, I accepted the likelihood was slim.

Our shoes click on the polished concrete floors as we walk from room to room and a new respect for Nico fills me as I watch him admire the dedication and talents of the different artists represented on the walls. He knows nothing about art. But that's the beauty of it. You don't need to understand the language for it to speak to you.

That's when I see it, and I stop walking, my mouth dropping open.

Feet rooted to the floor, I stare at the massive canvas painting on the wall in front of me.

"It's mine," I whisper.

Nico's voice is low and smooth. "Yeah, baby, it is."

It takes a moment for me to find the words because it's almost too surreal to understand what I am seeing.

I turn to look at my husband. "But how?"

"I spoke with Andrey—"

"Oh God, you didn't force him to sell you the gallery, did you?"

"No."

"You paid him to show it?"

"No. I simply mentioned that my wife was the most talented artist in New York City. He asked to see your work, so I invited him to view your pieces, and he loved them." He points at the abstract art of acrylic, rust, and patina on a textured surface of marble dust and plaster of Paris, I called, *Secret of the Sea Bed*. "He especially liked this one and asked if he could show it."

"Are you sure this transaction didn't involve a gun and some intimidating Mafia threats?" I ask almost light-hearted with happiness because my artwork is *actually* hanging in a gallery.

"Luckily for him, he loved your work, so I could keep my gun holstered." Amusement toys with his lips, then his face grows serious. "This is all you, Bella. I only showed your work to Andrey. Your talent did the heavy lifting and made him fall in love with it."

I feel giddy with excitement.

He hands me a business card. "Call him Monday. He would like to talk to you about your art and discuss viewing other pieces."

Stunned, I can only whisper, "Are you serious?"

Tears fill my eyes, and he grimaces. "You're not going to cry, are you?"

When I nod, he theatrically rolls his eyes as he pulls me in for a hug.

"This is the kindest thing anyone has ever done for me," I cry.

He pretends to be annoyed, but I know that somewhere in his black heart is a radiant piece of goodness.

"Just don't tell anyone that," he says. "Next thing I know, my rivals will be brokering peace treaties with fucking pinky swears and *do you like me, yes or no*, notes."

I look up at him through my tears and kiss him. "You pretend to be a monster, but you're not really."

His expression darkens.

"Oh, I am," he growls, trailing his thumb across my lips. "But I'm your monster, and I'll do whatever the fuck I have to do to keep you safe and make you happy."

I kiss him again and fumble with his shirt buttons.

"Does this mean we're back together?" he asks as I peel his shirt off his muscular form.

I keep my lips on his as I reply, "Oh yeah, you're stuck with me, Don De Kysa."

When I lower his zipper, he growls and hoists me in his powerful arms.

And as he fucks me against the wall of the art gallery next to the artwork I created in his penthouse, he obliterates any doubt I have about who I am and who I'm supposed to be with.

47

Bella

After calling Andrey the following Monday, the flamboyant art curator invited me to meet him over wine and brandy at a bar in Manhattan called *Poison Me*, and the two of us clicked like old friends

It turns out, he's crazy obsessed for textured abstract art and had already decided I was going to be his new star.

A month later, and here I am, about to attend the opening night of my very first exhibition.

It's crazy to even try to pull off a small exhibition in a month, but thanks to my ability to thrive in chaos and the steady support from my biggest fan, who I just happen to be married to, I've made it to opening night with my nerves intact and just a mild case of insanity.

Dressed in a short, glittering dress of shimmering white crystals, I stand in front of the gigantic mirror in our bedroom to put on a pair of chandelier earrings and clasp a thick Swarovski crystal bracelet around my wrist. Tonight's shoes are limited edition Louboutins which lift me three inches off the floor and make my legs look crazy good.

I know the moment my husband sees me in them, he'll get hard, because seeing me in a sexy pair of stilettos never fails to get him all worked up.

And of course, there is only one elixir for it.

Which wouldn't be such a bad idea right now, considering my nerves are tied up in knots and making me antsy. I could do with the distraction.

I hear the door to the bedroom open, and Nico looms up behind me, wrapping his strong arms around me. Just as I thought, dark appreciation flares in his eyes as he takes in my bare legs and high heels. "Goddamn, you are fine. Are they new shoes?"

I smile at him in the mirror. "Uh-huh."

I haven't told him yet, but I'm four days late. My period is usually always on time. But not this month, and the idea that I might be pregnant excites me. In fact, just thinking about it makes me crave his lovemaking even more.

I laugh as his big hands roam down my waist and hips to cup my ass.

"God, you smell good, too." He groans, drawing a deep breath in from the surface of my skin. "Fuck, everything about you makes me want you all the fucking time."

He slides a hand between my thighs, and I groan as his fingers slip beneath my panties. Sparks zap through me when they find my clit.

His voice is a low rasp in my ear. "You're already so wet for me. *Fuck*... you make me so goddamn hard." He dips a finger inside me, and my moan catches in my throat. His thumb presses against my clit, and the friction sends me weak behind the knees.

He takes my hand and guides it behind me, placing it over the rigid outline of his cock. "See what you do to me?" He nips at my earlobe. "See how fucking hard you get me?"

I moan and sink my teeth into my lip. "What are you going to do about it, villain?"

His chuckle is dark as he bends me over the edge of our bed and shreds my panties from my body.

He enters me roughly, his thick, long cock surging into me to the very hilt.

Stars cartwheel across my brain.

The day my husband stops wanting to take me because he's overcome with the need to be inside me is a day I don't ever want to see.

"Such a tight, sweet pussy," he groans, his groin slapping against my ass as he rocks in and out of my body. "Being inside you is everything... squeeze my cock, baby... yeah, like that... you're going to make me come so fucking hard."

Again, I think about the possibility of being pregnant, and my body throbs with excitement.

And if I'm not pregnant, I know I want to be.

Every thrust, every stroke, every thought of him filling me with his seed nudges me closer to coming.

"Come inside me," I beg.

He draws in air through flared nostrils and crushes his teeth into his bottom lip as he drives deeper and deeper. "*Goddamn..!*"

He stops thrusting and grabs my hips, letting out a rough, masculine growl as he comes, his cock pulsating against the walls of my sex, shooting his cum into the deepest part of me.

Make me pregnant, I pray, clenching his cock tightly as his hard strokes slow to a stop.

He exhales roughly, regaining his breath.

"Christ, what are you doing to me?" He slides his palms over my hips and pulls out, tucking his slick cock away before zipping his pants. He collapses on the bed with a groan. "I want to be inside you all the time. I'm becoming obsessed."

Standing in front of him, I straighten my dress and lean down to kiss him. "You passed *becoming* a long time ago. You're completely obsessed with me. Admit it."

He smiles, and my chest constricts at its beauty.

Standing, he reaches over to tuck a stray lock of hair behind my ear.

"You're my fucking world, Bella De Kysa."

"As you are mine, Don De Kysa."

Emotion shimmers in the space between us.

"Have I told you how proud of you I am?" he asks, taking me in his arms.

"All the time."

"Good. Because I am." He drops a kiss on my shoulder and nuzzles my neck. "Doesn't seem right that it's your night, and I'm the one who came. Tonight, I'm going to return the favor. Hard, slow, and fucking deep."

I smile and wrap my arms around him, enjoying being in his arms and looking forward to him fulfilling his promise.

How is it that life is this good?

The door buzzer breaks into our moment. Its Mateo letting us know he's downstairs.

The Devil's Den

With a reluctant growl, Nico moves away to slide on his dinner jacket. I grin as I take his arm. "Come on, villain. Let's go, and when we get home, you can have your way with me again."

∽

Leaving our apartment building, we step into the hot New York night.

The street is alive with activity. The sun is low, and the moon has already begun to rise in a sky streaked in red and gold.

Excitement and anticipation run hot through my veins.

This is really happening at last.

We're on our way to my exhibition, and it's a dream come true.

But as I step toward the limousine, a feminine voice calls my name.

Nico and I both turn to look.

Amélie stands on the curb beside us, looking desperate and disheveled. Her hair is unbrushed and tangled, her skin blotchy, her eyes wild as she points a gun at us.

At me.

"Why, Nico?" she cries. "Why her? Why not me?"

I feel Nico stiffen beside me. "What are you talking about, Amélie? We ended things a long time ago."

But she doesn't hear him. "She doesn't deserve you. She doesn't even love you! Can't you see that? She's lying to you when she says she does. But I love you, Nico. I've always loved you."

At that moment, everything seems to slow down. I look

for our security detail and see James running toward us from the entrance of the building. I see Nico step between Amélie and me just as she fires the gun.

Two gunshots crackle in the air around us, but they are quickly swallowed by the noisy New York street.

James dives for her, tackling her to the ground before she can fire a third.

But the damage is already done. Nico sags against me before sinking to the sidewalk, his eyes wide and unfocused, a bright red stain spreading across his white shirt.

I scream.

Amélie screams.

Both of us screaming for different reasons.

But Nico is silent.

His eyes close, and within seconds, his chest becomes still.

48

Bella

There was nothing they could do, the doctor says.

Despite their attempts, Nico died in surgery, and they could not save him.

The doctor gives me the news in a private room. My husband died less than an hour after he was shot.

I sag against him and collapse to the floor.

The doctor helps me to my feet and guides me over to a row of plastic chairs, where I wrap my arms around my body and brace myself for the onslaught of media attention. Outside, the flash of paparazzi cameras light up the night as they jostle for an image of Nico De Kysa's wife.

They don't know that the king is dead yet. But the fleeting glimpses of my pain that they are capturing speaks a thousand words.

By now, there will be speculation that he has died, and the right picture of me is all the confirmation they'll need.

And here I am, just in view of their lenses, giving it to them.

Exhausted, I lean forward and bury my face in my hands.

It's been a chaotic night. So many things have happened. My life has flipped on its ass. Everything is different, and a series of events out of my control have given birth to my new world.

Nico is dead.

I rub my temples, not sure what that means for me. I'm dazed and unsure and shattered. I feel like a broken crystal vase scattered across the floor.

Nico is dead.

How am I supposed to get used to those words?

Imogen appears moments later and gathers me into her arms while I stare lifelessly at nothing.

"How am I going to do this?" I finally ask her.

She wipes a curl from in front of my eyes. "If anyone can do this, Bella De Kysa, it's you."

~

They take me to see him in the morgue.

It's downstairs where it's quiet, and no one can see me but the handful of morgue technicians. The coroner greets me. Somewhere in his fifties, he offers me an empathetic look before taking me to where Nico lies dead on a cold slab.

My legs falter as I walk toward him. He's so still and pale. A sheet is pulled up to his shoulders, covering the bullet wounds that took his life. His face is sharp but slack. His hair combed off his face.

In death, Nico De Kysa is still beautiful.

I sit at a chair next to him and reach under the sheet to take his hand. His fingers are still warm, and it sends a small kick to my heart.

I raise them to my lips and kiss them softly. "I love you. I never told you that enough, I know that now."

In response, he is silent. Unmoving. *Dead.*

I hear a noise behind me and know I am being watched. Not by the coroner but by one or two of the morgue technicians. But I ignore them as I lean forward and rest my head on my husband's chest.

"I love you, Nico De Kysa. And not even death will change that."

∼

The days pass in a fog with excruciating slowness.

Plans are made. Pieces put in place to bury the man I love so desperately. My new life is forged in grief and pain in front of a world fascinated by the tragedy.

Amélie was detained at the scene but took another way out the moment she got the chance. A shard of a broken mirror. Her wrists. A lot of blood. *A life over.*

A search of her Upper East Side apartment revealed a deep obsession for Nico. She wanted to be his wife and hated me for taking him from her. High on pills and alcohol, she finally snapped. She wanted me dead, but instead, she ended Nico's life.

By the morning of his funeral, I'm exhausted.

"You've got this," I whisper to my reflection in the mirror over the sink.

I squeeze my eyes shut and suck in a deep breath to

steady my nerves. I grip the edge of the vanity, knowing what a mammoth task I have ahead.

Today, the world will be watching. Media teams with their TV cameras and long lenses will capture every morbid detail of the king being buried.

I travel with Massimo and Imogen to the funeral. I falter as I walk along the white path cutting through the immaculate lawns of the cemetery and take my seat across from Nico's gleaming coffin draped in flowers. People crowd the lawns. Politicians and criminals standing shoulder to shoulder in the cool November sunlight. Cameras flash. People sob. A somber cloud hangs in the air.

The presence of security is heavy. De Kysa enemies would see today as ripe for a massacre. But it won't happen. There are so many bodyguards and security mercenaries in place, no threat will pass undetected.

Nico's father isn't here. Too distraught to bury his son, he was taken to the hospital with chest pain and exhaustion.

My father sits behind me, a calm tower of strength. He's been to so many of these, I wonder if it ever gets any easier for him.

I remember the funerals of my mother and brothers. Of the three coffins lined up in a row. Three bodies but five lives destroyed by a car bomb meant for my father.

Death is so final. But sometimes it can be a rebirth. Their deaths paved the way to our new life in the US.

I don't even hear the priest. All I can do is keep focused on my tears and not let my nerves get the better of me. I feel sick and desperate for this to be over.

As Nico's coffin is lowered into the ground, Imogen reaches for my hand and squeezes. Across the lawn, paparazzi cameras hum and click and flash as they capture new fodder for their online magazines and blogs, and televised news reports.

One day, this will all be over—no paparazzi, no bodyguards, no suffocating fear of living in the world of the Mafia. I will sink into obscurity to live out my life in peace, and I feel a calmness settle into my soul at the thought.

When the fanfare is over, people line up to pay their respects, but it is all a blur. I shake hand after hand, and issue one thank-you after another until I don't think I can speak anymore.

Nico is no longer just dead. Now he is buried.

Gone forever.

Beside me, Massimo cuts a strong, supportive figure. His life has changed just as much as mine in the past five days.

Brotherless, he's now the new don of the De Kysa.

The cemetery begins to empty, but I remain in my chair and stare at the coffin lowered into its grave.

"Are you sure you don't want me to ride back with you to the apartment?" Imogen asks.

I shake my head. "I'll call you later."

She squeezes my hand. "You did really good today, Bella."

She brushes a kiss on my cheek and leaves.

Across the lawn, a black Escalade pulls in behind Massimo's parked car.

"It's time to go," he says.

Together, we walk away from Nico's grave and along the path leading to the road, both of us fully aware of lurking cameras.

We stop at the edge of the path, and he hugs me. "My

brother knew what he was doing when he picked you for a bride."

I smile through my tears. "You know he kidnapped me, right?"

"Semantics." He winks. "I'll see you soon, Bella De Kysa."

I walk toward the black Escalade with the black-out windows parked at the curb. I pause before I open the door and look over my shoulder in the direction of Nico's coffin gleaming in the late morning sunlight.

"Goodbye, my king," I whisper.

Sliding into the back seat, I close the door and let out the breath I was holding.

Beside me, my husband leans over and kisses me.

"Hello, my queen."

49

Nico

Five days earlier

I've been fucking shot.

I look at Bella, and I know I'm about to leave her, and it breaks my heart. I'm not afraid to die. But I am afraid to leave her.

Fuck, not now.

But the darkness sweeps over me, and I fall against her, the blood from my bullet wounds seeping onto her dress as I slide down her body and sink to the sidewalk.

I awaken to the sound of a machine beeping. It takes me a while, but I open my eyes, and all I see are the bright glow of lights. I slowly come to realize that I'm in the back of an ambulance.

Bella. I try to say her name, but there seems to be a

disconnect between my brain and my mouth. Finally, I'm able to rasp, "Bella?"

"Is that your girl?" the EMT asks me. He's an older guy. His thick accent is pure New York City. There's something comforting about him. "We couldn't bring her with us, buddy. I need all the room back here so I can help you."

I struggle to remember what happened. I was shot.

Fuck.

"Am I going to die?"

He smiles as he fills a syringe. "Not on my watch, you ain't."

But the darkness calls to me again, and I'm unable to fight it. Feeling heavy, I slip back into its nothingness.

I wake up under another bright light God knows how long afterward, only vaguely aware of the people moving around me. I feel dreamy, like I'm floating. I feel good, and I know it's because my blood is thick with drugs.

Blindly, I reach out and grab onto the first person I can. "Get me my brother."

~

I'm going to live.

But I've made up my mind that I'm also going to die.

The only thing that I want from my old life is my wife. But other than that, I want out. I don't want to be Domenico anymore. I want to be Bella's Nico.

I want to soak up the sun on a tropical beach somewhere and spend my days with sandy toes and margarita highs. I want to live in baggy beach shorts and take midmorning naps, then feast on fresh lobster taken right out of the ocean near where we live. I want to play with my future babies in the sand dunes with the tangy sea air on our lips, and the saltiness of the ocean in our hair. And when the sun goes down, I want to worship my queen with every single inch of my body until she can't take the pleasure anymore and begs me to stop.

Facing your mortality reveals your true priorities, and in those final moments before I died, none of my priorities involved anything but Bella and our life together. Money. Power. Ruling my kingdom. They are nothing in the face of death—while my queen is everything.

I don't want this city.

I don't want to be king anymore.

I haven't for some time.

Hell, I've fantasized about giving it all up more times than I care to remember.

I never told Bella the truth about how I felt. Never really had the chance to. The only person I ever confided in was my brother.

"The first chance I get, Massimo, I'm escaping. I don't know how it will happen, but I will recognize the opportunity when it arrives."

Today, two 9mm bullets delivered that opportunity.

Now I know for sure... Domenico De Kysa must die.

50

Bella

Five Days Earlier

I burst through the front doors of the hospital.

Because of how critical Nico was, they wouldn't let me travel with him in the back of the ambulance, which terrified me.

Mateo drove me, cutting through the heavy New York traffic with cutthroat expertise while I called Massimo and shouted a conversation at him that I can't even remember.

Being closer to the hospital, he made it there before me, while I sat in the back of the Escalade with my heart in my throat and my ears still ringing from the gunshots.

"Where is he?" I cry when I see Massimo.

Adrenaline courses through me at the speed of light.

"He's in surgery."

"He's alive?" I sob.

"Bella, we need to talk." He takes me by the shoulders, I'm assuming to calm down the titanic emotional response I am having in the middle of the hospital, but I can't stand his serious tone, so I begin to cry harder.

"Oh God, he's going to die, isn't he?"

Massimo's lips stay together, igniting my fear.

Finally, he says, "There are things we need to discuss." He glances over my shoulder at the gathering crowd outside the hospital. "But not here."

He guides me away from the triage reception, and I blindly follow him down a long, brightly lit corridor. I feel sick. Sucked into a sudden fog and unsure of a way out.

The squeak of our shoes against the linoleum becomes a mantra in my head as I scramble to make sense of the past hour.

How is it that less than sixty minutes ago my husband was so virile and alive as he fucked me over the edge of the bed... and now he's in surgery with two bullets in him?

My steps falter when I think of him lying in a pool of blood on the sidewalk, and I have to draw in a breath to steady myself.

Massimo leads me into a small supply room off to the left and closes the door. He starts looking around, and it suddenly occurs to me that he is looking for any surveillance equipment.

My brows knit together. "Massimo, what's going on?"

His alert eyes scan every line and angle of the ceiling. "Nico is alive, and as far as I know, he intends to stay that way."

"Oh, thank God." I sag with relief. "He's out of danger?"

"Yes."

"And you know this for sure?"

"Yes."

More relief.

"Then why have you dragged me in here? What's with all the secrecy?"

"Because what I am about to tell you requires it." He stops looking around the room and focuses on me. "Your future with Nico depends on no one hearing what I am about to say next."

"Then you'd better tell me what the fuck is happening right the fuck now."

His expression tightens, his eyes serious. "Nico wants to die so he can give you the life you deserve. He wants out, Bella."

My mouth drops open in disbelief.

And that fog from earlier, it gets even thicker as my mind struggles to wade through it.

"He's going to fake his death?" I ask.

"To have a life with you, yes."

All I can do is stare at my brother-in-law.

I'm as still as a church mouse, but in my head a tropical storm is whipping up violent chaos.

"I only spoke to him briefly before he went into surgery. While I waited for you to arrive, I put a few chess pieces in play."

It's like I'm having an out-of-body experience, and all I can do is nod.

Luckily, Massimo is fully present and firing with all pistons.

"We keep this on the down low, and we keep it tight.

Only those who need to know will know. No one outside the inner sanctum will be privy to it."

I let out a shaky breath. "What do you need me to do?"

"We need to convince the world that he is dead before we do anything else. Unfortunately, Bella, you'll have to carry the heavy load right out of the gate. The paparazzi are already lined up out in front of the hospital. I have a trusted associate who will deliver the news to you just in view of the cameras outside. You will react with the grief of a woman who has just learned she is a widow."

I nod, still hardly believing what is happening. "I can do that."

"But it won't be enough to satiate the press's thirst for a good tragic story. They'll bribe hospital employees for information."

"Meaning?"

"Meaning you and Nico are going to have to put on a performance for them too." He thinks for a moment, then adds, "Nico will be taken to the morgue. We have to follow usual procedures, or someone might get wind of something fishy in the air. I will arrange for you to visit him in the morgue to say goodbye. But I will make sure as many people as possible know about it. You will say your goodbyes. He will be transported to the funeral home of our choice. We have one we use. It's attached to a crematorium that we've used in the past."

I'm not confused enough to miss what he means by that. When you create corpses, I guess having a crematorium in your back pocket is handy.

"I'll organize private healthcare for Nico, and he can recuperate in a secret location."

Massimo's ability to come up with this plan so effortlessly on the spot tells me he'll make a great don.

Which is what he will be once Nico is officially declared dead.

Which makes me ask, "What about the surgeon and nurses keeping him alive? Aren't they a liability? I mean, someone has to declare him dead."

"They will be none the wiser. It will be the coroner who declares him dead."

"And you know the coroner?"

"Money meet bank account. We've used him before. He will declare Nico dead from a sudden complication following surgery. He's trustworthy."

I blow out a deep breath. "Wow, you really know your stuff."

He grins. "Thank you."

"You and Anastacia should collaborate," I mutter. "I think you two could rule the world."

"Do you feel up to this?" he asks.

"Do I have a choice?"

"No, I was being polite."

"What happens after we leave the hospital?"

"We can work out the semantics later, but for now, we need to keep this simple, and we need to keep it real. Nico is going to die tonight, and you are going to play the role of the grieving widow."

He's so confident it makes me believe we might be able to get away with it.

His phone vibrates in his breast pocket. It's a message.

"Nico is out of surgery. Everything went well." He gives me a reassuring smile. "It's showtime."

An hour later, Massimo leads me into a private room where Nico lies in a hospital bed under a gleaming golden light. Trusted bodyguards are everywhere, inside and outside of the room.

When he sees me, he tries to sit up, but winces and collapses against the pillows. Gauze bandages hug his torso, covering his wounds.

I take his hand, savoring its warmth because it means his heart is beating and his blood is flowing through his veins. "If this is your way of getting me to run away with you and live on an island, then it's overkill. You could've just asked."

His smile is lazy and heavy with drugs. "You know me, go big or go home."

Tears prick at my eyes as my adrenaline slowly drains from my body, and I start to realize the enormity of the situation.

A lump forms in my throat. Things could have turned out very differently.

Nico reaches for my face. "Kiss me, hellcat."

"You need some rest, brother," Massimo says behind me.

But Nico isn't interested in rest.

"Stop being a mother hen and let me kiss my bride." He pulls me down for a kiss and groans as our lips meet. When he breaks it off, he groans again. "Goddamn, I needed that."

Now that my adrenaline wanes, relief floods every muscle and fiber. I push my fingers through his thick hair, feeling grateful, feeling love.

"Massimo has filled you in?" he asks me, his voice hoarse.

"Yes, he's been busy." I give my brother-in-law a grateful smile. "He's very good at this whole faking-your-death thing. I think we might actually get away with it."

Nico glances at his brother, and I'm surprised by the affection on his face. Maybe it's the drugs. Or maybe things are changing faster than I anticipated, and Nico is letting go of his stony facade.

"I appreciate it," he says to Massimo. "More than I could ever tell you."

Massimo seems just as surprised but quickly covers it.

"Don't be getting soft on me, brother," he replies.

Nico's eyes lower. "Don't worry. My heart might still be beating, but it's still dark and thorny."

"Just the way we like it," Massimo says.

I lean down and kiss my husband. "I love you, villain."

"You'd fucking better," he growls.

Beside us, Massimo shakes his head wearily. "Now that your girl has agreed to run away with you, can you please get some fucking rest?"

51

Bella

Massimo leans against the railing and stares out at the ocean as the boat carves a white-tipped path through the blue waves. "This is your last chance to back out. Are you sure you want to go through with it?"

"If you ask me that one more time, I will throw you overboard," Nico growls at his brother.

Massimo ignores his threat, preoccupied by the enormity of what we are doing. Even if we weren't sure, it's too late now. Domenico De Kysa is dead.

According to media sources, I am in Italy visiting relatives.

While Nico's role is done, I still have to play the part of the grieving widow. It's important they see me struggling to cope with my sudden, tragic loss.

Unfortunately, I can't move from New York City yet. There would be too many questions, and questions lead to inquiries, and an investigation could blow this entire plan to smithereens. If a journalist starts scratching around and uncovers the truth, it could be deadly for Nico. Because if his enemies discover he is still alive, they'll come looking to wash the streets with De Kysa blood.

So I will stay in our New York penthouse a little longer until the world sees I have moved on and their interest in me and my tragedy wanes. I'll even relaunch my exhibition, the one we never made it to the night Nico was shot. I'm even considering opening my own boutique gallery where I can help launch up-and-coming artists.

With a new life stretching ahead of me on the horizon, the possibilities are endless.

It will be hard to be away from Nico, even if it does secure a harmonious future free from organized crime, bloodshed, and violence.

To make it work, I will disappear from public view to visit Nico on the island, only to reappear a couple of weeks later in the city as the grieving widow, visiting certain paparazzi hotspots to ensure they plaster my grief across their headlines and pages.

It's going to take months, maybe even a year or two before I can leave.

Well, that was the plan.

Until this morning when two little pink lines told me my world was about to be shaken up even more.

Not believing it at first, I had Arianna purchase another three tests from the drug store for me (paparazzi are a bitch), and all three were positive.

With everything happening, I'd forgotten my period was late.

Shocked, I'd made Arianna promise not to say a word to her brothers. But she's so excited about being an auntie she's already online shopping and bound to let it slip.

Now we are on our way to the island hideaway via an indistinguishable boat, and I'm trying to find the words to tell Nico that our life is about to flip again.

We never talked about children.

Hell, I don't even know if he wants children.

My hand slides to my belly.

But I do, baby.

I want you more than what I know what to do with.

I feel the heat of Nico's gaze along my skin, and when I look up, I see him looking at me.

He moves away from Massimo and takes my hand, leading me off the boat's deck and down the stairs into the cabin.

He takes me in his arms and kisses me.

"What are you up to?" I ask.

"I want some alone time with my wife."

The look he gives me warms me everywhere.

"You're about to get that in spades," I say. "I believe island life is quite lazy, and there isn't much to do but lie in the sun, drink wine, and fuck."

"Sounds perfect." He turns me so my back is pressed to his chest. "But this sea air is making me needy for my wife right now."

He begins nibbling along my throat. Beneath his lips, my skin pebbles. "Here?"

His lips reach my ear. "Everywhere."

His hands glide down my body to lift the hem of my

dress. My legs part, and his fingers slide beneath my panties, making me gasp as they begin teasing my clit.

Up on deck, Massimo laughs at something Mateo said. Then they both laugh and start talking again.

While below deck, my husband conjures my orgasm with ridiculous ease.

He drags his lips up my neck to the base of my ear. "When were you going to tell me?"

"Tell you what?" I bite back a moan as his finger continues to torture the nub of nerves, rubbing it back and forth, bringing me to the brink. If he keeps it up, I'm going to come hard and fast.

"That you're pregnant," he says smoothly.

My eyes fly open. "How did you know?"

His lips brush my ear. "I know everything."

Grinning, I reach backward to wind my arms around his neck as he continues to rub my pussy. "What gave it away?"

"The shine in your eyes. The glow on your skin. The way your hand moves to your belly." His breath is hot on my skin. His fingers work frantically while I rock my hips to meet the much-needed pressure of his palm against my clit. "I want you to come now, and after that, I'm going to take you to the bedroom and spend the afternoon making you come again and again and again."

My head falls back as my orgasm crashes through me.

"That's it, baby, let go." He circles my clit with relentless pressure, turning my bones soft and making me weak. "Goddamn, I love feeling you come."

When I'm nothing but a rag doll, he spins me around and presses me to the wall, caging me in his arms and his intoxicating heat. My gaze falls into the molten heat of his as he asks, "So you're definitely pregnant?"

"Yes."

His lips twitch. "Is it mine?"

I shrug. "I mean, I suppose."

He smiles, but then his eyes darken, and a possessiveness gleams in them.

"Tell me I'm going to be a father."

His words make my heart swell. "You're going to be a father."

I watch his jaw tighten with emotion. And for the tiniest moment, I see a hint of vulnerability in his eyes. But then it's gone and replaced with an unquestionable love.

He places his hands on my belly, his expression unguarded and emotional.

"Hello, baby. I'm your papa, and I'm going to make it my purpose in life to make you as happy as your beautiful mama makes me."

And kneeling in front of me, he places a kiss on my belly.

EPILOGUE

Nico

The sand is as soft as powdered sugar between my toes, and the late afternoon sun is warm on my back. A gentle, salty breeze whispers against my skin and reminds me that a summer storm is supposed to blow in later tonight.

I hear a giggle and turn to see my four-year-old son trying to walk in my sandy footprints behind me, leaping from one to the other, and laughing when he gets the wobbles.

Sitting on my shoulders, my three-year-old daughter giggles at her brother.

I grin at my son, pride swelling in my chest. "If you keep growing up so fast, your feet will be bigger than mine in no time."

He leaps onto a new footprint and falls onto his butt in the sand, laughing as a gentle wave rolls over him.

My wife walks beside me, her long, red hair tangling in

the sea breeze. *My queen.* She's dressed in a white summer dress, the floaty, thin fabric wrapping around her big belly and fluttering about her legs. Our second son is due any day now, and I have to kick myself to make sure this life is not a dream.

Sometimes I wonder if I deserve this.

If this is too good to be true.

But then I realize that is the old Nico talking because some habits are hard to break.

I will never regret my decision to walk away. To turn my back on the dark life and step into the light with my wife at my side.

We etch out a simple life. One that doesn't need the sheen and sparkle of glamour and power.

One that doesn't have us looking over our shoulders.

One that isn't sheathed in the darkness of blood and murder.

Our home is carved into the white cliffs of the island, open-plan and breezy, with stunning sunrises and golden sunsets, and views for as far as the eye can see.

We etch out a life rich with art and knowledge, and gratitude for the peace that had eluded me all of my adult life. The outside world is just one laptop away, so I'm able to run businesses incognito. And when I feel the need for more space, I simply close my computer and walk away. No one knows I'm here. No one will ever know I'm here. I own this island and know everyone who steps onto its white sand shores.

Here we are safe at last, and my bambinos will grow up without knowing the taste of blood and hate, and Mafia rivalry.

Following my death, Massimo took over running the De Kysa syndicate, and a few times a year, he makes it to our island, arriving under the dark veil of night. He loves his niece and nephew and loves to spend days soaking up the sun and the simple but satisfying joy of island life. We don't talk about the family, the past, or anything remotely related to my old life. We only look forward.

To help maintain the facade of my death, Bella visits her father in New York several times a year, and when she returns and tells me about the city where I had once reigned, I look out the window and see our home, and I hear my babies giggle and my wife laugh, and I realize I don't miss a thing about my old life.

I have all that I need.

I know I've been a bad man.

But I hope that if I love Bella with a pure heart every single day, I can redeem myself for the sins of my past life.

I'll never understand why Amélie did what she did. There was never anything more than sex between us. But apparently, her obsession ran deep. Her private journals were a portal into a tortured woman crazed by a fixation for me.

The old me would want revenge on her for trying to hurt Bella. But the new me is able to find it in his heart to forgive her.

I'm trying to be a better man.

I want to be.

My wife slips her hand into mine, bringing me back to the present. "Something on your mind?"

I take in her big blue-green eyes and sun-kissed face.

"Only how good my life is."

"Well, it's about to get real good." She grins wickedly as she leans closer and whispers, "These two munchkins are due for their afternoon nap, and I'm feeling needy for my husband. What do you say we get these kids home, and you and I get naked?"

"I say we better start walking faster."

She grins, and despite her big round belly, she runs ahead, chasing our son who runs along the sandy shore.

I smile after them.

I've never been so happy in my fucking life.

Nothing in the world could compete with what I have now.

My name is Nico.

And it's a fucking pleasure to meet you.

Continue onto book two in the series
The Devil's Lair

ABOUT THE AUTHOR

Penny Dee writes contemporary romance about rock stars, bikers, hockey players, mafia kings, and everyone in-between. Her stories bring the suspense, the feels, and a whole lot of heat.

She found her happily ever after with an Australian hottie who she met on a blind date.

ALSO BY PENNY DEE

The Kings of Mayhem Original Series

Kings of Mayhem

Brothers in Arms

Biker Baby

Hell on Wheels

Off Limits

Bull

The Kings of Mayhem Tennessee Series

Jack

Doc

Ares

Printed in Great Britain
by Amazon